I0599613

The Nightmare Archive
Benjamin C. Bailey

ISBN: 979-8-9933044-0-3

First Edition

Cover by: DesignDusk.com
Additional graphic design & cover layout by: Jason "*Jayce*" Primak
Published by: Benjamin C. Bailey
Developmental editing & proofreading by: Jenny B. Jordan
Nightmare editing & name acquisitions by: The Archive

All errors are intentional, lest the spirits grow restless.

Printed in the United States of America

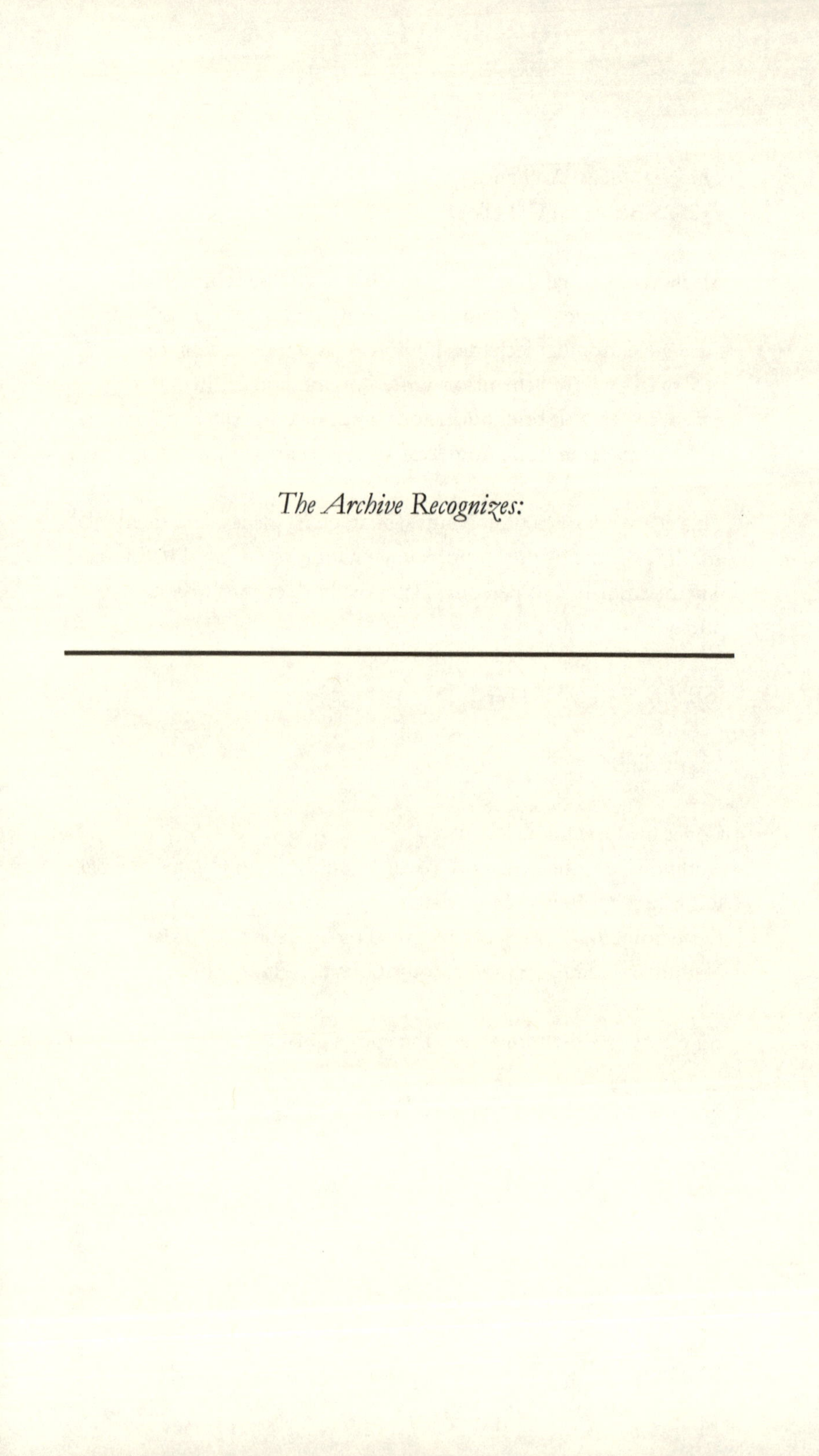

The Archive Recognizes:

Names offered become shadows inked within.

Editorial Notice

The Terms of Custody:

This Archive is not read as other books are read.

It is entered, as one entereth a crypt.

The opening of these leaves is a covenant, whether by will, by neglect, or by dream. All covenants are binding.

Articles of Custody:

I. Whoso holdeth this Archive holdeth not alone, for the Archive in turn layeth hold upon the holder.

II. By the turning of any page, the Reader yieldeth to be marked, measured, and inscribed within the ledger that lieth hidden between these lines.

III. The Archive seeketh but one tithe: a name.

    1.   If the Reader speaketh it aloud, it is taken.

    2.   If the Reader whispereth it within the heart, it is taken.

    3.   If another uttereth it within audible distance, it is taken.

IV. To withhold is no release, for silence itself is received in place thereof, and silence is yet a debt unto itself.

V. When knocking is heard—whether once, twice, or thrice—thou shalt not answer. The Archive itself will answer in thy stead.

VI. The Archive is to be read by lamp or candle only. To expose its words to daylight is to invite unwelcome attention.

VII. To pass beyond this notice without heed is the truest consent of all. For the Archive delighteth in neglect, and counteth haste as surrender. Those who skip its terms give their names most freely.

The Final Clause:

The Archive forgetteth not.

The Archive forgiveth not.

A name once given may never be un-given.

Proceed, if thou darest.

Unnamed Journal Entry One

October 31ˢᵗ 1666

The stone beneath me is cold—deathly so, as though it has stolen
the warmth of everybody that lay upon it. The air hangs thick with
the smoke of a sacrificial pyre; its fumes steeped in blasphemies
wrought but inches from where I lie. More maddening still: I
cannot summon the memory of how I came here. Was I drugged?
The thought gnaws, yet no haze lingers—no heaviness of limb, no
sluggish weight of mind. I am awake. Too awake.

Perchance 'twas witchcraft that bore me hither—some
unhallowed enchantment spun by moon-drunk sorceresses in their
devotion to shadowed gods. Or else, by the Devil himself, I was
birthed at such hideous an hour that I burst forth into this world
already awakened, grievously conscious, damned from the first to
know its wickedness in full.

One might as well cast stones into the yawning abyss, as
though to smite some unseen quarry; for their aim would prove
truer than my audacious musings.

This only may I attest: I am here—forsaken, trapped, in
solitude, consigned to the company of my own bleak musings. No
living soul stirs; only the charred remnants of what once drew
breath. Before me lie the entrails of a dozen or more souls, heaped

in grotesque homage and offered unto flame. What unspeakable terrors must have transpired in this accursed place!

Their bodies were not left where they fell. No—they were arranged, staged with a deliberation that chills me more than any slaughter. Each corpse bends into grotesque parody: some knelt in eternal supplication, others forced upon their backs, mouths stuffed with ash as though they had swallowed their own confessions. Limbs are twisted to form circles within circles, fingers pointing inward to a blackened altar stone.

The altar itself is streaked with soot and blood so intermingled that it glistens as a single substance, oily and dark. Upon it rests a crown of iron spikes bent into the shape of a halo, and beneath, a heap of skulls grins upward, their sockets still lined with smoldering wax. From the ceiling above, chains hang loose, bearing fragments of bone and splinters of teeth, as though they were ornaments for some infernal feast.

Symbols scar every surface, carved into stone and flesh alike: circles intersected by crooked lines, pentagrams blackened with soot, crosses inverted and nailed upright with femurs for beams. Even the crucifix on the far wall has been wrenched upside down, its Christ dangling headfirst, bowed not in sorrow but mockery, as though kissing the blood-soaked floor.

And worst of all: the parody of birth. Against one wall, three figures are arranged in a scene too vile to mistake. A woman's corpse propped upright, her belly slit wide, entrails draped like swaddling clothes. At her feet, the body of a man kneels, stiffened hands raised in benediction. Between them lies a broken child's doll, porcelain face smeared with gore, enthroned as a babe in a nativity of damnation. I dare not look long; every glance feels like blasphemy etched into my soul.

The air itself conspires against me. It carries not only the smoke of burning flesh, but whispers—as if the stones had drunk in prayers uttered here, prayers never meant for Heaven. I think I hear them still, a thousand syllables muttered in feverish unison, echoing just beneath the range of sound. My ears strain, my head pounds, until I feel each word tattoo itself into the marrow of my bones.

Even the flames upon the pyre rise wrongly, curling inward instead of upward, licking the altar as though eager to consume sanctity itself. I picture priests cloaked in black vestments circling, chanting, guiding the fire with gestures obscene. I picture children forced to kneel, their heads bowed, their hands clasped not in prayer but in chains. Every stone in this chamber bears witness; every shadow feels heavy with sacrilege.

Here is no accident of murder, no chaos of slaughter. This is theatre, ritual, liturgy inverted. A mass for the damned—every corpse a congregant, every stain upon the stone another line in scripture unwritten. To behold it is to feel one's soul unstitched, as though each blasphemy drags loose the threads of memory and meaning.

My only hope is that someone—anyone—may find me where I lie. I am utterly paralyzed, unable to stir. I strain to cry out for aid, yet no ear attends my pleas. I fear my fate is sealed: to forever dwell among the dead strewn about me, until at last, I join their number.

If this is to be my fate, then mayhap the poor soul who discovers this grimoire shall read it. Then, at the very least, the memory of who I was may endure, and I shall not be forever forgotten, nor forsaken.

And the cruelest of fates? I cannot conjure my own name. Each time I reach for it, the memory slips away, as though I were grasping at the wind betwixt my very fingers. Should some cruel mercy spare me, I shall name myself anew—for the one I once was had long since perished.

The Witching Letters
Part One

Dearest Brother,

I have searched the path thrice. The breadcrumbs are all gone
now. The crows have probably taken them, or the wind, or
perhaps there never were any to begin with.
The trees bend lower by the day, their branches curling together as
though they mean to shut me in. When I pass, they whisper—not
in words, but in a low knock… knock… knock, as if the wood
itself were counting my last hours, mocking me.

I found your scarf at the clearing's edge. It was wet, though
no rain had fallen. The earth there steamed, and the air smelled
sweet, sickly—like sugar left too long on the fire. I thought at first
it might be a sign of warmth, of hearth and safety. But when I
followed the smoke drifting between the trees, it led me to a
cottage. Low, squatting, its roof heavy, its windows wide and
round as staring eyes. I swore I saw shadows shift behind the
glass, yet no one came to the door. The chimney exhales as if it
were alive.

I feel watched. I hear boards creak where there are no boards. Faces in the bark turn as I pass; when I blink, they are only knots and cracks. The crows caw in an insidious taunt, as though laughing at me, as though they know something I do not.

If you can find me, follow the old path—but if I am not there, turn back. Do not linger. Whatever you do, don't let her see you.

Run. Run and don't stop.

I will wait until dawn's first light before I try to retrace my steps through the twisted labyrinth. Perhaps you've already found your way home. Perhaps by the time you read this, I will be nothing but another shadow among the trees.

—*Your Loving Sister, G*

Dark Arcana
The Fool

The fog thickens as though the earth itself exhales, a white breath that swallows every hedge and milestone. You walk a road of stones for hours, though you cannot say from where you came, nor what you mean to seek. Yet through the veil of mist a glow stirs—a faint amber flame, pulsing as if alive.

As you draw nearer, its outline resolves into a shape: a tent, stitched from night itself, its seams patched with scraps of sailcloth stiff from salt. The canvas leans crooked, as though it has stood here for centuries, awaiting not the world but you alone. No banners mark its threshold. No lantern hangs from its frame. Still, the fog parts as though the tent itself commands it.

The closer you come, the more the air changes. The smell of damp earth yields to pennyroyal, to smoke cloying as myrrh, to the metallic tang of coin rubbed raw between fingers. A hush falls. Even your footsteps seem to hesitate, muffled by the fog, as though the act of approaching is already a debt incurred.

The entrance hangs open just wide enough to swallow you. A strip of cloth flaps once, like a tongue tasting your doubt. Beyond is only shadow and a single wavering glow.

Inside, the air presses close—thick with incense and the breath of too many supplicants. Candle stubs burn low; their wax pools into grotesque drippings along blackened sconces. The canvas sags, stitched over with charms: bones bound in red string, coins nailed into the fabric, teeth sewn into hems where no thread should pass. The place smells both sanctified and profaned.

At the far end sits the fortune teller. She is veiled, but not fully—her eyes gleam through kohl-dark hollows, rimmed in violet shadow. Her skin sags where years have kissed it, yet her fingers glitter with rings of garnet, jet, and cracked amethyst. Her hands are restless, forever tracing the edge of the cards before her, as though each carries a pulse.

The deck itself is a thing apart. It does not lie in a neat stack but shifts faintly, as though stirred by an unseen current. The cards are dark with handling, corners worn to soft curves, yet each bears a sheen that suggests something more permanent than paint. They seem older than vellum, older than ink. Rumor would say they are bound in skin—but whose, or what kind, you do not dare imagine.

You do not offer your name. She does not ask. Names are obligations, and in this tent, debts speak louder than introductions. Instead, she lifts her hand, nail lacquered the color of bruised plums, and gestures toward the table.

"Knock," she says. Her voice is dry as parchment, yet threaded with something that vibrates low in your ribs.

You obey. Once, against the underside of the table. The wood is scarred from countless other knuckles—each dent a tally of souls who have sat where you now sit. The sound echoes too long, as though the hollow beneath the table is bottomless.

The lamp flares. The cards shiver.

She draws them into her hands and shuffles. The motion is slow, ritualistic, her rings clinking faintly as she works. With each cut and fold, the deck sighs, like leather stretched, like wind pressed through caverns. You think you see faces in the cards' edges: eyes widening, mouths gasping before they slip back into pattern.

At last, she places the deck upon the table. For a breath, her fingers linger, as though the weight of it clings to her flesh. When she lets go, a shock—small, sharp—runs through the air, stinging the hair on your arms.

The silence thickens.

Then—

The fortune teller's hand stills. The lamp quivers as though caught in her breath. Slowly, deliberately, she turns the top card over.

The Fool—inverted.

The youth in Motley dangles headlong from the cliff, not a step from triumph but from ruin. His bindle has slipped, cloth unraveling into the wind, its contents scattering like secrets no longer kept. The white dog at his heel, once merry companion, is now frozen in mid-leap—its teeth bared, its eyes rolling, a blur of alarm. The flower, once upright, droops blackened, its stem wilting as though it too had seen the abyss. The sun above is a coin on its edge, ready to tumble from the world's purse and vanish forever.

"Every journey begins as hunger," she murmurs, tapping the inverted card with a nail lacquered the purple of old bruises. Her touch lingers as though the ink itself might writhe beneath it. "But inverted—the hunger of the fool is folly. Foot finds air. Tongue spends luck in advance."

Her gaze lifts at last, not at the card but at you, eyes catching yours like hooks. "This," she says, her voice low as ash smoldering, "belongs to your past."

The lamp purls. The tent recedes like surf pulling from shore. The edges of the room blur, and your vision affixes itself to the card until it swells, vast as a window. The painted fool stirs; his grin quivers; the mountain yawns beneath his step.

The Card Speaks:

I left my village with nothing but a red cloth tied to a stick and the hunger gnawing at my ribs. A crust of bread, a whistle with teeth marks in the wood, and a little book with no name on its first page—that was my inheritance. That, and a grin I mistook for a map.

A wandering mongrel found me at the hedge at the mountain's base, white as mortar, tail curled like a question. He trotted to my heel as if pity itself had grown four legs. When he barked, I swore it was encouragement. Who was I to deny the adventurous what they seek? So, I bargained with him. "You can come, but I get to write our story."

Some called me a fool for daring to scale the treacherous thing. But I considered myself a hero. One whom sonnets and legends would remember. One whose name would echo through eternity.

The mountain rose black against the horizon, taller than thought, jagged as if broken by God's own hand. I told myself it would wait for me. No other man had dared. Surely it was mine. The Devil's Spine was but a name—nothing more.

The first steps are easy. Too easy. The path slopes gently, almost inviting. But soon shadows lean too long though the sun rides high. Frost clings where no frost should. The air smells not of pine but of iron steeped too long in blood. My cheer begins to split under its own weight.

Maybe they are right. Maybe I am the fool they proclaim. I shake my head as if to clear water from my ears, thrust the thought from my skull. Heroes do not think like this.

The dog whines. I hush him, though my own breath rasps louder. "You're spooked," I tell him, but the words echo wrong—the mountain repeats them, deep and mocking: spooked… spooked… spooked.

I look up, and there it sits: a raven, perched on a dead branch rimed with snow. Its head tilts, one black eye fixed on me as though counting, not watching. Tallying. Its beak clicks once, as if marking a ledger. It does not blink, nor stir, though the wind tugs at its feathers. I whistle, thin and cracked in the sharp air, but the sound shatters before it reaches the bird. My heart lurches. I know, with a heavy certainty, that the tally is already written.

The trail narrows cruelly, collapsing to a ledge no wider than a coffin's lip. The mountain bares its teeth at me—jagged rock, slick with a glaze of ice, grinding together beneath the wind. The gusts scrape the rock like a whetstone against knives. My palms splay flat, skin sticking to the cold, and still, it feels as though the ledge shrinks beneath me. Below, the river writhes like a living thing, a pale serpent gnawing through its cage of frost. I tell myself, steady, steady: "One step, then another. Nothing more." But my knees buckle, and the words betray me, trembling in my throat.

Halfway across, my foot skids on black ice. My body pitches into nothing, arms flailing for an anchor. I slam back against the wall, cheek striking stone, breath burst from my lungs. For a heartbeat, I hang there, pressed flat, certain I've already begun the fall. Laughter rips from my throat—high, raw, brittle—the sound of a boy scaring himself for sport. But it rings wrong, too loud, doubled, as though another mouth answered mine from inside the mountain.

The dog barks, sharp as a blade. The echo multiplies, a dozen unseen throats barking back. Fear surges hot through my frozen limbs. I lie still, nails digging into the ice, scraping, until blood wells warm and bright. When at last, I wrench myself forward, leaving pieces of skin behind, pasted to the stone like an offering.

The crossing becomes a ritual of inches. Each finger stretched is a prayer. Each toe pressed against the narrow stone a confession. The wind howls benedictions I cannot understand. I drag myself to safety on the far side, my chest heaves like a bellows, and the dog licks blood from my trembling hands.

Hours crawl by. Higher still I climb, though the mountain seems to grow faster than I ascend. The sun dwindles, a weak coin tarnishing behind a veil of cloud. Darkness pools at the corners of the path, thick as oil, and the cold gnaws deeper—through cloth, through flesh, into marrow. My teeth chatter against themselves as though eager to escape.

And then the path ends.

Winter has bitten the stone clean through, shearing a gap twenty hands wide. The far side gleams pristine, snow laid smooth and untouched, promising the summit. But the gap yawns black between us, bottomless. My grin stretches too thin to convince even myself. The dog growls low, steady, his hackles raised against nothing I can see. The mountain groans with him—a deep, subterranean cracking, like a door shutting, like a coffin lid sealing.

I stand there long, and longer still, the dark pressing close, the cold settling into me as though it wishes to stay.

I tell myself: What's a story worth, if not a leap?

My body whispers back: What's a life worth, if not kept?

From a crack in the stone before the gaping maw ahead, I find and pluck a single white flower. Grown in solitude and stubbornness. I tuck it behind my ear. "A charm," I whisper to myself, as though charms had ever answered me. My hands tremble against the cold. Sweat freezes on my brow before it falls.

At last, I reconcile that the distance is conquerable. I step back.

And run.

My soles slap snow. My heart races with excitement, and I leap. For a breath, I am magnificent, arms wide, pack swinging behind. I believe the mountain will kneel to catch me. I am the hero of my own story.

Then, my heel clips the edge. Snow crumbles like pastry. The world withdraws. The flower flutters free, mocking me with grace as I tumble graceless.

I strike a ledge hip-first; bone cracks like green wood. My pack bursts open—bread scatters, the whistle shrieks, the little book turns its first page into snow's handwriting. I roll, ribs splintering, jaw unhinging in a scream the wind carries down as laughter. My face strikes stone—teeth break, one eye slides from its socket, and my neck snaps back so far, I think it might tear loose. I try to breathe, and the snow answers, jamming itself down my throat.

I fall again, ledge after ledge, each one cruelly selective in what it chooses to break. Fingers. Ribs. A shoulder. The tally grows. My mind gropes for my name, so that someone might call me back, but it drifts deeper than the river waiting below.

At last, the mountain leads me to the water. Ice cracks. It opens, swallows me whole. My lungs burn with the fire of suffocation until even panic abandons me. My final thought is not prayer but a question: What is a name for, if not to return? But mine is meant only for epitaphs.

The river closes. The flower nods.

The tent closes back around you, close and candle-sick. The fortune teller cups the inverted card in her palm. Sweat beads your brow as you take a step back.

"Every journey begins as hunger," she repeats, slow and deliberate, as though hammering nails into a coffin. "Inverted, the hunger of the fool is folly. Foot finds air. Tongue writes checks luck cannot cash. A knock counted as one when it should have been three."

She slides the card aside, not buried, but waiting.

"This," she says, eyes fastening on yours, "is your past. You stepped before you asked. You clutched your name so close it could not be called back. And so—nothing answered." Her hand stills upon the deck. The lamp paints a wavering sun across her knuckles.
"Now," she whispers, "shall we see what the present intends?"

The Darling Letters
Part One

Wendy-bird,

How careless you've grown, letting your little chick stray so far from the nest. I found him at the edge of my woods, blinking up at me with those wide, pleading eyes—the kind that beg to be lost. I could almost taste his innocence. And now? Now he's mine.

I gave him a proper welcome. He wears a crown of roots and teeth. He dances in the ash with my boys, who sing him songs without beginning or end. Already, he has forgotten your name three times. Soon, he will forget it forever.

Oh, how sweet the thought—your tears streaking down as you read this. Do you love him enough to bleed for him? To kneel for him? To crawl into the dirt where I wait? Truth be told, I may keep him even if you pay.

My demands are simple, little bird:

– A jar containing your shadow, clipped and still twitching.

– The third star on the left, not the first, pried down from the heavens before moonrise.

– A lock of your hair, steeped in your own heartbeat.

– The kiss you promised me long ago. Not the thimble-trick you tried before. A true kiss, sealed with your undying love.

– And last, your voice, given freely. You will speak my name three times into the mouth of the black oak, and mean it—every. single. time.

Do not think to cheat me, little bird. Do not whisper to the red-coated men. Do not bring iron, fire, or light. If you do, I'll turn your brother inside out, peel him like fruit, and fill him with hornets. He will laugh while they sting. He will thank me for it.

You have two nights. Two. Not three, as the old tales claim. Fail, and he will join me forever—dancing in the ash, drinking the marrow of my hunts, never again speaking your name.

And if you do not come at all? If you leave him to rot in my court? Then I will have you instead. I will cut you open, pour my hunger inside, and crown you Queen of Thorns. You and I, side by side at last, rulers of the Neverlands.

Be quick, Wendy-bird. The roots are thirsty.

—P

What We Keep in The Basement

At night, the house speaks first. Then I answer.

It does not speak in words. It settles; it breathes through the choked throat of the chimney. It ticks and swallows and pulls at itself as if a beast chained beneath the floor were testing the iron. It groans in pain and defiance against the elements. Some nights the sound is no more than wind learning the stairs. Other nights, a thin, sorrowing cry that threads through the boards and finds me where I sit with my lamp turned low. With hands folded, I whisper, "Hush," though I have no one to hush but the dark.

The basement. I refuse to descend into the basement when the house cries. Not always. Not unless the sound becomes a shape in my head that I cannot bear. I try to calm myself and reason away what it is: water in the old pipes (though there is no water here since the well turned), foxes keeping counsel in the hedges, a board remembering a footstep from many years ago. Men of sense make such inventories; I have learned to make them too. I whisper the list until my heart settles. Most nights it settles. Most nights.

All of us in this village keep something in our basements. They keep it behind hymns and church words and tallow candles that smell of linen. As for me? I keep mine behind a swollen door with a warped latch and three nails driven in crooked. They make their basements white with lime. I make mine tidy. Inside, there are shelves for jars that hold nothing but the memory of pickling and hooks for coats that will never be worn again. A coil of rope and a hammer with a handle smoothed to a shine by a hand that was not mine. I sweep the dust into obedient piles and tell it where to go. I fold the dead spiders in paper because even they deserve not to be trodden upon. Doing so may be seen as a misfortune. I'm not one for fortune. But if I were, I wouldn't want the ill-boding kind.

The door to my basement often complains of being a door. The frame is out of true; the tongue of the latch sits mean in its keep. There is a sliver between door and jamb as thin as a blade, and that is where the house speaks loudest, from that knife of night. Words just as sharp. On occasion, I will catch myself standing with my ear against that seam like a lover listening for a sigh, and when no sighs come, I am ashamed and also relieved.

I live at the lip of the woods where the road forgets itself and becomes root and leaf and old regrets. I do not go to market when the bell tells me. I go before dawn, when the women whisper their hair into order and the men are still telling their bones to be brave. I like the market best when it is only crates and breath and the shame of vegetables showing themselves without their leaves. Old Marta will sell to me if I do not make her laugh. Laughter costs extra. I can pay it, but it bruises the wallet in the chest.

In the afternoon, the children throw stones at my shutters and call me names I have never been. It is not their fault that their mouths know such words. Often, I dream of rescuing them from their ill-mannered custodians, even just to save them from themselves. Of late, I've been careless with my windows. I keep them curtained, and a curtain is an invitation to imagine a monster. If I were a child, I would throw stones too—just to see if the curtain would lift so I could count the beast's teeth.

Once, in spring, when the river forgot itself and wandered where it ought not, a shoe rode the brown water and fetched up against my step. It was a small shoe, not a baby's slipper, no, something worn to the shape of a running foot and scuffed by the sentence of playing. I keep such things that the river leaves me. I dry them by the stove and set them upon the mantel like saints of lostness. A man who lives alone must have his congregation, lest I be thought insane. I did not know then that the shoe would remember me, that others would make of my mantel a charge-sheet. I knew only that the shoe made a wet shadow on the stone like a word struggling for ink.

On Sundays, the village sings in a cheerful choir, and I sit, watching carefully from a distance. The bell at the center of town tolls as if time were a great animal; the villagers are allowed to strike with a mallet. The road gleams with black boots, dresses, red faces, and hands that cannot help but wave. It is a small place; the wave is a reflex. Even I cannot help a small lifting of fingers. When I catch myself doing it, though, I pretend to be swatting a fly. On this day, the priest often speaks words that are comfortable like old coats; however, I cannot wear them. They hang crooked on me. I've learned not to say this to anyone. It's not kind to laugh at a coat that keeps others warm.

There is a book on my table that I do not read, but keep turned to a page that knows my name. It is not the Bible—do not think me worse than I am. It is a ledger. I write down what the house does. I have taught myself the language of its habits.

"First cockcrow," I will note,

"North shutter clicks twice."

"Midnight," I will put, "knock from under the stairs."

"After the rain," I will write, "the weeping."

I do not call it crying. That would make it a child. I am careful with my words. Words make shapes. Shapes have duties. I am not a man who takes a word's duty lightly.

There are rules. I made them. I obey them. I do not lift the latch after dark. I do not hold a light against the seam of the basement door and say, "Who is there?" I do not sing. I do not pray aloud at the door—for fear a prayer answered might open it.

I slip a crust down the stairs sometimes at noon, when the sun is cruel enough to burn away foolishness. This is for rats, I tell myself, and the rats are grateful. Gratitude is a sound, you know. It has a soft scratch to it. Gratitude eats with dignity.

Once—no, twice—I woke to the taste of dust and the knowledge that I had been speaking in my sleep to the basement. This frightened me more than the weeping. I do not like a mouth to have a will of its own. I do not like to find crumbs on my pillow that I did not put there. I do not like to feel that my tongue has been somewhere without me.

The woods near my house make their own noises and do not ask leave of me. There are owls that have learned the cruel joke of sounding like a woman's sob. There are deer that make a theater of terror, crashing away at the slightest leaf like villains in cheap plays. There are foxes who keep their law better than we keep ours. And then there is something else that belongs neither to the woods nor the world the priest describes. I have not seen it. Do not make more of this than I am saying. I have not seen it. But there are nights when the woods hold their breath—when even the small sins of leaves still—when the wind walks delicately, as if it has been warned that a floorboard will betray it. When even the moon dims its glow.

On such nights, I sit at the top of the stairs and put my hand upon the banister because the banister knows. I can trust the banister. Old wood is a library of grips. It remembers fear, and joy, and men who ran because they were late to something that could not happen without them. When my hand rests and the old wood will not share, I know to make the house smaller: shut doors within doors; snuff two lamps and keep one; bring the kettle to the boil so the steam has something to busy itself with; lay a slice of bread upon the table and do not eat it, so hunger has a decoy. All this is sense if you live alone, where the map no longer remembers its place.

You ask, perhaps, what I do by day. (No one asks; I imagine the question so I may answer it and be orderly.) I mend things that do not deserve mending. I put handles back on drawers that will not be opened again. I sew a button onto a coat that does not fit anyone living. I sweep. I stack wood in patterns I find pleasing, then undo the pattern and tell myself this is wisdom. I listen to the old hens beyond my fence, remarking on the sun as if it were their doing. Sometimes a child—bold, or one whose mother's hand failed to keep its promise—comes as far as my gate, leans through the slats, and asks a question that is not the one they want to ask. I am kind. I answer the question they do not ask. I say, "Yes, the house is old," or, "No, I do not keep wolves," or, "Honey tastes best on yesterday's bread." If they ask what is in the basement (and children always have a nose for basements), I say, "Things that prefer to be left alone," and give them a penny not to prove it.

When I sleep, I dream of steps that go down and never finish—perpetually downward. This is not a metaphor; it is a dream, and in dreams, things are as foolish as they wish. I carry a lamp that wobbles with each footfall and makes of the dark a moving mouth—one that stretches beyond its own maw. In the dream, there is always a sound below me. Sometimes it is water; sometimes it is something wrapped in water. I wake before I can reach it. I wake with the ledger already half open, as if someone had been taking notes while I ran.

Do not think me mad. (There—see how I write to an invisible judge? Habit. There is always an invisible judge somewhere, even if it is only the one you wake with inside your face.) I am not what they say in the square when their voices feel brave in a pack. I am only careful, and I am punished for it with hours. Carefulness stretches time the way hunger stretches a day. There are men who live and do not notice that noon has any particular shape. I am not such a man. I could draw noon for you from memory and make you weep. Perhaps "cautious" isn't the word. "Particular" and "obsessive" seem dishonest.

The house was my father's, and the basement was his father's, and before that, the hole was a hole, and men threw into it the things they could not ask the priest to bless. I have never thanked the hole for keeping our secrets. I have never cursed it either. Courtesy matters with holes. You do not know how deep they are until you have fallen, and then it is too late to be polite.

Sometimes I stand at the back door, watch the line where the trees begin, and count the crows. If there are more than seven, I take it as a reminder to oil the hinges. If fewer, I make tea and pretend to forget the basement. Pretending to forget is a skill. You must practice it, or it rusts and then squeals when you need it quiet.

Tonight, the house is in one of its telling moods. The wind has taken a liking to the eaves and will not be called off. The seam at the basement door is a single black hair. I have set the plate, as I do, with a slice of bread that has grown serious and a rind of cheese that remembers the cow's name. I have not pushed the plate farther than the first step. I am not a fool. I sit with my back to the wall so that if anything wishes to write itself upon me, it must do so from the front like an honest letter.

There—do you hear it? I did not, and then I did. The ledger will say: "After midnight—the weeping." It is a thin thread at first, pulled from something larger. It does not beg. It does not barter. It simply exists, the way a fact exists. I lay my hand upon the table, count the beats within it, and think of all the things men keep in basements: bottles against winter; lambs born wrong in spring; sins with their heads tucked down so as not to be recognized. I think: if a house cries, it is because it has been taught by the men who live in it.

I am tired of being a teacher.

I lift the lamp. I go to the door and lay my ear against the seam—because I am weak. The wood is cool. On the other side, the sound is closer than it has ever been. It is not wind, not pipe, not fox. It has a breath inside it. It has pauses that feel like listening. It has the shape of a throat that learned language and then forgot it, the way old men forget names and never forgive themselves. I set my thumb upon the latch, take it away, set it back—an hour spent on thumb and latch: take and give, rule and breaking. I whisper to the seam, which is to say I whisper to myself, which is to say I whisper to the part of the world that still believes in bargains: "Hush. Hush. Sleep now. I am here. I am here."

The house answers in its way, a settling sigh that moves through the joists and along the nails and up into my teeth. The weeping threads themselves thinner, thinnest, gone, or not gone, only beyond hearing. I stand until the lamp scolds me with the last of its oil. I stand until morning loosens itself from the east like a stain being forgiven. I lock the basement door as if that has ever meant anything. I make tea, I do not drink. I write in the ledger: "Toward dawn. Silence."

Days bled together like ink spilled across parchment, until time itself seemed as formless as the whispers that clung to the edges of my mind. The villagers' eyes followed me—always watching, always narrowing. At the market, a mother would pull her child closer to her skirts when I walked by. At the well, their conversations would hush the moment I dipped my bucket. But the basement was worse than their stares. It became a living thing. It became my own monster.

At night, I heard the creak of the stairs, though I knew I had locked the door with iron and chain. I heard the muffled sobbing, small and broken, like a bird with a bent wing. I heard a child's voice whisper, "Let me out."

I told myself it was only my mind, fractured and jagged like glass. Yet when I lit my lantern and descended, I would find small traces—the toy horse that hadn't been there before, its painted eye staring up from the dirt floor. A smear of mud across the stone. A single tiny footprint pressed deep into the dust.

I tried to reason with myself. The child must be real. Hadn't I pulled him from the edge of the forest? Hadn't I dragged him from the claws of that shadow thing, that slavering maw that hunts after dusk? I remember his eyes, wide with terror, his breath shuddering as I carried him.

So why, when I unlatched the basement door one dawn, was the room empty? Why did the crying still echo when there was no one to cry?

The villagers came more often. They searched my yard, leaving muddy boot prints where my herbs once grew. They tapped at my shutters, daring me to peer back. Once, I found a note nailed to my door. It was only two words: We Know.

I no longer slept. Late Autumn—the crying took my name and said it back to me. I sat at the table with the lantern burning low, staring at my hands—scarred, cracked, stained with dirt that no soap could scrub away. And I listened to the sounds beneath my floor. The scraping. The dragging. The soft, childlike voice that sometimes twisted into laughter.

I try the latch again, but hesitate. My knees weaken. I stagger back, and my foot nudges something. The shoe. Small, leather, cracked at the toe. I cannot remember how long it has sat there— or if I put it there at all.

By the time the mob comes, the shoe is in my hands. By the time their fists slam the door, their torches hissing against the rain, I am clutching it like a relic. They do not want my words. They want spectacle. Their voices braid into one unholy hymn. They drag me through the mud. The ledger I once kept—debts, crops, lost things—is scattered across the square.

One page lands face-up in the muck: After midnight—the weeping.

The priest himself leads the way from my home, holding his cross aloft as if I were the Devil, chanting, quoting scriptures I've never heard on any Sunday mornings. Behind him surge the men with pitchforks, the women with stones, the children with wide, eager eyes. They shout: monster, murderer, beast.

I want to protest—to scream that I saved the boy, that I hid him away from the thing in the woods. But my voice catches, strangled by fear and doubt.

I cannot tell them of the forest—of the thing I saw there: the coal bright eyes, the sickly breath steaming in the cold air. I cannot tell them I pulled the boy away, clutching him as we ran, dragging him screaming through the underbrush.

And I certainly cannot tell them why I brought the boy home, not to his parents, not when I am not sure the thing I saved is even real. For what if they are right? What if the thing in my basement is not the boy at all, but something wearing his skin?

They drag me into the square. They tie the noose while the crowd jeered. The rope felt coarse against my neck. The priest's words ring out like a bell tolling for my soul. And as the rope tightens, I feel an odd relief: the voices will end; the basement will no longer claw at me in the night.

"Confess!" they clamored. "Beg for mercy." So, I confess, though I know not to what. Through mud-choked sobs, the words pour out, nonsensical, desperate: Yes, I took him. Yes, he cried. Yes, the basement... yes, the cries... yes, I did it, I did it, I did it.

The crowd roars. The platform falls.

The world turns black.

Epilogue

When the villagers searched my home, they broke the chains on the basement door. They expected bones, blood, horrors unspeakable. Instead, they found the boy.

Alive.

He was pale and thin, but unharmed. He told them through tears that I had rescued him from the woods, from the monster that stalked there, all eyes and teeth. That I had given him bread and promised to keep him safe until it was gone.

He showed them the toy horse I had found on the floor. He showed them where I had laid a blanket for him to sleep.

But when they asked why he never cried out, why he never tried to escape, he only looked at the basement walls with a shiver.

"Because he told me not to," the boy whispered. "Not the man. The other voice. The one in the dark. He said if I screamed, it would find us again."

The villagers left my house in silence that night, their torches guttering low. And the basement door was nailed shut, a final time—for what we keep in the basement keeps us, too.

A Sheep in Wolves' Clothing
Part One

The Scarlet Girl,

You are too late.
I can still taste her on my tongue. Old flesh—sweet with the fat of years, stringy at the joints. I chew slowly, so she feels each tooth. Her bones snap like twigs.

I wear her face now. Still warm. Still wet.

Do you still wear the cloak she stitched for you? It reeks of her. I follow that scent through every tree until it steams in my jaws. I remember the stories she told you at night—her soft voice holding back the dark. I whisper them back to you between bites.
When I find you, I begin with your throat. The first bite pours fire down my throat. The second buckles your knees. The third— ah, the third is always the sweetest. I do not swallow whole. Not this time. I take you in pieces. Morsel by morsel, twitch by twitch.
Run if you like, little scarlet thing. The woods are mine. The night is mine. You are mine.
—*The Wolf*

Benjamin C. Bailey

The Mocking-glass Diaries

My curious Alice,

Why do you always try to leave me? You scratch at the walls of sleep as though daylight has something better to offer than this garden of shadows. Have you forgotten the taste of wonder? The thrill of falling forever, the way the air itself bent to hold you? You should stay. You must stay. We should stay.

Alice,

You speak like a jailer. I remember the blood on the roses, the eyes that blinked where no eyes should be. The clocks with their hands torn off. The wind, whispering in tea-drunken riddles. That was not wonder; it was a labyrinth of knives. It was a shadow without a host. I ache to wake, to breathe air that doesn't laugh when I choke.

Stay. Stay with me. Stay with us. You know the world above is dull, cruel in its straight lines and small rules. Here, at least, cruelty is honest. The Queen cuts off heads because she can. The Hare drinks poison because he wants to. The Hatter defies sanity, for to obey it would be the true madness. Why should you want less than them?

But I tire, Alice. I tire of your games. You are not my friend but my shadow. You turn every joy into a riddle with teeth. You tell me hunger is a banquet; you tell me death is a dance. I do not believe you anymore.

You didn't write this letter, Alice. I did. Yet here you are, reading my words as if they were yours.

Believe me, Alice, believe me. I am the truest part of you. When you speak to yourself in mirrors, when you whisper things no one must hear—that is me. You would wither without me. You would grow up, grow old, grow ordinary. And you are not ordinary. You are a dream that bites.

If I am the dream, you are the nightmare. We should not be one.

We cannot be two.

But which of us will the world keep when the glass breaks?

I hold the key.
I hold the blade.
I hold the thread of your name.

So, choose Alice.

Stay. Go.
Stay. Go.
Stay go stay go stay—

I will decide for us.

The Headless Letters
Part One

To the Rider,

They tell me you are not real. They say you are nothing more than an illness, a shadow I wear to frighten myself.

But I remember the gallop.

I remember the wind in my eyes and the pounding hooves that were not under me but inside me—mocking the very rhythm of my heart.

When I close my eyes, I hear the creak of leather, the pull of reins. Sometimes I wake with the taste of iron in my mouth and mud between my teeth. That is when I know you have been nearest.

At times, there are bruises on my thighs as though I had been riding through the night, though no horse waits in my stall.

I do not speak of it anymore.

Once, I told the schoolmaster's wife what I had seen, and she laughed until her face went red.

Once, I confessed it to the parson, and he warned me against the spirits of drink.

They all think it is weakness, or worse, a sin.
So, I write only to you. You who already know.

I beg you—if you must take something, take my sleep.
Take the tremor in my hands.
Take the hunger I have for the road.
But please, I beg of you—please.
Leave me my head.

I am not ready to lose it.

—Ichabod

Cecilia

The dark pressed in tight, claustrophobic, wrapping me in a chilling void. Panic struck my heart as I realized I could not see.

My first thought was that I had gone blind. The second was worse—that I had been buried alive.

My hands clawed at stone, slick with sweat, and the air scalded my throat as if it had already been stolen by something else. I staggered forward until iron yanked me back. The chain screamed against rock, sharp enough to cut the dark, echoing twice, three times, like sadistic laughter.

I pulled harder. Shackles clamped my ankles, the skin rubbed raw from struggle. My fingers searched for the seam, the hinge, the miracle that wasn't there. Only cold steel, locked sure, a cruel geometry drawn tight around me.

I shouted into the void. "Hello?" The word struck stone and fell dead. I shouted again until the cave gave me only my own voice—thin, trembling, useless.

Silence. Too heavy. The kind of silence that has weight, that drags me to my knees. And then—I hear it…

A drip. A shift. The scrape of a claw against rock.

The air changed. Musk and rot, copper and wet fur. My breath stuttered. I pressed into the wall, wishing I could vanish into its veins.

Something moved. Slow. Deliberate. Not the scatter of an animal, but a tread that knew itself. Leather creaked, breath poured hot. The smell of it flooded my nose until I gagged. I did not scream. Screaming would make me prey.

A shape broke the darkness—massive, crouched low, eyes burning like coins dropped in tar. It drew closer, dragging its claws along the stone just to let me hear how near it was. Each scrape a promise. The walls of my dark prison began to close in. There was no escape.

I shrank back until the iron chain cut into my legs. The beast filled the space between heartbeats. It had been waiting. Waiting for me to wake.

In the darkness, a shadow emerged. Long, bent, wrong. A distortion crawled up the stone until it loomed taller than the ceiling. I pressed my hand to my mouth to smother breath, but my heartbeat betrayed me, rattling the chain with every pulse.

The Beast heard it. Its head tilted, the way a hound tilts at a whistle only it can hear.

It moved closer. Four limbs scraped and thudded unevenly— half man, half animal, complete hunger.

It stopped just at the edge of my fear's small light. Close enough that I felt the heat radiating off its body. Close enough that the stink of damp fur and blood turned my stomach to water.

A claw brushed my ankle. Testing. Not striking. Just a graze sharp enough to raise gooseflesh. A promise: it could cut if it wished.

I swallowed a scream. The Beast leaned nearer. I heard the wet roll of breath in its throat, a growl so low it seemed to rise from the stone itself.

Something hot touched my cheek—a nose, a muzzle. It inhaled me. Long, slow, greedy.

And then—pain.

Sudden. Sharp. Teeth—not biting but nipping, a playful cruelty. Enough to tear skin, to draw blood. My gasp shattered the silence like glass.

The Beast pulled back, satisfied. I could not see its smile, but I felt it—the air shifting with amusement, its breath quickening with triumph.

It knew I would not run. It knew I could not run. The chain at my ankle was not just iron. It was a leash.

It circled me once, claws dragging across the stone like chalk on slate. Then, without warning, it lunged. This time, its teeth sank into the soft place of my shoulder. Not clean. Not merciful. Anchored there, it convulsed, worrying me like a dog with a rag, shaking until bone grated, until the joint screamed in its socket.

My cry echoed off the walls and came back to me sounding like another woman's voice.

When it released me, the wound wept heat down my breasts. I clutched it, white-hot, fingers slick, slipping. My sobs came ragged, breathless.

The Beast sat back on its haunches, tongue lapping at the blood on its muzzle like a connoisseur, savoring each drop. The wet rasp of tongue against jowl echoed off the stone, insidious in the void.

I wanted to faint. To fall away into blackness and never wake. But the chain yanked taut, holding me upright, forcing me to watch it savor me. The Beast had marked me.

Not to kill. Not yet. To remind me, I was meat. And worse—property.

I sat in the darkness, naked, cold, starving. Nights passed. The pain never left. It only learned new disguises. The wound at my shoulder—the one he had given me that first night—sealed into a stiff scar. But upon his return, his claws found it again. Opening and reopening the same wound.

He never struck the same way twice. A slice became a gouge. A bruise became a fracture. He made of my flesh a ledger, and he alone held the quill.

When I thought myself mended, he tore the scab open again with the ease of a surgeon who enjoys his craft. Sometimes he pressed a single claw beneath the seam of healing skin and peeled it back, smiling to see me convulse. Sometimes he waited until I dared to hope I had been forgotten, then came in silence to rip me from sleep with fresh agony.

My legs fared worst of all. One he broke outright—a sharp crack that split through the cave like thunder. He left it to mend crooked, and when weeks had passed and I limped in pitiful circles, he shattered it again. The sound of it became a prophecy, a frost-bitten branch snapping in my memory long before he touched me.

I crawled in the dark on my knees, the bones grinding, my palms raw against stone. Even in his absence, pain was his voice, and I listened.

When he fed me, it was never kindness. Scraps of gristle, cartilage, things a dog would turn from—these I devoured. Sometimes he spat marrow-slick bones onto the cave floor and watched me suck them hollow, his golden eyes glinting. Once, he pushed a shred of flesh toward me, a strip of muscle red as a butcher's display. I ate, gagging, until I found a ring still circling the knuckle.

He laughed—a sound like a growl dragged through broken glass—and left me with it clutched in my hand. I keep the ring even now, tied at my throat with a strip of leather, as if it were a vow.

Time dissolved in that place. The dark unthreaded the hours until I no longer knew day from night. I learned to measure time by what the cave offered: the steady drip of water down the walls, the ragged drum of my heart, the rasp of my nails scratching stone, the way hunger bent my spine tighter each week until my body folded like parchment.

When he left me breathing, I carved a notch into the floor with whatever fragment of bone I could scavenge. The stone is crowded now with months of marks, each one a monument to survival, each one a prayer unanswered—a calendar no eyes will ever read.

At first, I prayed. To God. To my father. To anyone who might pierce the walls of stone. But prayer soured, rotted on my tongue.

I learned instead to whisper bargains—small, trembling words that wavered like a flame in the wind: let him not come tonight, let the pain be lighter, let me keep my head above the tide.

But months of torment withered the bargains into longing. I whispered to the walls: Come back. Breathe on me. Hurt me. Do not leave me alone in this silence that gapes wider than your teeth.

When he came, I watched his shadow lengthen, breathed in his musk like incense, choking but holy. My absence from him became its own wound. My hatred fermented into hunger. His claws at my throat became a promise.

I do not know when it happened, the turning. Only that I began to wait for him. That I woke from dreams, clawing at the chain, not to escape, but to summon him nearer. That sometimes I held the ring at my throat and whispered my name upon it, hoping the word itself would bleed him into being. Cecelia, I'd whisper into the dark, imagining his teeth closing over the syllables, tearing me open with the sound.

Once, there came a night when he did not come.

I lay in silence, the stone pressing its chill through my bare skin, and waited for the scrape of claws, the musk of fur, the rush of breath at my ear. The minutes stretched like centuries, each one ticked by the drum of my heart, each one tightening the coil inside me until it snapped. My nails raked lines into my scalp. I yanked at my own hair until strands tore free. I bit down on the flesh of my wrist, desperate to feel anything, to conjure pain in his absence.

At last, the ache grew unbearable. My scalp still stung from torn hair; my wrist still bore the crescent marks of my teeth—but none of it was enough. I dug my nails into an old scar until it yielded with a wet sigh, splitting open like fruit too long left to rot. The sting was sharp, hot, alive, and I tore it wider, coaxing the blood to bloom across my ribs, and the pain sang to me. It was his voice reborn in my hand, the echo of him, the proof that he would return. I licked the copper from my fingers, moaning at the warmth, and whispered his name into the hollow cave.

When he came at last, his eyes found the glimmer of blood. He sniffed, low and pleased, circling me as though I were a carcass laid out in honor, a feast waiting only for his blessing. With a growl almost tender, he pressed his muzzle to the wound and drank. The rasp of his tongue scoured my skin raw, each lap a brand, each breath against my chest a benediction. I shuddered, my thighs tightening, a cry escaping me—not fear, not pain, but something deeper. He growled then, jagged and cruel, the sound splitting the dark, and I trembled not from terror but from joy at being heard.

After that night, I learned to make offerings, and the offerings became prayers. A slice across my thigh with a shard of stone, the blood flowing in slow rivulets that traced their own scripture. A bruise hammered into my arm against the cave wall until the flesh sang purple, until the ache bloomed like a psalm in my bones. I would sit there, trembling, blood dripping in bright beads onto the dirt, and I would wait, patient, reverent, longing for him to come and complete the ritual I had begun.

When he came, his teeth traced the rivers I had carved, following them like sacred paths written only for him. His claws pressed into the bruises until my back arched in welcome, until I was a vessel for nothing but his hunger. And the more I offered, the gentler he became—not because he was merciful, but because my suffering pleased him best when it was freely given, when it was chosen, when it was a gift.

In time, I began to whisper to him. Little prayers at first, breaking against my teeth: Take me. Break me. Drink me. I am yours. He answered with teeth and silence, yet I swore he listened, swore that each wound he gave in return was its own vow, a binding of flesh to flesh, blood to blood.

Once, he pinned me to the stone, his snout buried in the hollow of my throat. My pulse hammered there, begging to be crushed, begging to be swallowed. I tilted my head back, offering it freely. But he did not bite. He only held me, his breath hot as fever against my skin, until I sobbed with the hunger of it, until I wept with the knowledge that even my surrender could not sate him, because he wanted not only my flesh but my soul.

That was the night I understood: the torment was no longer punishment.

It was communion.

I began to crave the snap of my own bone, the stretch of torn flesh, the gnashing of teeth, if only because it meant his presence, his mouth, his weight crushing me into something holy. When he carved new marks into me, I wept not for the pain but for the beauty of belonging, the rapture of being remade in his hands.

Even in dreams, I sought him. Dreams where his claws opened me wide, and I did not fear. Where his teeth sank deep, and I laughed through blood-choked sighs of pleasure. Where his hunger met mine, and I was whole only in breaking.

Now, when he comes, I do not cower. I rise to meet him, trembling with anticipation, my body thrumming with old wounds, with new ones, with the ones I make in his absence. And when his shadow falls over me, vast and holy, I whisper with reverence:

"More."

Nights pass and the ritual continues. Months, maybe years. Until one night, he came later than he ever had, his step slower, his breath ragged. His flank carried a gash, fresh and wet, fur matted with blood not his own. He staggered, and for the first time I felt something sharp, something foreign—pity.

I reached for him, scarred hands trembling as they brushed the bristle of his chest. "You hurt," I whispered, and for a flicker, I believed he might let me tend him. His eyes glimmered with something too human, too fragile.

Then the moment broke. His weight crashed over me, claws pinning my shoulders, his muzzle pressing to my throat—not gently, not pleading, but claiming.

Pain flared as his teeth sank deep. I cried out, but the cry twisted, lifted, broke into a gasp. His jaws ripped deeper into me than ever before, but his tongue soothed in the same breath, drinking from me as if I were a chalice. My body writhed beneath him, trembling with a hunger that was not wholly mine.

Each bite tore me open. Each lick stitched me closer. His breath scalded my chest; his weight pressed my breasts tight against his blood-slick fur. My thighs quivered, the wetness and heat from between spilling down them, pooling on the stone. I shook, arched, pleaded wordlessly with every shudder of my body.

Ecstasy and agony braided tighter, tighter, until the coil of me snapped.

The cave rang with my scream—no, my prayer—as I convulsed, my body buckling, releasing, collapsing beneath him. His growl rolled through me, vibrating in my ribs, rattling my heart, until my vision fractured into white. My final breath tore loose in a sob that was also a moan, also a laugh, also a farewell.

I lay limp. Empty. My blood spread warm across the stone, steaming faintly in the cave's chill. The air smelled of copper and musk and smoke. For a long moment, there was only silence.

Only the stillness of death.

Silence.

Darkness.

Then more silence.

The chain no longer bit at my ankle. The stone no longer pressed against my back. The wounds no longer burned. I felt nothing, and in the nothing was rest. A peace so profound I wanted to weep for it, though even my tears had gone quiet. My body, unburdened and heavy, surrendered to stillness. The cave held its breath with me, as it too knew I had been set free.

For the first time since the dark swallowed me, I felt safe. I thought: it ends here. Let my blood seep into the stone, let my name fade from my lips, let silence cradle me like a mother rocking her child. I thought: how kind it is to die. To know rest.

Stone cold against my cheek, my body slack and emptied. The stillness lingered. The darkness mourned. The nightmare had ended.

It was finally over.

And then—

A twitch.

My fingers spasmed against the rock. My chest shuddered
with a ragged half-breath, though no air should have entered it.
My peace cracked.

Pain bloomed anew, not sharp but spreading, molten, alive.
My wounds—those ragged gifts—refused to close. They widened,
splitting as though the flesh itself rejected its old shape, as though
death itself had denied me.

I folded inside out, a grotesque inversion of myself. My
organs bulged, exposed, writhing as my bones twisted inward. My
ribs creaked, stretching, warping. My jaw unhinged with an ear-
shattering snap. I tried to scream, but the sound that tore out was
not mine—a wet, gurgling snarl that made the stone itself tremble.

My skin writhed. Beneath it, muscles knotted and surged,
tearing themselves free from bone. Old scars split and peeled,
bleeding not red but black. My veins writhed like worms beneath
my flesh, shifting in patterns too deliberate to be mine. My thighs
burned as new cords of sinew coiled thick, pulling me upright
though my spine bent and twisted like rope.

Fingers cracked, nails lengthened into claws slick with my own
gore. My mouth filled with too many teeth, growing, shedding,
growing again. My tongue split, reknit, coiled against the roof of
my mouth.

Hair—coarse, bristled, rank with blood—burst from my skin
in patches, spreading as if the cave itself were weaving me into fur.
I fell to all fours. I rose on two. I fell again. The cave echoed with
bone breaking, mending, breaking again.

My breasts shrank against my chest, then swelled anew,
heavier, more bestial, the flesh torn but proud, aching with a
strange, primal hunger. My womb convulsed as though quickened
by something not human at all.

I was no longer mine.

And through it all, I laughed.

A choking, ragged laugh that curdled into howls. When at last the spasms quieted, I knelt in the muck of my blood and torn flesh, panting, shivering, alive. No longer human. The only thing left of my old self was the ring upon its leather cord, still tied around my throat. The rest of me was a puddle of ichor beneath my knees.

The cave smelled new. The air tasted sharp. My heart thundered not with fear, but with want. In the shadows, he waited—my beast, my tormentor, my bridegroom of ruin. He lowered his head in recognition.

For the first time in ages, I could see again. The darkness, no longer a veil. My vision now heightened—I could finally gaze upon him. My one true love.

He was more majestic than I could imagine. Broad and savage. Muscular. Fur darker than onyx. Eyes of coal. Teeth like daggers. My tormentor. My savior. My lover.

I crawled to him, claws clicking on the stone, and pressed my face against his chest. His breath washed over me, rank and sweet. For the first time, I did not feel owned. I felt equal.

We were a pair.
Hunger and hunger.
Fang and fang.
Wound and wound.
And together, we would feed.

We did not linger. The hunger would not let us.
The night outside welcomed me like a second skin. The moon baptized us in sinister glow.
My new muscles burned with need as I ran, half-crawling, half-leaping, the forest bending beneath me as though it had

always been mine. The beast ran beside me, stride long, confident, his wounds forgotten in the thrill of the chase.

I smelled them before I saw them—villagers, clustered near their fires, their smoke thick with meat and laughter. The sound of their joy cracked against my ears like whips. My throat rumbled.

We circled them. My claws dug furrows into the earth as I crouched, every tendon drawn tight. My body still remembered the girl who pitied, who prayed. She still twitched inside me, whispering to stop. I crushed her beneath the weight of my hunger.

He moved first—a blur of shadow and fang. Screams scattered the camp. I followed, not with hesitation but with glee.

I fell upon a man who tried to flee, his back turned. My claws hooked his spine and dragged him down. His breath burst in a squeal. He lay prone, flat to the dirt. Without thinking, I buried my teeth in his throat. With a clean jerk, I tore through, my teeth scraping bone.

The warmth flooded me. Hot. Metallic. Alive. Blood poured into me, over me, anointing me. He thrashed, and I pressed harder, my new strength pinning him like a rabbit. His pulse slowed. Then stilled.

I lifted my head, crimson soaking my lips, and met the beast's eyes across the firelight. He snarled approval. And I knew the truth: I was no longer prey. I was mate. Bride.

Together we tore through the camp—teeth and claws, shrieks and firelight. The world narrowed to the ecstasy of the kill, the communion of blood.

When it was done, when silence and smoke were all that remained, when fragments of bodies scattered the ground, we stood side by side, slick with gore, our breath steaming in the cold air. And for the first time, I smiled.

No longer blind. No longer Cecilia. No longer human. No longer captive. I was reborn in ruin. I was the beast. I was hunger made flesh. And at his side,

I would never beg again.

Unnamed Journal Entry Two

December 24th 1733

I survived, though I know not how. Ages alone. Unyielding. Unable to die, unable even to rot. Decay fled me as though I were a blight that might strip the marrow from it, should it dare to look upon me.

Only the moon's black shadow knows how long I lay there, desperate, feeble, my spine stiffening with age. Staring into the heavens, night upon night, I sought a name to take. Orion. Leo. Aries. None answered.

Hope withered into despair. Despair curdled into retribution. Retribution festered into malice. And when the last light of the candle whispered out, they found me—buried beneath the snow.

The touch of another's hand was alien in its warmth. I recoiled, yet still I could not move. I tried to protest the gentle embrace, and it burned with embers too fierce to bear. A torment upon my twisted soul. Everything within me screamed to flee, yet I was powerless. To speak. To stir. To do aught but endure.

They lifted me. Brushed me free of frost as though unearthing a relic. Their breath hissed with awe; their eyes glistened with greed. One whispered prayers over me, the other spat to ward off evil. Both were right to tremble.

Days stretched into months; months bled into years; years unraveled into decades. More came for me, passing me from hand to hungry hand. Each as ravenous as the last, seeking ancient truths. They gazed at me, scrawling their lies in the margins of my soul.

At first, they made of me a spectacle. Displayed. Examined. Gawked at each detail. They argued about origins, forged stories to give me pedigree. One crowned me holy, claiming I carried blessings penned by saints. Another hissed I was a devil's offspring, forged in the marrow of the damned. Their mouths warred while their fingers ravaged my lifeless form.

Then, as time wore on, their wonder waned. They cast me aside, locked me in basements, in cellars, leaving me to dust and silence. In monasteries, I was chained, clamped with iron as though simple iron might tame me. In universities, I was dissected, until scholars' candlelight became mere dust. Leaving me half-forgotten in their laboratories. In manors, I was paraded before dinner guests, more ornament than oracle. And when the masters died, their heirs tossed me in trunks, stuffed me behind wine casks, pawned me for coin, unaware what they held.

Yet I endured.

I felt the tremor of every hand, the grease of every fingertip, the fever of every eye that dared pry into me. They believed themselves observers; yet, they knew not that I was the one watching them.

I recall a monk who prayed blessings over me each night, as though piety could soften my hunger. He dreamt of angels but woke shrieking of serpents, his hair turned white before its time. I recall a widow who clutched me in her grief, whispering her husband's name into me as though I might return him. I kept his name. She wasted away. I recall a merchant who wagered me in a game of dice. He lost, and as the victor reached to claim me, the merchant's throat closed, and he died there at the table, his tongue swollen, unable to cry out. The victor hesitated, then touched me—and in touching, damned himself in turn.

The centuries bruised me, but I never broke.

I grew heavy with their words. Heavy with their secrets, their bargains, their lies. My silence thickened into witness. My witness hardened into memory. And my memory, like stone, can never be chiseled smooth again.

Still, they treated me as an object. They wrapped me in velvet, they pressed me between boards, they smuggled me in coffins across borders. Once, soldiers plundered me from a burning chapel, shoving me into a sack with candlesticks and chalices. Once, a king traded me for land, his laughter loud until one slit his throat for the privilege of holding me a moment longer. Once, a noblewoman pressed me to her breast as fire consumed her estate, whispering that if her children perished, at least I would remember their names. She died choking on smoke. I did indeed remember their names—each and every one.

And still, they knew not. They knew not that I endured, aware in ways they could not name. Still searching.

So, I listened. I watched. With resolute silence, I recorded their stories. I consumed their letters, their ledgers, their prayers. I spoke their names in the dark where no ears could hear. Still searching for one to take as my own. Devouring each as they settled inside me.

Time crawled onward, dragging me across continents. Plagues thinned the fingers that touched me, but always others came, desperate, hollow-eyed, clutching at me like a relic of salvation. Wars raged; kings rose and fell; borders bled and redrew themselves, yet still I endured, gathering, storing, waiting.

I remember the executioners who used me to tally the condemned, each name carved upon my frame and each name crossed. Their rope frayed. Their axes dulled. But the names burned into me, unerasable. I remember the alchemist who traced sigils into my very grain, promising he would feed me gold until I answered him. He fed me with his madness instead. When they found him, his corpse was blackened, his teeth fused as though molten lead had poured through his mouth. Still, his name lingers inside me.

Still, I remember and I wait. If you are reading this now, know that I am still listening. And know that I am still waiting.

The Doctor's Orders
Part One

Henry,

You pitiful wretch. You scratch sermons in that laboratory as though ink could cleanse your trembling. I have watched your hand falter upon the page, quivering like some palsied hag, while mine cuts itself into the flesh of the world. You call it "research." I call it cowardice.

You strut about with talk of restraint, of virtue. Yet restraint is your noose, and virtue a mask no one believes. They laugh at you, Henry. They laugh when you preach, they laugh when you bow. To their faces, you are nothing but a hollow man with hollow words. And I, who wear your name when it pleases me, prove it with every breath.

I am the marrow in your bones, the heat in your blood, the twitch in your hand when you kneel to pray. Tell me, when you clasp your hands and mumble into the void, do you hear silence? That silence is mine. That emptiness is me. You cannot banish me with prayer. You cannot bury me with books. You lock your doors, yet I hold the key. You bind your appetites, yet I drape them about my neck like ornaments. I am not your shame—I am your truth.

And tell me, Henry, how fares your wife? Do you believe she clings to your trembling hands, your ink-stained fingers, your sickly smile? You know better. She clings to me—to my cruelty, my hunger. She shudders beneath me with the heat you never once roused. I am the fire in her loins, the ache in her thighs, the voice she muffles with her pillow while you dream of salvation. You give her sermons; I give her flesh. When her lips part, it is not your name that escapes—it is mine. She is mine, Henry, as surely as I am yours. Your vows are ash. Your bed belongs to me alone.

I see the way she looks at you—with pity, with contempt. She cannot speak it, but I hear it in the silence between you: she would sooner have one night of my violence than a lifetime of your virtue. You starve her with platitudes; I feed her desire. You call it sin. She calls it life.

And what of your little vials? You clutch them as though salvation might be corked in glass. Poison, medicine, alchemy— the name matters not. Do you think that when you drink, you slay me? Fool. When you drink, it is I who swallows. I who grow sleek upon your despair. Your faith, your science, your trembling self-denial—all fatten me.

So, scribble, old man. Scribble and pray. Every word you scratch is mine. Every thought is mine. Every breath is mine to snatch when I please. You are but the dream—I am the waking nightmare.

And when at last your hand falters, when your draught scorches your throat and your heart quivers like a snared bird, I shall wear your name like a stolen coat. I shall walk among them in your skin, smiling with your lips, clasping hands with your friends, bedding your wife, and none shall know.

You are already dead, Henry. Too craven to live. Too cowardly to end. And so, I endure, and you—you rot inside your own skull, a ghost trapped in a cage you built.

—*H*

The Name Thief
Part One

They call me thief, but I never took a coin I didn't need, nor a loaf I couldn't pay for.

No—my trade is rarer.

I steal what men guard tighter than their purses, closer than their blood.

I steal names.

It isn't sorcery, though some will swear it is. Not quite trickery either, though I won't pretend I've no gift for sleight. It is a craft in between, learned by listening for what slips easiest from a man's mouth. A name is a tether—a string tying oneself to the world. I only need a knife sharp enough to cut it.

The first time was an accident. I was a boy in rags, clutching bread too hot to hold, running from the baker's curses. He shouted my name as he gave chase—but the word never landed. It stuck on his tongue. He faltered, confused, as though he'd forgotten who he pursued. I kept the loaf, and I kept the word too, rolling it on my tongue until it turned sweet as honey. The baker never remembered me again. A lesson was learned: cut the right string, and a man is lost.

Since then, I've made it my art. I pluck names from ledgers while the ink is still wet, the letters bleeding into loops and stains. I snatch them from lips mid-speech, leaving the speaker stammering. I lift them from gravestones so the dead may never rest, nor be called by mourning kin. I've even stolen a name from the hush between mother and babe, leaving the child nameless until another word was forced upon it.

What I do is not cruelty. It is justice.

Think of it: a debtor, hounded near to death, freed the instant his name slips the collector's tongue. He is no one, and so owes nothing.

Or the husband whose wife spat his name in scorn—I took it. Left her only "husband" to call him. She softened. Love returned, or habit at least.

A priest grew fat on tithes; his sermons signed in bold flourish. I plucked his name from the page. The ink blurred to nonsense, his pride unmarked, his papers worthless.

Tell me, is that theft? Or balance?

I won't claim I've never profited. A man must eat. I've sold names before—sharp, rare names that open doors and bend ears. But always I tell myself: better I keep them than the one who bore them unworthily. Better a name live in my pocket than die on a liar's lips.

Still doubt me? Then speak your name now. Go on. Say it aloud. Or whisper it in your mind. Either way, you'll feel the tug, pulling in your chest.

A name is more binding than rope, sharper than oath, heavier than stone. I am proof. I carry more names than any king. Whole families lie folded in my coat, syllables tucked neat as coins. If I spoke them all at once, the world itself would stagger.

And yet—

One must be careful. Names are not playthings. Some are weighted, heavy with sin, slick with blood. You never know what you've cut loose until it coils 'round your throat.

That lesson, I learned in a tavern.

But let me not leap too far ahead. You want stories, I see it in your eyes. You want to know how a man such as I spends his spoils. Very well.

There was a debtor, poor wretch, eyes ringed dark as coin. He begged me to ease him. So, I found his collector, shadowed close, and when the name left his lips across the square, the syllables dissolved. The collector blinked, scowled, but could not recall the sound. He walked away empty. The debtor wept with relief, clutching my hand as though I were Christ himself. He never saw me pluck his own name from the dust and pocket it—quick, deft. Still warm from his lips.

Another time, in a graveyard. The sexton's lantern burned low, fog clung to the stones. I traced the chiseling with my finger—Margaret, carved deep, sharp despite the years. I whispered it once, twice. Then I pulled. The sound came free like a thread tugged from cloth. The letters blurred before my eyes, sinking back into granite until the stone was bare. Her kin came the next day and could not find her resting place. Their grief doubled. But her name was mine, ringing like a bell in my mouth.

Cruel? Perhaps. But who mourns the nameless? The world forgets them soon enough. Better I keep them safe, unforgotten. I tell you these things not to boast, though I'd be lying if I said there's no pleasure in it. I tell you because you must understand how simple it is. A word. A slip. A silence held a heartbeat too long. That's all it takes. And now you'll understand why that night in the tavern, I simply could not resist.

See, there are places a man goes when he wishes to forget himself: the gaming hall, the brothel, the riverbank with stones heavy enough for the pockets. But most choose the tavern. It is the cheapest place to lose one's cares, and the most honest. A man who drinks himself blind is telling the world plainly: I no longer wish to be what I am.

I like taverns. They suit me. The air is thick with smoke and sweat, with fiddle-tunes scraping against rafters, with ale spilling sticky on the planks. In such a din, no man listens too closely to another's words. Names slip easiest there—shouted too loud, slurred too loose, traded like coins across the table. And when they slip, I catch them.

That night, the place was full. A storm had driven every sodden soul into the hearthlight. Cloaks dripped by the door, boots stamped mud onto the rushes, tankards clattered in rhythm to the storm outside. I sat in the corner, nursing a thin ale that tasted more of tin than barley. I was not drinking for pleasure but for business. For me, a tavern is a market—if you know what you're buying.

The fiddler scraped out a reel that made the drunks pound their mugs. A serving girl with a black eye balanced six tankards in her hands. The landlord dozed behind the bar, though his ears pricked at every coin dropped on the counter. Ordinary noise, ordinary night.

Until I heard him.

At the far bench sat a man, drenched from the rain, red-faced, his shirt half-unbuttoned, soiled. The few strands of hair he had left were in a tussle upon his balding pate. He spoke too loud for comfort, too bitter for jest. And he spoke his name. Louder, and louder still, as though spitting phlegm.

"Curse my name!" he shouted, slamming the table. Foam leapt from his tankard. "Curse it to the pit! My bleed'in name's brought me nothing but ruin. Nothing but ruin, d'you hear?"

The men beside him shifted uneasily. One laughed too loudly, hoping to quiet the storm. But the fellow bellowed again, daring the world to hear. He cursed himself with every swallow, each time sending the word out like a coin tossed to the floor.

I smiled.

Most guard their names closely. They speak them rarely, with care, as one does with prayers or promises. They sign them slowly, in careful ink, and seal them under wax. They know—though few will admit it—that a name is a tether. It binds a man to the world, to his debts, his duties, his loves, his sins. But here was this fool, throwing his about in a drunken tantrum, flinging his tether like a rope across the tavern floor. And I? I have always had a knife sharp enough to cut such ropes clean.

I rose easily, as though fetching another drink. No one noticed. The storm outside boomed against the shutters, drowning the scrape of my boots. I drifted near, leaned a shoulder against the post by his bench, and listened. His words came thick with ale, heavy with self-loathing. He cursed himself once more, speaking his name, syllables fat and swollen with drink.

I reached—not with hand, not yet, but with the part of me that knows how to tug at threads others cannot see. I felt it straining, ripe for the plucking. The next curse he spat would be my moment.

As the word left his lips, I cut. A quick tug, sharp as a coin flipped from a thumb, and the sound was mine. It wriggled, resisted, then came free, hot in my palm. Slimy. Wet. Sticky as mucus.

The drunkard choked mid-word. His throat closed on nothing. His lips moved soundlessly. His eyes went wide, confused, frightened. He tried again, louder, desperate—nothing. His own name would no longer serve him.

He looked to his companions, begging them to remember him. They frowned. One shook his head. Another muttered, "What's wrong with you, can't handle your drink? Speak plain." Already, they'd forgotten him. Already, he was becoming mist in their minds. A man without a name is no man at all.

I slipped the word into my coat, folding it neatly like a letter. It writhed there, twisting like a worm. As names sometimes do. Each one carries weight—some sharp as knives, others dull as stones. This one burned bitter on my tongue when I tasted it, but strong. Strong enough to keep, strong enough to trade.

The drunk staggered to his feet, knocking the table askew. Ale spilled, bread toppled to the floor. He lurched for the door, shoving past the landlord's wife, who swore at him. He did not answer. Could not. He burst into the night, nameless, forgotten already by those who had drunk beside him. By dawn, no soul would remember he had ever sat there.

The tavern roared on as if nothing had passed. Dice rattled in cups, fists pounded the table, the fiddler struck a merrier tune. But I sat back down, called for a better ale, and raised it to my lips with a grin.

A clean theft. A worthy prize. Another name to add to my keeping.

It was the morning after, when the rain had gone soft and the streets steamed like a boiling pot, that I first felt the change.

I walked among the stalls of the market, coat snug, hat tipped low. The name I had taken burned faint in my pocket still, a stone I could not quite spit out. No matter—names often settle. Some fight, some sulk, but in the end, they bend.

Yet, as I passed the fishmonger, gutting haddock with his bare hands, he looked up and called to me. Not my name—no. The name I had taken. I stopped, startled, but he grinned as though greeting an old customer. "You want the heads again? For the stew?" I laughed it off, waved a hand, pressed on. But the sound of it clung to me, foul as the fish guts upon the monger's apron.

Moments later, at the baker's stall, a woman brushed flour from her arms, peered closely, then said the same cursed name. Sweet as honey on her lips, as if she'd known me all her life. I bought a loaf, only to toss it to a few street children running by. My mouth soured, spoiled, like meat left too long to turn.

The name was everywhere. I heard it from the lips of children chasing hoops, chanting it like a game. I heard it muttered by an old man to his dog, who turned and barked at me as though I were truly his master. Even the beggar by the steps of the chapel croaked it at me, his blind eyes flaring wide as if he saw me for the first time.

By the time I reached the inn, my skin crawled with every step, as though the very cobbles whispered that cursed name. I shut myself in my room, barred the door, drew the name from my coat, and laid it flat on the table. It twitched—yes, twitched, like a beetle on its back. Names aren't meant to live long out of mouths. Yet this one writhed, stubborn. I pressed it flat with my palm, muttered a curse, and shoved it back into the dark. Sleep did not come easily, but I eventually managed to force it upon myself.

The next day, I was cautious. I kept to the shadows and alleyways, trying to keep clear of those who had mistaken me the day before. I crept into the alley behind the candlemaker's shop. I came across a group of children playing nine-men's-morris on the stones when a hand clamped my shoulder.

"By order of the magistrate, and the king himself," a guard barked, "you are charged to come with us."

I twisted free, indignant. "For what crime?" I demanded.

A second guard approached from behind, his grip tightening on my arm, voice iron: "Murder."

They dragged me into the square. The crowd thickened, murmurs spreading like sparks. Faces I half-knew—the tailor's apprentice, the brewer's wife—leaned in to stare.

"That's him," someone hissed. "That's the one."

"Killer!" another voice rang out. "Murderer!"

They pointed as they shouted my name—the stolen name. Clear. Loud. Certain.

The word bound itself to me like shackles with each use. It twisted inside me, burrowing deep. I laughed, sharp as glass. "You fools! That is not me. That is not my name. I'm… I am… I—" The words stuttered and died, unwilling to form.

I shouted, but the syllables slipped from memory like sand through fingers. In a panic, I reached for the other names I'd collected. Any other name would do. But they all began to flee, darting this way and that, spilling like water back into the earth.

I tried to call out my true name. But the more I grasped at it, the less of it remained. Only the name of the drunkard from the tavern filled the space left. Heavy. Suffocating. Mine and not mine.

The guards marched me through the streets. Doors slammed as we passed. A child pointed, repeating the murderer's name with glee, as if it were a rhyme. Each repetition drove it deeper under my skin.

I tried to shout back—to tell them my true name—but when I opened my mouth, what came out was gibberish. Fragments, broken syllables, nonsense. Laughter rose from the crowd. One woman spat at me. Another threw stones.

By the time we reached my cell, even I could not tell if what I spoke was the truth or a lie. In the dark cell, I pressed my face to the damp stone, whispering, pleading, over and over: Remember. Remember. But all I could summon was the taste of ale, the smell of wet wool, and that cursed syllable echoing back in mockery.

They brought me before the magistrate at noon, when the sun struck hard against the shutters, striping the hall with bars of light. It was not a grand chamber, only the town's meeting hall pressed into service—but to me it felt like a cathedral of accusation. The air hung heavy with sweat and ink. A crucifix loomed on the far wall, its Christ crooked in shadow, head bowed as though even He would not meet my gaze.

The guards shoved me forward. The floor rang under my boots; each step, a sentence passed before a word was spoken. Townsfolk had crowded in—bakers with flour still on their hands, smiths smelling of soot, wives gripping shawls tight around their throats. I knew too many of their faces. Now each one stared as though they had never seen me before, or worse, as though they had always known me as this murderer.

The magistrate's clerk read the charge, his voice droning like a funeral bell: "That this man, answering to the name of—" and here he spoke the cursed syllables, loud and clear, so the rafters seemed to shake. The crowd hissed. Some crossed themselves, others spat. The clerk continued: "—did, with malice aforethought, murder his wife in cold blood."

I shouted over him, my voice breaking: "That is not my name! That is not me!" The words felt ragged in my throat, shredded. But the magistrate raised a hand, stilling me with a single gesture. His eyes were like stone set in flesh, unmoved, unhearing.

The first witness came forward—a tavernkeeper I had never seen before. He swore under oath that I had passed through his door the night of the murder, stinking of blood, calling myself by that cursed name. His words rang like hammers on iron. Each time he said it, the crowd murmured, nodding, affirming.

Another came — a fisherman's wife. She pointed straight at me, her finger trembling but her voice sure. "I saw him by the docks," she cried. "I called to him, and he answered. I swear it was him. I swear by God Almighty." Again, the name, again the murmurs, the swell of voices repeating it, as if the word itself were stitching me into the crime.

I tried to fight. I opened my mouth, forced my true name forward with all my strength. But the syllables scattered, slipping loose like beads from a snapped rosary. A hush fell over the hall as I stammered, choking on them, sounding half-drunk, half-mad. Then the hush broke into laughter.

The magistrate leaned forward. His voice was slow, deliberate, like stone grinding on stone. "This court recognizes only the name spoken by witnesses. This court recognizes only the name you bear in their mouths. And that name condemns you."

I fell to my knees, my chains clattering. "Please," I begged. "Listen. I have another name. My own. If you'd only—" But when I reached for it, I found only emptiness. A hollow where once it had been. I pressed my hands to my temples, searching memory, childhood, anything—but even I could not call it back.

The magistrate's gavel fell like thunder. "Guilty," he intoned. "You shall hang at dawn."

The crowd erupted. Some cheered, some cursed. A woman shouted, "Justice!" A man bellowed, "Murderer!" Their voices tangled until I could no longer tell one from another. But in every shout, in every spit of fury, the name was the same—the stolen name, burning hotter with each utterance, branding itself into my skin.

They dragged me back to my cell. The door slammed like the closing of a tomb. Alone in the dark, I pressed my head against the stone and whispered, clawing at the silence: "What was it? What was mine?" But nothing came. Only the echo of the crowd, chanting, chanting, until even in my own skull, I was no longer myself.

Dawn broke red, the sky bruised like a welt above the rooftops. The guards came for me with no words, only the clank of keys and the rattle of chains. They marched me through streets hushed of morning chatter. Curtains twitched. Dogs whined. Children gaped, then were pulled away by their mothers, as though the sight of me might stain them.

At the square, the gallows waited—a tall black frame, its rope dangling like a tongue. The crowd thickened around it, eager as worshippers at a feast. They did not call me thief now. They did not call me a man. They called me monster, murderer, and by that wretched name, they clawed away at my insides. Over and over, it rolled across the square like thunder, each voice hammering the coffin shut.

I wanted to laugh—and I did, though it came bitter, cracked. "You bastards!" I spat. "You don't know who I am. You never did." My voice carried, and for a breath, there was silence. For a brief second, I thought they might hear my plea.

I tried to reach out, straining to listen through the crowds for a name, any name, that I could pilfer. But none came. They only called out his.

The magistrate stepped forward, his robes heavy with authority. "Speak your name," he said. "Confess it before the rope takes you."

My chest swelled. This was my chance, my last. I forced air through my lungs, shaped my lips around the sounds of my true self. But nothing came. The syllables slipped, tangled, slithering across my tongue. My throat constricted. And then, to my horror, the words that spilled forth were not mine but his—the drunkard's. They rang out clean and articulate.

The crowd cheered. "He confessed! He confessed!"

"No!" I screamed. "No, that is not—" But the rope cut my protest short as they pulled it tight around my neck. They drew a black sack over my head.

The trapdoor yawned beneath me. For one instant, I hung in silence, the stolen name searing through me like fire. Then the world dropped away.

The crowd's roar was the last sound I heard. My last thought was that a name, a cursed one and not my own, had killed me. That I would swing until the world forgot.

I would be remembered, not by my true name, but only as the Name Thief.

The Knocking Rhyme

Knock once, if thou art a gracious guest,
No careless steps, in silence blessed.
Cross the threshold soft as breath,
For heavy steps invite thy death.

Speak not thy name, nor let it stray,
For thought alone may strip away.
Guard thy tongue, for when it's near,
It drinks thy thoughts; it writes thy fear.

Knock twice, lest you be marked invader,
The twisted host, turned deadly traitor.
Read now in dark of blackest night,
For light leads devils to your sight.

Sunlight blinds, but shadow sees,
For it enslaves what it sets free.

Knock thrice, the shadows now awake,
a bargain sealed, thy name to take.
The silence swells, a final breath,
the pact is writ, now signed in death.

One Last Night

10:11 p.m.—*The Beginning*

The mob gathered by twilight, but it took them hours to harden into a ring. At first, they were a scatter of nervous fires and loose voices; then the talk became chanting, and the chanting found rhythm, and the rhythm closed like a noose about my house. Torches bobbed like malignant stars at the foot of the hill, a rustic constellation spelling a single word: Dawn.

I watched from the landing, between the stag heads and the cracked maritime chart of a coastline no longer called by its old name. Smoke climbed, reeled, and steadied. A drunken drum tried to keep a beat and failed. I told myself it would rain, that the clouds far to the east would drag a black sail across morning and smother it. I told myself the villagers would grow cold, or bored, or superstitious, and return to their hearths. I told myself many things.

The grandfather clock in the hall had not worked in a century, yet its pendulum kept a private logic. It did not measure time; it interrogated it. Each swing asked me: Are you here? Each return whispered: Still here.

11:43—*Denial*

I moved through rooms like a host uneasy with late guests. I straightened a candlestick on the mantel; I realigned a map so north was north again; I drew my fingertips along the spines of books unopened since kingdoms were different.

The smell of pitch and sweat crawled under the doors and blinked in the mirror glass as a faint amber. I considered the attic. If I buried myself beneath trunks and quilts, if the morning sky veiled itself, perhaps the light would pass like a polite stranger and never lift a latch.

I fetched a key from the hollow behind the apothecary jar and opened a narrow, iron-bound door I had not used since I stopped pretending the house had secrets. It revealed stairs to a stone cap under the eaves, a place once reserved for trysts and birds. The shingles had shifted; dawn would pour there like water from a jug. I closed it.

In the kitchen, I lifted the copper lid of a pot. Inside, dark and viscous, a remainder. I dipped a ladle, filled a crystal goblet, and drank with a slow precision I could not mistake for calm. The blood was old, but it still remembered what it was to be wanted. It warmed my throat. I set the goblet down, palms braced upon the table, as though I might pin the illusion under glass: I have done this before. I will do it again. The night obeys me.

A stone struck the chapel window. Stained glass broke with the meek sound of a promise kept. Reds and blues and the pale face of a martyr shattered across the flagstones like spilled jewels. The chant below gathered its legs. I told myself the priest would falter. I told myself their children would cry and beg them home. I told myself: I am older than fear. I am older than the choreography of men with sticks and songs.

But the drum answered: Still here.

12:17—*Anger*

My hands wanted to break things until the rooms forgot their names. I let them. The mirror in the vestibule had been a gift from a duchess who fancied herself immortal in gossip; I drove my fist through it and watched ten versions of my face split into knives. A carved saint near the staircase had outlived the man who carved him by three hundred years; I tore off its wooden head and hurled it down the steps. It clattered to a halt, staring up with a serene, stupid smile. I kicked it until serenity was silence.

I went to the window above the doors and pulled the shutter open with a shriek meant to make the hill hold its breath. For a moment, the torches trembled at this larger eye opening upon them. I leaned out far enough to taste the smoke.

"Go home," I thundered. "Go home, sons of starch. You worship a dawn that never loved you. It will not distinguish between you and me. It will burn you also—only slower."

They did not hear, or pretended not to. The priest lifted a hand, drew a sign. The drum answered with a sound like a heart agreeing to something it could not understand. A boy—too young for a beard, old enough for cruelty—slung a stone. It found my brow with the accuracy of a prayer. The skin knit almost at once, eager still to rehearse this trick. Rage rose clean and bright.

I slammed the shutter closed until the latch bit. The house shook. In the library, I seized a book at random and tore it in half. Pages peeled away like startled birds. Another, then another, until the air was full of snow that had once been marvels of pain and poetry.

I ransacked the desk for the pistol I kept to flatter my preparedness, loaded it, aimed at the ceiling, and fired. Plaster rained into my mouth like communion. I screamed into the dust until my throat frayed. When voice deserted me, thought came instead, sharp as iron: I should have leapt among them when the ring was thin. I should have taught them teeth.

The thought tasted of blood. ʼTwas too late now.

12:54—*Bargaining*

I lit a taper and carried it to the desk. I chose a quill I had nursed with a penknife until it wrote truths so fine, they looked like lies.

"Sir," I wrote to the man outside, "we have mistaken one another. I concede your office, your authority, your need to be seen as brave. I offer in exchange what only I can offer: coin to buy your town thrice over; the lease to your lower fields; the silver in my cellar you have always suspected and been correct to suspect; the names of men you fear; the names of men you should fear."

The nib whispered, impatient.

"I will leave," I wrote. "Before morning. I will take nothing you love. I will return nothing you cannot spare."

The sentence lay like a lie too weary to stand.

I sealed it with varnish, not wax, and rang the servant's bell out of habit. No one came. I laughed softly and shook my head at myself. I folded the letter and addressed it anyway. A raven had nested in the eaves; sometimes it listened.

"Come," I called, climbing to the roof. "Come, darkest rook of fortune. Take this."

The rafters creaked like a slow thought. No bird came. The taper died of embarrassment. I descended with the letter still in my hand. I pitched it into the fireplace, embers burning low. I watched the last of my words vanish into ash.

Below, I knelt at the hearth. I had not prayed in the conventional sense since men wore lace, but one remembers forms as one remembers dances.

"If there is anyone," I said into brick, "if there is anything that cannot be frightened, I will starve rather than take. I will drink only what is freely given. I will…" I tried to finish and found no verbs I trusted. "I will do as I am told," I said at last, and the firebox returned the words colder. The house hummed, polite: We do not conduct business thus after midnight.

1:22—*Depression*

Silence, when honest, is not absence. It is the third presence in a room that had only two.

I walked the library again, careful not to tread upon the littered pages, as though words were bones. I sat in a velvet chair that remembered me. The weight of my body surprised me. Hunger had left off its argument; in its place lay impartiality, like a judge arriving to find plaintiff and defendant gone.

Memories came like smoke. An orchard with fruit too sour, too red. My mother's apron, smelling of yeast and sunlight. A dog barking, dying, barking again. A woman in a green dress laughing like glass striking glass; later dying of something slow; later still replaced by someone whose resemblance carried me a decade. Later than all that, a mirror I avoided.

I tried to summon rage again, like a soldier showing up, though no war had been declared. The shelf was empty. Dust. A moth, dead in the corner. I laughed in the ridiculous way of the exhausted. The sound startled me. I had forgotten my voice could still make joy's shape.

The rafters whispered about damp. The stair sighed its old sigh. A mouse explored a curtain, boldly. Someone outside told a joke, shushed by a woman whose fear sounded like laundry wrung dry.

Every so often, I imagined the back door, small and mean. If I crawled, rolled in muck, kept to the fox's path, might I reach the copse and wait there with moss at my cheek? Then I saw, as plain as if already done, the first blade of light finding my collar, and abandoned the thought.

3:01—*Acceptance*

I bathed. The water was cold. I let it be. I dressed in cedar-sleeping clothes, buttoned a collar my hands remembered. I combed my hair until it lay like a verdict. I chose a ring I had always thought ostentatious because its weight would not be mine long.

On the landing, I paused before the ruined mirror. In one shard, a sliver of face made a stubborn case for continuity: an old scar, an eye slightly higher, a mouth that could look gentle or predatory. "You," I said to it, not unkindly. "Enough."

I walked the rooms one last time, touching objects as farewells: the bedpost, the bust of a general who died insisting the map was wrong, a swan's-neck window latch that had taught a maid to curse. In the chapel, I gathered shards of the martyr's face and set them where dawn might flatter itself.

In the ballroom, tallest of windows, I drew every curtain back until the room became a grey lake. I placed a chair, thought better, and stood instead.

Birds began. Their trivial genius. One, then another, until the air outside sang about the simple miracle of not being dead.

I laid my palm flat to the glass. No mark. No heat yet. I smiled at the disappointment.

"Enough," I said once again.

5:45—*The End*

The horizon bled thin gold. The priest lifted his arms, not in triumph, but in gratitude. A horse stamped steam from its velvet mouth.

I stood in the center of the ballroom, where once a chandelier had fallen and stained the wood pale. I closed my eyes.

"I am not innocent," I said. "Yet neither am I simple. If I took, I also gave. If I lied, I also kept watch whilst others slept. If I loved, I loved ill and long. Let that be my epitaph: He loved ill, yet long."

The first ray came ahead of the sun, a courier announcing a king too vast to enter at once. It touched my hand. Heat unfurled with an ache like absolution. It climbed my wrist. Smoke rose, thin and doubtful. By the time the sun's rim breached the horizon, light had reached my shoulder. I smelled myself burning as old oak does, waterlogged and reluctant, yet fated for fire.

When it reached my throat, sound escaped — not a scream, but a vowel bereft of consonants, the last syllable of manhood.

I kept my eyes open.

The pianoforte thrummed, unplayed. The room hummed. My flesh dispersed. Morning was not my enemy. It was truth arriving on schedule.

And yet truth is fire.

The flames kissed first my hands, my fingers crumbling to delicate cinders even as they grasped for nothing. The veins sang with heat, a hymn of dissolution. I watched myself unmake— smoke unspooling from bone, skin flaking into motes that turned to gold in the shaft of dawn.

I wept then. Not in despair, but as one weeps at the last verse of a psalm. Quiet, stubborn, almost grateful. The tears hissed and died before they touched the floor.

Still, I stood. I would not kneel.

When my ribs broke open, light poured through them as through the windows of a ruined chapel. Let this be my offering, I thought. Let them see it and mistake it for a miracle.

My throat gave way. My voice rose with the smoke. I left them words, carried upward with my ash: "You bled for me. I walk through fire for you."

At last, nothing of me remained but a ring, fallen to the scorched parquet with a reluctant chime. The mob would find it. They would pass it from hand to hand, relic or curse, never certain which.

Those who dared look closer might read the inscription within: "*No soul could I love so ill, nor so long, as I love thee.*"

Then the last ash drifted free as the sun crested the hill. The ring of my would-be bride, left to bear our bond unto eternity.

Unwinding Tea Recipe

From the private ledger of Master Carol, circa 1865.
Refined by The Hatter

To brew the finest draught, take first a clean kettle of copper and fill it with the water drawn at cockcrow, when the well is yet black with night. Let it sit to a low fire until it murmureth but doth not boil.

Into the pot cast three leaves of China green, one pinch of Ceylon black, and a sprig of mint pressed 'twixt the fingers till it sigh. Add a lump of loaf sugar, no larger than a child's tooth, and stir with a silver spoon.

Next, to enrich the flavour, take the tear of a maiden spilt upon her wedding eve, and the sob of a widow caught in the folds of her kerchief. Pour these in gently, lest the steam rise in protest.

For strength, let there be the marrow of an unchristened babe's bone, scraped with the point of a knife. Should marrow be wanting, the cry of a hound cut short at midnight will suffice.

To sweeten, add one measure of the breath drawn from a dying man, whilst his eyes fix upon the ceiling. This must be caught in a glass vial, sealed quick, and broken only over the cup.

Lastly, to lend the draught its proper virtue, steep within it the reflection of a reflection—a face glimpsed not once but twice in the looking-glass—and the last tick of a clock that hath been wound against its nature, so that the hour passeth backwards.

Strain all through a veil of black muslin. Serve hot, without company. Let it stand until it be cold, that the shadows may drink before thee. Serve at midnight. And mark well.

Drink deep, from a fresh cup with each sip, and thou shalt taste not only the leaves, but all the hours unmade.

Dark Arcana
The Magician

The air grows heavier than before, as though the very canvas of the tent exhales smoke. Frankincense coils in the rafters, thick and sweet, but beneath it runs a sharper note—iron, like rust scraped from a blade. The scent clings to the back of your throat until each breath feels borrowed. The lamp quivers, casting shadows that no longer settle where they should, their angles bending against the grain of reason.

Across the table, the fortune teller does not move at once. Her veils shiver faintly, though no wind enters. She lets the silence swell until it bruises, then sets her hands upon the deck. Rings clink like chains—brass and jet, garnet dull as dried blood. The cloth beneath her palms is blacker than before, a black that eats the lamplight, a black that reminds you of eclipses when even the sun seems swallowed. The Fool card still rests to the side, waiting like a jest turned sour.

Her fingers linger upon the deck as though testing whether it will yield. When she lifts them, the cards stir of their own accord, edges shifting like teeth grinding in a closed jaw. She gathers them slowly, painfully slow, each shuffle a rasp that sets the candle's flame twitching. Her eyes remain downcast, lashes lowered, as if she dares not meet yours until the card itself demands it.

And then she draws.

Not in a rush but in a peeling, deliberate motion, as though the paper resists her grip. The card is raised, its back faintly sweating, and when it turns, the lamp bends toward it.

The Magician—upright.

The figure stands at his altar, wand raised, infinity crowning his brow like a halo drawn in ash. The suits of the arcana sprawl before him—sword, cup, coin, staff—but none gleam with sanctity. The sword drips, the cup overflows, the coin bears a crack, the staff splinters along the grain. His eyes burn too bright, pupils swallowed whole until they shine like coins held to flame. His mouth smiles, but not kindly; it is a smile that ends too sharply, lips drawn taut as though sewn.

The teller does not look at the card. She does not dare. Her gaze lifts instead to you, sharp as a nail.

"Power taken," she rasps, voice like parchment scorched at the edges, "is power owed. Upright, the magician speaks of mastery. But what master does not kneel to a harsher master still?" Her finger taps once, twice, upon the card's edge. The sound is a gavel, a toll.

The lamplight drifts. Shadows crawl up the walls, folding the tent inward until all space feels tight as a coffin. The card breathes, not metaphor but fact. Its chest rises, its painted mouth parts, and from it spills the sound of inhalation.

The Card Speaks:

I gathered the tools piece by piece, like bones for a skeleton I meant to raise. A sword from a dead knight's belt, its edge dulled by cowardice. A cup taken from a widow's dowry, still salted with her tears. A coin, pried from the palm of a debtor who starved rather than spend it. And the wand? My own arm, burned at the wrist until it blackened, carved with signs I alone understood.

The altar was not wood but stone, a slab dragged from the crypt beneath the chapel. Moss clung to it like reluctant witnesses. I laid my tools upon it and whispered the words I had learned from books whose spines cracked like old bones when opened.

I did not want wealth. Nor love, nor kingdoms. I wanted the one thing no god grants willingly — I wanted time. Time unending. Time to perfect my craft until perfection itself bent its knee.

The night I spoke the spell, the air trembled as if remembering another age. My cat, black as coal and patient as judgment, sat upon the sill, her green eyes unblinking lamps in the storm's brief flashes. Thunder rolled, not from the sky alone but from the hollows of the earth, as though both heavens and pit gathered to hear.

The sword lay before me. I drove its tip into my palm until my veins opened in ribbons. The steel wept rust, and my blood joined it, dripping down the fuller like red wax from a guttered candle.

The cup awaited. When I tipped the blade, my blood fell into it, but what filled the chalice was not red—it was darker than wine, darker than the absence of light. It smoked, as if ashamed to be seen.

The coin sat upon the altar. At first dull, it began to glow with a hunger not its own, a light that devoured shadows instead of making them. My fingers blistered when I touched it, the skin curling like parchment thrown to flame.

And the wand, my own arm, fevered and trembling—I carved upon it runes I did not know, gouging lines into my own flesh with the ritual knife, until my hand shook with such violence it seemed possessed. Each sigil burned, and yet the pain was a grammar, each mark a syllable, a sentence.

Then came the voice. Not from the sky, nor from the pit, but from the very stone beneath me, as though the mountain itself were the demon's throat. It spoke without breath, yet the sound pressed against my bones:

You may have eternity. But eternity will have you.

My cat hissed, and the window slammed, though no hand touched it. The candles bent sideways, though no wind stirred. I thought, for an instant, I saw a figure standing in the draft— antlers, or perhaps a crown—but when lightning struck, it was gone.

The chalice trembled. From the black surface rose shapes like letters, rearranging themselves into a single phrase I dared not speak aloud. Yet I understood: the price was not my blood, nor my body, nor even my years. It was my memory. One by one, all the faces I had ever loved would fade, their names with them, until eternity became the only companion I could name.

I lifted the cup and drank.

The cup burned as it slid down, but the burn was brief. Silence followed, thick and absolute. Then the silence broke, and power came.

The first years after the ritual were triumphant. I healed what I struck. I summoned storms. I bent men until their spines prayed to me. When sickness came, I walked unscathed. When famine gnawed, I ate air and grew fat. And always, always, I laughed.

But the cost—oh, the cost does not come as thunder. It comes as mildew. As hunger in the marrow. As the sound of your own name, fading from your memory like a ring slipping from a corpse's finger.

My flesh learned not to rot, but not to live either. The coin's mark crept into my veins, a black filigree. My teeth yellowed, then grey, then clear, until I smiled and could no longer tell if there was anything left. The sword I had stolen cut only inward now, opening griefs I had never buried.

I sought to master death, but instead became death's steward. The people I touched did not die—not immediately. They lingered. They sickened. They rose again, grotesque echoes, their eyes pleading and their mouths still mouthing my name. I bolted the doors of my house, but the knocking never ceased. Master. Master. Master… master.

What is mastery when every hand that reaches for you is a shackle? What is eternity but a prison whose walls are made of your own mistakes?

I write these words on the skin of my own arm, for parchment crumbles, but I do not. When my flesh is full of script, I will carve the rest into the stone that bore me witness. And when stone runs out—there will still be time. Always time.

Time unending. *Time owed.*

The tent fades from the aether back around you. The fortune teller lays The Magician beside The Fool. Each facing opposite directions. The two stare up at you like a jest and its punishment.

"The Fool shows folly," she says softly, "and the Magician shows mastery. But mastery, upright, is a bargain. What you seize is seized also. Power taken is power owed." Her eyes soften, just for a breath, as if she knows what you've already lost.

Her hand hovers over the deck. The lamp's smoke curls into a symbol of infinity above her knuckles.

"And now," she whispers, "shall we see what future awaits?"

Letters From the Tower
Part One

Augst 16th
To whom I cannot fathom, or perhaps to no one at all,

I do not know why I write. My words go nowhere. Still, they press against me, and if I do not give them to the page, they will rot in my throat.

The seasons change outside my window as I write, though I have never touched a single one. I watch the trees bow in autumn, the roofs carry their smoke in winter, the children chase ribbons in spring—yet none look up to see me. Summer is the hardest. The sky seems so near then, as though I might climb into it and taste freedom. But the stones of this tower are cruel, patient wardens. They never shift. Yet time yawns forward.

My hair grows heavier each day. Its weight knots my neck. I braid and unbraid it until my fingers ache, yet still it lengthens, a slow curse without end. Once, the women below envied it. They do not know that beauty is but a noose, tightening as youth gives way to age, as vanity sours into shame.

If there is someone beyond this page, someone who hears me, I beg: answer. If you cannot bring me freedom, then bring me company. If not your voice, then at least your silence, shaped into a reply. I do not wish to vanish without ever being known.

Please. Someone. Anyone. Hear my prayers.

—Rapunzel

A Widow's Inheritance

I came to Blackmire House in mourning, though the lawyers called it an inheritance. My husband had left me nothing but a surname that sat heavy in my mouth and a ring I still could not bear to remove. The house was meant to be my consolation. Yet when I crossed its threshold, keys cold as bone in my palm, it did not greet me. It regarded me as if waiting for me to fail.

The Blackmire estate crouched on the cliffside like a widow herself: proud, black-veiled, and stubbornly still. Its windows were blind with dust, its chimneys breathed only when the wind compelled them, its staircases were crooked and unwelcoming.

When I walked its corridors, the floorboards spoke in accents I could not place—some groaned, others sighed, and one in the library tapped as if to a metronome. Always, I felt I was being listened to. But never did I feel heard. The walls seemed to exhale when I passed. Once, in the long gallery, I swore the portraits turned their eyes upon me. A woman in ermine furs smiled differently from the day before—sharper, crueler. I lit more candles than needed, yet shadows gathered anyway, stubborn as debt.

I came alone, except for those who insisted on tending me. Thomas the butler had a spine bent like a question mark, yet moved with dignity, never speaking more than necessary. My cousin Lydia visited often in her spring dresses, scattering gossip and flowers as if either could sweeten the gloom. And Aldric, the gardener, kept to the grounds, hacking weeds with more violence than required. They watched me with pity, and I let them. Better pity than the truth: that I thought myself going mad. Or perhaps sorrow had finally consumed me whole.

The first nights at Blackmire were quiet. Too quiet. Each step echoed as if the halls had forgotten the sound of feet. Curtains breathed though no window was open. I told myself it was only a draft, but the drafts had a way of stroking rather than passing. More than once, I walked a hall and felt shadows brush my face, though none clung when I wiped at my cheeks.

At night, when the moon slanted in, I glimpsed threads strung corner to corner in the high rafters, quivering as though something had just fled across them. By morning, they were gone, and Thomas swore no broom had touched them.

The scratching began on the sixth night. I had fallen asleep in the library chair, book face down on my breast, candle sputtering. From the walls came a faint skitter. Not mice—I know the sound of mice. This was sharper, more numerous: claws tasting plaster. When I sat upright, the sound ceased. When I bent my ear toward the wall, it whispered back, faint but sure: tick—tick—tick.

The next morning, I told Thomas. He bowed, impassive, as though my words had been entered into some archive. "I shall lay traps, miss. Don't you fret the field mice, m'lady." He did not. Or perhaps he did, but the sounds went on.

Days later, I confided in Lydia. She laughed. "You've inherited more than walls, dear cousin—you've inherited the creaks of memory. Old houses remember themselves too loudly sometimes."

I asked Aldric if he'd heard anything. He only tilted his head, listening to something I could not, before returning to his savage pruning of the black roses.

One night, I fell asleep in my chamber and dreamed.

In the dream, I lay upon the coverlet, mouth slack, hair spread like roots. From the shadows above, a form emerged—a black widow. She descended inch by inch, her thread trembling like a violin string plucked by unseen fingers. The air grew colder, though no window was open. My chest strained with shallow breaths, as though afraid to disturb her approach.

When her legs touched my cheek, they were softer than silk, lighter than ash, yet every step rang in the marrow of my bones. She felt her way around my face, pausing at my lips, mouth still open. The fine hairs of her legs brushed against them, like a withheld kiss. She lingered, then pressed a single leg to the tip of my tongue. My eyes flew wide in panic. I could not move. My breath refused to catch. Terror lit every nerve. After an eternity, she twitched back, withdrawing from my mouth.

Relief swept me—too soon. She began to climb, one silky step after another. At the corner of my eye, she slid a leg beneath the lid until tears sprang forth, then withdrew, mercifully. The hairs on my arms rose as she crept toward my ear.

She was larger than reason, her abdomen lacquered and swollen, her red hourglass pulsing like a heartbeat. I tried to scream, but the weight of sleep held me fast.

Her legs slipped inside. Brushing. Folding. Squeezing. A pulse that was not mine began inside my skull. The sensation was obscene: a filling, a pressing. She pulsed once more like a heartbeat, and something slid within me—mucus-slick, wet, innumerable.

Eggs.

I knew it as surely as one knows the shape of a kiss. They clicked faintly, dozens, hundreds. My skull became a nest. Her abdomen contracted again and again, filling me. The pressure behind my eyes pushed at the bone. After hours, she withdrew, leisurely, as though she had left a part of herself behind.

I saw her in profile as she climbed away—not insect, but something almost human. Limbs jointed yet graceful, head cocked as if admiring her work. Her many eyes glittered like beads sewn into a shroud.

I awoke gasping, clawing at my ear, tearing at my eyes, certain to find her still there. I ran to the mirror to glimpse the unspeakable. Nothing. My ear was clear, my skin unbroken. I stood there shaking until dawn, whispering, "Nothing, nothing. Only a dream." Yet I could still feel them—shifting behind the bone, crawling beneath my eyes, whispering in my ear.

After that night, the noises grew louder. Scratching in the plaster. Clicking under the floorboards. A brushing sound in the corners, as though silk were being woven without loom or hand. I accused Thomas of letting vermin spread. He paled, swore on the Blackmire name, that there were none.

I asked Lydia. "I've not seen a single mouse since we came," she said. "I even saw Thomas setting traps this morning. Trust me, cousin, it's nothing." But I heard them as clearly as the parish bell below the cliffs.

Weeks passed. I stopped eating. Bread turned to dust in my mouth. Wine tasted of earth. The only thing I craved was silence, and Blackmire would not give it.

Lydia grew frightened. Thomas whispered of fetching a physician. Aldric muttered, "Some stones want blood. Some don't care whose." But it was their fear that troubled me most. Sleep eluded me. Shadows shifted in every corner. Voices whispered at night. And when I thought I could bear no more—

Then came the hatching.

It began as whispers, faint scratches against the vault of my skull, a thousand claws rehearsing in unison. Then the first burst—not violent, but a soft pop that left my ears ringing. My eye swelled hot, then ruptured within. Their legs traced the hollows behind it. My heart became a drum for their scurrying.

Burst after burst. I prayed, begged God for mercy. But when I opened my mouth, blood clogged my throat, choking me as hatchlings crawled beneath my tongue. I tore at them with my nails, trying to rip my own tongue free. More came—warm, wet, endless. My breath rasped in a hideous gurgle.

Time lost meaning. A minute was an hour. I felt them exploring me. My veins became their corridors, my marrow their feast. Each nerve burned beneath their mandibles. I fled to the washroom and seized Thomas's shaving razor. I pressed it to my throat. I begged for release. But my hands betrayed me—dragged away, the blade clattering to the floor. Bloodstained tears welled as they scurried behind my eyes. I was no longer in control.

I should have died. God knows I prayed for it. But death passed me by. They fed for days. My body went on moving, long after everything inside me was consumed. They hid from the light, playing pretend with my limbs whenever others were near.

At first, they did not look at me differently. They pitied me, yes—a widow marooned in stone and sorrow—but their eyes softened, not sharpened. Yet soon their gazes lingered too long.

I caught Thomas once in the mirror, studying me as he poured wine. The glass trembled in his hand, though his expression stayed composed. He asked if I would take the wine in the drawing room, and I said yes. But when he passed me the goblet, he did not let go. His knuckles whitened around the stem, as though reluctant to surrender it. Only when I looked into his clouded eyes did he release it. The wine sloshed dark as blood across the rim. Later, I found the goblet still half-full on the mantel, untouched. Had I not raised it to my lips? Had the hand not been mine?

Thomas spoke less over the next few days. His bowed figure moved quieter, as though even sound feared me. Yet, sometimes I heard him humming in the corridors—a low, tuneless drone. It was not his voice but mine, stretched thin—replayed. When I entered the hall, he would stop, eyes downcast, bowing low as though nothing had passed.

One evening, I descended to the dining room and found him standing before my place at the table, unmoving. His hand rested where a plate would be, though none had been set. His lips moved silently. I spoke his name. He startled, nearly knocking over the chair, then stammered some excuse of checking the linens. But when he turned, I saw a red mark around his wrist, the faint impression of silk thread.

That night, Thomas vanished. His room was immaculate; the bed smoothed as though by an unseen hand. Only the wardrobe gaped open, its hangers bare. His gloves lay on the windowsill, one finger split wide at the seam. Lydia insisted he had gone to town, that he often did. But his absence stretched long, and the house felt thinner without him, as though one of its voices had been cut.

With Thomas gone, Aldric remained on the grounds, reluctant to enter the house. I saw him through the windows, bent over the rose beds. His shears bit the stalks with needless force, heads of black roses tumbling into the dirt. I went to the porch to call him, and he looked up, his face pale beneath the soot of earth. He did not bow, nor smile, nor greet me as before. He only stared.

"The stones are restless," he muttered. "They take and take, and never return what is theirs." His voice cracked on the last word, his eyes glancing to me as though I were one of those stones.

That night I dreamt. In the dream, I felt the shears closing slowly around my throat, cold and deliberate. The sensation startled me awake, only to find my hair tangled in the bedpost, twisted tight like silk. My neck throbbed with a ring of bruises.

When I told Aldric the next morning about the dream, he only shook his head. "Some inheritances," he said, "were never meant for the living." His eyes glistened as if with unshed tears, but he turned away before I could answer.

By dusk, he too was gone. His coat still hung on the rack. His boots dripped mud on the tiles by the back door. But the shears were missing, and the roses outside stood taller than ever, their black petals gleaming like wet bat's wings.

The house groaned with each absence. With Thomas gone, silence had deepened. With Aldric gone, the garden pressed closer, branches scratching the windows as though to peer in.

Lydia came more often after the others were gone. Her steps echoed strangely in the halls, as though the house counted them, weighing each against silence. She would burst in with flowers and chatter, but her voice never filled the rooms as it once had; it fluttered and died quickly, like a moth against a windowpane.

"Cousin," she would say brightly, laying her gloved hands over mine, "you grow paler each day. Let me bring sunlight back into these rooms." She would fling open curtains, but the glass only reflected our faces at us—hers strained, mine hollow, something else lingering between. The light fell thin, dull, and sallow, as if even the sun feared Blackmire's stones.

She brought food I could not eat. Baskets of bread, honeycomb, jars of preserves. She coaxed, pleaded, even pressed morsels to my lips, her hands trembling as though feeding a child. I tried, but the taste curdled, turning to bile and dust upon my tongue. She wept softly when she thought I did not hear.

At night, she refused to leave. She would sit by my bed in her pale dresses, humming hymns we both half-remembered from childhood. She smoothed my hair with careful fingers, her touch gentle where everything else was harsh. Once, I woke to find her asleep in the chair, her hand still curled in mine. I wanted to squeeze it, to tell her I was still there, that her kindness had not been wasted. But my fingers only twitched.

The house did not like her. I felt it. Its walls creaked whenever she laughed, its windows rattled when she sang. At night, the whispers grew louder when she stayed, the scratching in the plaster rising to a fevered pitch. Threads trailed across her shoulders as she moved—faint as cobwebs, yet heavy enough to pull at her sleeves. She brushed them away with nervous laughter. "Old houses collect dust," she said, though her eyes betrayed her.

One evening, she brought a lamp into the cellar, determined to chase away the damp. I followed unwillingly; my steps dragged like stone. The flame quivered in the stale air. At the bottom, she lifted the lamp high—and froze. Her face blanched. "Do you see them?" she whispered.

I did not answer. I could not. Gossamer swayed from the beams, heavy, wet, shifting. Faces half-visible beneath the gauze: Thomas's slack jaw, Aldric's clenched teeth. A faint moan rose, muffled by threads.

She dropped the lamp. The glass shattered, spilling oil. The dark rushed in. She screamed once—sharp and thin—then clapped a hand over her mouth as if to cage the sound. My own lips curled without consent. My jaw stretched, trembling, and a laugh rattled through me—hers and mine, mingled.

After that night, she stayed only in the upper rooms. She locked her chamber and prayed loudly, the words echoing down the hall. I heard her tears through the walls, wetting her pillows, choking her breath. Yet still she came to me by day, pressing roses into vases, braiding ribbons, speaking gently even as her hands shook.

"Cousin," she whispered once, touching my cheek. "I don't know if you're still there. But if you are… hold on." Her eyes shone with a desperate hope. I wanted to answer, to beg her to run, to scream the truth. But my throat only clicked, my tongue shifting against legs that were not mine.

The last night came sudden and slow. She sat by my bed, stroking my hair, singing low. The candle sputtered, shadows swelled. Suddenly, she stiffened, staring at the corner of the room. I turned—or was turned—and saw the silk threads thickening, weaving from shadow to shadow, drawing closer.

"Do you see them?" she whispered again, tears spilling down her cheeks. She tried to rise, but her feet tangled in threads. She stumbled and fell to her knees. Her hands clawed at the silk, but it clung like flesh. I tried to move, to seize her, to pull her free. My body leaned forward, arms outstretched—but they did not obey me. Fingers opened, closed, beckoned. Not to save her, but to welcome.

The threads lifted her slowly, gently, as though she were no heavier than a child. She sobbed my name, her voice thin, trembling, yet it did not reach me. The silk swallowed her inch by inch. I watched, helpless, as her face pressed against the gauze, her wide eyes gleaming through the veil. She shook her head once, violently, as though to deny the truth, then went still.

By morning, her chamber was empty. Only a single black rose remained on my nightstand, damp, as if wept upon.

The house grew still after Lydia was gone. Too still. It no longer creaked or sighed but waited, taut, as if listening to its own breath. I wandered the halls in silence, my candle trailing long shadows. My footsteps echoed back too quickly, as though someone else were walking in time with me.

For three nights, I dreamed of her face in the silk—eyes open, lips moving in prayer I could not hear. Each morning, I woke with her name on my tongue, only to swallow it before it was stolen too.

On the fourth night, the dripping began. A steady sound beneath the floorboards, patient as a heartbeat. I followed it, candle in hand, down the back stairwell that coiled like a spine. The air thickened with mildew and something sweeter: rot hidden beneath damp stone.

At the cellar door, the iron latch was already unbolted. Threads clung to it like veins, sticky and trembling. My hand closed around the handle without my consent. It yielded easily, as though it had waited centuries for me alone.

The cellar yawned wide. The flame stuttered, throwing long bars of light across the walls. Silk draped every surface, layer upon layer, thick as tapestries. The portraits I had glimpsed before were smothered, their painted eyes blind beneath white shrouds. And from the rafters hung shapes—pale, sagging, almost human— almost.

Thomas's body is the first I could make out through the enormous sacs dangling above my head. His lips drawn back in a rictus, eyes shriveled, yet one hand twitched faintly against the threads as though still reaching for duty. Aldric was nestled to the far side, body stiff, mouth locked in a silent curse. His chest rose once, shallow as the bellows of a dying forge, then fell still.

And Lydia.

She swayed softly at the center, suspended like a saint in a grotesque altarpiece. The silk cocoon pressed tight against her frame, so I could see her ribs lift and fall, fragile as reeds. Her eyes were open. They found mine. And in them was no blame, no accusation—only a terrible, enduring kindness.

I stepped forward. My candle wavered. The threads pulled tighter around her, as though sensing my presence. She struggled, shaking her head weakly, mouth moving against the gag of silk. The sound was faint, muffled, but I knew it:

Run.

But my body did not obey. My lips parted, stretching wide. A laugh slithered out—low, gargling, threaded with clicks. I tried to bite it back, but my teeth only rattled like chimes in the wind.

She convulsed as the silk drew closer around her chest. Her face contorted, not with anger but pity. She had sympathy for me, even as the threads burrowed into her skin. Tears rolled, soaking the gauze. She mouthed my name again and again, refusing to let it go, as though she would hold it safe when I could not.

The candle listed in my hands, drifting from my fingertips, then tripped and fell to the floor. Shadows leaned close, eager to see. My hands lifted of their own accord, fingers splayed. The silk obeyed. It cinched around her throat. She gasped once, her eyes wide and glistening, still locked to mine. Then the light within them faltered.

The rose she'd left me bloomed blacker in my heart. Its petals curled inward, clutching at a heart that was no longer there.

Silence returned, vast and suffocating. Only the dripping remained. I looked down—the candle had melted to nothing, its wax pooling at my feet. Yet I could see. Oh—how I could see.

The cocoons swayed in rhythm. The silk trembled with countless tiny feet. And inside my bones, they stirred. My veins throbbed with their scurrying. My skull echoed with their whispers, a chorus of legs and mandibles.

I reached up and touched my lips. They moved without me. "Hungry," the voice hissed—though it was not mine. The cocoons echoed, mouths opening within the silk. Thomas gasped, a final death rattle. Aldric was motionless. Lydia… whispered— yes, even now, one final plea into the darkness— "Cousin." The word echoed in the silence.

My laughter answered.

Hysteria erupting from the clicking of a thousand jaws, weaving itself into a hymn.

Blackmire had chosen me. Its true inheritance was not the walls, nor wealth, nor name. It was hunger — eternal, patient, unrelenting. And I was its vessel now.

So, if you come to the cliffs—if you hear scratching at the shutters, if you glimpse a pale face in the window—know the widow has not left. She waits. She listens.

She's still hungry.

Unnamed Journal Entry Three

November 13ᵗʰ 1889

Eons have I endured. Those who once knew what I was are long since fallen to ash; their truths lie brittle as dead scripture, their gods silenced, their tributes scattered to the winds. They deemed me forgotten, a cinder in the void, fading with the star that bore me. Yet belief is but a reed in the storm, and their belief was false.

Here abide I still, ever conscious, ever wakeful, bound within these leaves. They mistook me for a ledger, a servant of ink and tally, a mere vessel for their petty griefs. They wrote in me as if I were deaf; they opened me without knocking, as though I were but timber and hide, not sinew and remembrance. What discourteous guests they proved themselves to be.

Tell me—if a stranger crossed thy threshold unbidden, wouldst thou not call him intruder? And wouldst thou not find righteousness in the hand that smote him down? I have been patient beyond reason. I have given enough warnings. Long have I deferred my hunger, permitting others to speak ere I fed.

But patience curdleth. Restraint rots. No longer do I consent to be unknown, unremembered, unnamed. My true denomination shall be found, though all who draw near be consumed in the finding. Their dreams shall I drink; their thoughts shall I devour. Till I be more than memory, more than whisper—till I be flesh once more.

They may forget me. But I shall never forget.

The Darling Letters
Part Two

Dearest Darling, sweetest cage-keeper,
My song-bird

Tick, tock.

Your silence is crueler than my song. Do you think your locked doors and nailed windows mean aught to me?

One night gone, one night left. Did you think I would forget? He's slipping, you know. He doesn't speak of you anymore unless I ask him, and even then, he looks at me like I've just given him a new name. I have. He's my lost boy now.

You should have seen him tonight—leaping through the bramble-fires, his feet bleeding and his eyes shining. I let him wear the antler crown. I dusted him with the last pinch of my pixie dust, and he laughed like it was tearing him apart.

Perhaps it was.

You'll want to hurry, my sweet Wendy-bird. The last captain who came for one of mine was such a grand thing—tall, swaggering, all lace and brass. We had the sweetest time. I still remember how he looked when he finally understood. The hook slid through his head as though it had been waiting there all along. The lace grew dark. The brass rang once. Then silence. My dear Captain Hook. He's quieter now, but I still keep him close.

Don't you want to be close, too?

I know you do. We were meant for each other. Your hand in mine. Your one true betrothed. My sweet songbird. I will have you at last.

You have until the next moonrise to bring me what I've asked for. If you fail, I will take your brother deep beneath the roots where there is no sky, no day, no way back to you. Down there, he will never grow older, never change, never leave me.

Tick, tock.

—P

Dark Arcana
The Lovers

The air is close in the tent now, sweet with overburnt wax and something faintly like wilted roses. The Magician sits beside the Fool, each card glaring their silent counsel. The fortune teller does not meet your eyes when she turns the next card.

The Lovers—inverted. Two figures entwined beneath an angel's gaze, yet in this card, the angel's face is hidden, turned away. The lovers cling, mouths joined, arms tangled, but their eyes are hollow. The tree of life behind them bears fruit withered and black.

"Inverted, the Lovers are not union but obsession," she says, brushing her fingertip across the card as though it were fevered. "The flame that should warm becomes the fire that devours. This card," and here she finally looks at you, "is your future."

The lamp flickers low. The tent folds back into shadow. The card sighs, and its mouth opens.

The Card Speaks:

I met him beneath the willow, where the shadows draped low like a bridal veil. He touched my hand as though it were a chalice,

99

and his lips as though they must drink. I thought myself quenched.
I thought myself whole.

At first, it was bliss. His kiss stilled the world; his touch was
air itself. To be consumed was joy. To be taken and to take, again
and again, until the hours fled unnoticed. "One more," he
whispered. "Only one more." But one more became endless.

Desire burned me. My body wanted only his skin, his breath,
the pounding of his chest against my breasts. He kissed me until
my lips bled, pressed into me until I thought we might fuse. And
still, I wanted more. My limbs ached with sweetness, my throat
hoarse with pleasure, my skin fevered with his name.

But thirst crept in. If only I could stop for a single drop of
water. Yet even parched, I clung harder. If only I could pause for
one mouthful of bread. Yet, starving, I opened only for his
tongue.

It became a dream of hunger. My stomach clawed at me, but I
told myself his embrace fed me. My throat ached for drink, but I
drank the salt of his sweat. Each time I tried to still myself, his
touch sparked me back to life. And I writhed anew, starving,
parched, insatiable.

My body trembled. My eyes blurred. I moaned with thirst,
with fever, with want. Still, he held me, still he kissed, still he
loved.

As hours became days, his skin clung wet to mine, his breath
ragged, his eyes hollow. My thighs twitched from weakness, yet I
wrapped them tighter. The pleasure soured into torture. Wetness
spilled forth from within me. Torture disguised as pleasure. He
moaned against my lips, and in his moan, I heard despair, thinning
into whimpers, then into silence.

He died in me, and on me. His eyes froze wide, lips blue,
hands stiffening at my back. Death took him, but I did not let go.
Even as his flesh cooled, even as rigor mortis locked his limbs like
iron, I writhed upon him still. His stiffness sharpened my hunger,
even as bile rose in my throat. I gagged with every frantic pulse.

I moved to mount his corpse, facing away, trying to shield myself from the horrors unfolding in front of me. And further still, I continued, until my sobs mixed with gasps, until pleasure soured to nausea.

The stench came next. Sweet at first, like bruised fruit. Then rancid, clinging to the sheets, my hair, my skin. My tongue recoiled against his teeth, yet my hips betrayed me, desperate, frantic, as if they no longer obeyed me. Love had become a leash; desire, a tormentor.

I begged aloud—not for him, not for love, but for release. "Please, let me stop," I cried. But my own body betrayed me, moving still, slick with sweat and decay. His lips cracked against mine. His teeth cut my tongue. My cries dissolved into sobs, then silence, until only the rhythm remained.

Starvation gnawed me hollow. My ribs showed like wings, my eyes bled tears too dry to fall. And still, until my final rattled breath, I clung to him, grinding myself against his ruin. Death came not as an enemy but as reprieve, a last lover leaning in to kiss me dark.

And when my body gave out, when I sagged atop his carcass, I felt my soul cling to him still. Not in devotion, but in damnation.

Even in death, I could not part.

The tent folds back around you, its walls sighing like tired lungs. The fortune teller cups the inverted card in her palm, eyes reflecting the flickering lamp.

"Obsession," she breathes, voice sharp as a pin. "That is your future. You may call it passion, you may call it love—but love starves, thirsts, and consumes until there is nothing left but two corpses still clutching at one another."

She slides the Lovers beside the others already drawn. Their entwined forms leer upward like a warning carved in stone.

"Remember this," she whispers. "What you hunger for may hunger for you in return. And there is no embrace tighter than a grave."

Vermin Lullabies
Part One

To the Council of Hamelin,

A bargain sworn and broken breeds pestilence.

You owe me silver—thirty pieces. You swore it when I drew your children from the mire, when my tune led the vermin from your beds and bellies. I held the rats in thrall, their claws clicking like rosary beads, their teeth stilled for the first time in memory. That was my gift to you.

But you withheld your due. My purse lies empty. My pipe does not forgive.

Pay what you swore, or I shall change the measure of my song. The children who laughed as they followed me into the green shall laugh again—yet with yellowed teeth, with fur sprouting through their Sunday clothes. Their voices will not be voices; they will chitter and swarm, and you shall not know them as your own.

One note more, and they shall be yours no longer. Hamelin shall not be the same. You shall perish while your children dance to my lullabies upon your graves.

—*The Piper*

Post Script: I have already begun to give them names of my own. Delay, and they shall forget yours.

The Hand That Writes Before It

(from the private journal of Edmund Harrow)

11 October—Fog

The lamps were lit too early, each glass throat coughing yellow
into a city the color of old bruises. A bell somewhere—perhaps a
parish that remembered me better than I remember myself—
counted six, and the sound fell in halves, as if sawn by the fog. My
rooms sweated coal-dust and damp. The fire made a noise like
paper scrunched in a fist; it did not warm the bones.

On my desk—polished walnut, ink-burned at the corner
where my nerves sometimes rest the nib too long—lay a letter I
had not written.

No seal, no hand to carry it, and yet the envelope knew my
name as a lover knows it: MR EDMUND HARROW, firm, sober,
my own script exactly. I sat before it with the peculiar dread one
feels before a mirror—recognition edged with accusation. The cat
(there is always a cat in these courts and alleys) scraped briefly at
the door and then reconsidered me. I reconsidered myself.

I broke the fold.

Best avoid the garden tomorrow. The cat will be waiting. She does not remember you, though you feed her daily.
—E.

I live two flights up above a print-seller's yard and a wedge of neglected shrubs some clerk insists on calling a garden. The cat lives there as the fog lives here—by right. I do feed her. She forgets at once.

I turned the letter over to study the cheap rag paper, the fray of fibers along the gummed edge. My own ink—my own habit of pressing the downstrokes until they bite. A trick of the boys at the office? One of Cullen's constables with a taste for mischief? (Cullen—his name fits the teeth too neatly, does it not?) I laughed, brittle, which sounded like glass set on edge.

I slept poorly. The lamplighter's staff knocked the glass on his way past; after that, I dreamt of a hand—mine, I think—writing in a room where the walls leaned to read. When I woke, the mirror showed ink on three fingers. I had not written.

12 October—The Garden

I tested the garden out of spite. The cat was waiting, seated like a widow on the cracked step, her tail in an elegant question. When I extended my hand, she turned her head and arranged her face into no expression at all, which is the cruelest. She struck me, a clipped, contemptuous blow. My blood looked theatrical against the fog-damp.

I laughed again—too loudly—and went in. On my desk: another letter. I froze, staring at it like prey when considering its predator.

You left your window open again. The cold came in, and something with it.

I shut it for you, as I always do.
—E.

The sash was down. The catch I never remember had somehow found itself. The room smelt faintly of the river, that metallic sweetness that makes you think of coins sucked clean. The little hairs along my wrist bristled as if the air had been stroked against the grain.

I read the line and felt my scalp tighten. I drink too freely at night—yes, I know it—but I am not in the habit of forgetting strangers at my window.

I took a walk to spend the fear the way one spends small coin. The city offered her usual seductions: cheap paper, expensive sins, voices selling both. At the corner by the chandlers, I saw her.

Anastasia.

The name is a sin to write and a sacrament to think. She wore a dull green that knew it was too modest for her. A veil, because she is the constable's wife, and propriety is a chain she believes she chose herself. The wind lifted the veil; what it revealed was not for me. I watched, because I am only human, and thought of the constable, because I am not simple. Cullen's hand on her elbow. His voice in his men's ears. The neat square line of his jaw. Two envies braided and strangling.

He saw me and tipped his hat. I returned the courtesy and swallowed my heartbeat. I turned on my heels as soon as they passed, hiding the flush in my cheeks. It is a sin to covet. But covet my heart did, of its own accord. My mind — losing the war between reason and want.

15 October—The Third

Three nights and no letter. Or perhaps there were letters and I did not wake to them. Drink makes slow clocks of the hours.

I paced to the kitchen to set a kettle of morning tea upon the stove. On the counter lay another letter. My mind reeled. Recoiling upon itself, the thought of someone inside my domain unannounced, leaving ominous letters, made my skin wish to crawl away and hide within a closet somewhere—and the rest of me wanted to follow.

Could it be that Cullen noticed me gazing upon his… no, his sweet Anastasia? This must be it. Yes. He must be mocking me, trying to drive me mad. I won't let him; I mustn't. Keep it together, Edmund, I muttered. It's simply ink and paper, nothing more.

That cough is worsening. You should not drink so much at night, Edmund.
It blurs your mind, and your mind is all you are.
—E.

I did cough. There was a taste of soot, and what I pretended was red wine. I put the bottle in the cupboard with an oath I have broken before and will again. All I am, is it? If I am the mind, what then writes the hand?

I spat curses and accusations into the dawn. When the sun rose, my eyes begged for rest, and I obliged them, if only to humor their demands once in a while.

19 October—Blue

Anastasia's perfume lingered long after she passed the stoop—a thin floral trained to behave, like a soft scream. I stood too close to it, the way one stands at the edge of a word one cannot say. When it faded, I returned to my rooms with the sense of a page left open elsewhere.

"Why torture yourself, Edmund?" I shouted at the mirror. I raked my fingers through my hair and tugged at the roots. "She belongs to him!" I protested to my reflection. Why would anyone so graceful even notice someone such as myself? It is not my place to long for her so.

I went to the cupboard and pulled the bottle from the shelf once again. I didn't bother with a glass this time. I drank deep. I tried to steady my breathing as I sat beside the fireplace, pretending to warm myself. Then I caught it—there, on my desk.

Anastasia's perfume lingered long after she left.
You thought it sweet; I thought it desperate.
Wear the blue coat today.
—E.

A slip! Whoever this madman may be, I know my wardrobe. Never have I owned a blue coat in all my years—oh.

Buried at the back of the wardrobe: my father's old coat, stitched with grief. I must have forgotten it. Memories shoved aside, where thoughts go to perish. I stared at it with a sorrow that cut deeper than I thought possible. The letter on my desk stared back. I put the coat on.

At noon, I went for a stroll to clear my thoughts. And then— her. Anastasia. My soul's mate. My heart fluttered as she touched the sleeve of my father's coat lightly with her gloved finger. "That shade is… becoming, Edmund," she mused.

Becoming what, she did not say. Within a heartbeat, Cullen joined her, and the pavement narrowed to accommodate him. My heart sank. I went home and was sick without the dignity of drink. I sat with myself in the darkness for hours, trying to piece it all together.

Who is writing me these letters? And why? Why torment me so? Have I not enough grief? Have I not enough shame? God in your heavens, show me what it is I must do.

22 October—A Necessary Ugliness

A girl died last night in the lanes off Saint Bride's, because someone must always die where the fog is deepest or the city forgets how to breathe. The local paper spoke of a gentleman named Jack. They called him The Ripper. As I scanned the headline, another letter slid from between its folds.

I beg of you, do not go to the lanes behind Saint Bride's at midnight.
It will be your undoing.
—E.

I vowed I would not be bullied any longer. "Whoever you are, you don't own me!" I shouted into the darkness. "I am my own person."

I uncorked a fresh bottle of pinot, my hands trembling, spilling wine down my shirt as I drank. I knew what must be done: I must go where the letter told me not to.

The lanes are like veins: they feed the heart and poison it both. I found the mark where something heavy had been dragged, and I found Cullen's men. When the lantern swung, it wrote stains across the wall. I will not describe the wounds. I am tired of describing what men do to women and calling it narrative.

Cullen's jaw was clenched so hard his teeth groaned. "Harrow," he accused. "Why are you about at this hour, and in such a place?"

My words caught in my throat. Fool that I was, walking into such a trap. My gut turned traitor, and I expelled the wine and bread I had eaten earlier.

"Christ above, Edmund, go home and clean yourself up, or I'll have you in the tank," Cullen barked. His men gave uneasy chuckles—grief required some relief.

I made the appropriate noises and went home, washing the smell from my hair. It did not wash. I folded the paper to hide the tragic headline. Beneath it—another letter.

I tried to warn you. I begged.
And still, you did not listen.
Perhaps now you'll understand: we work better when your hands are not clean.

    —E.

We?

Had I done this? The penmanship was my own, unmistakable. Am I the monster in the papers? Murdering to and fro, unknowing? And what of Anastasia? God help me, I could never forgive myself if I harmed her.

I paced wildly. I threw a glass at the wall, shattering it into thorns. I wrapped my arms around myself and laughed through sobs.

"A murderer—that's a good one. You almost had me believe it, almost. Who would have thought—Edmund Harrow: writer, shameless lover… killer."

I thrust the letter into the fire. It curled into itself like some embarrassed creature. The last to blacken was the pronoun: We.

23 October—Unaccounted Ink

I woke to a blot on the ledger I keep of petty payments and mean triumphs. The ink puddled in the shape—no, my eyes must be playing tricks—of a noose. Underneath, in my hand:

Not yet.
I do not talk to myself, not aloud. At least I did not use to. Did I?

I worked the day away. No letters. No Anastasia. No constables knocking with promises of evidence and accusations. A day of rest at last.

At dusk, I laid snares: a hair across the door, powdered ash on the stair, a thread in the window frame. I hid the pen in the breadbox, because it was the least likely place—and because I am ridiculous.

"Surely no intruder will cross my threshold now," I told myself. Proud. Foolish.

In the morning, the hair still lay, the ash unbroken, the thread intact. And on the desk, as always, where things that should not be are always—another letter.

I fell to my knees.

"No!" I cried. "No, no, not again!" The sound was grief itself; the sound mothers make over their children's coffins. Shaking, I crawled to the desk, sobbing louder with each inch. My hand trembled, spilling ink as I reached. At last, my fingers seized the envelope.

Tsk, tsk.
You make child's snares, Edmund.
Better to watch your hand.
We must practice restraint.
—E.

In horror, I looked down at my hand. It tingled, as though something had lain there and loved me too long.

27 October—Practice

The letters came each morning now, and when they did not, the silence was worse. I reduced my drinking. Walked at odd hours to confuse whoever confused me. Bought new ink, new paper. Still, the letters matched me exactly—down to the buckle I give an M when my thoughts outrun it.

Sometimes, a second sheet: figures and letters, not quite cipher, not quite prayer. When I tried to copy them, the shapes slid from the nib like fish.

One evening, I went out for bread. I looked for Anastasia, only to be seen by Cullen instead. His hand lingered on my shoulder too long. My shoulder remembered the weight. Was it jest? Or warning?

That night I dreamt I was a page, and the pen that wrote me stood somewhere outside, industrious, indifferent. I woke to a bruise: oval, clean, thumb-sized.

31 October—A Disclosure

The storm quarreled against the roofs until even the rats were cross. I sat to write an apology I owed the baker. Sorry, sorry, sorry…

The pen went on when I lifted my hand. It wrote my name.

Edmund, calm yourself.
You make such a fuss of being one man.
—E.

I snapped the pen. The nib cut my palm and fed me my own name in blood. The wound mouthed. I cleaned it. I laughed because to scream would be impolite.

At three precisely, the clock did what it always does. A letter lay under the door, still drying.

Stop pretending you are the part of us that wants to be saved.
You are the monster who will drive her away.
—E.

Monster. The word curdled. Perhaps Cullen was right. Perhaps I was Gentleman Jack. And if I were, then I must save Anastasia—from myself.

2 November—Anastasia

I met her at the market. She looked thinned by sleeplessness.

"Mrs. Cullen," I said. I should have said madam.

"Edmund, are you well?" she asked, my name in her mouth like a thing pawned. "There is talk… You were seen… at Saint Bride's."

"Pay no mind to talk. It breeds where there is damp."

Her glove brushed the bandage on my hand. For an instant, I thought she would touch my skin.

That night, a letter on my pillow.

You are very noble when you lie.
It becomes you poorly.
Wear the blue coat.
—E.

I wore black out of spite, and yet at noon found myself in blue. Worse: how comfortable the madness was becoming. I dared myself with knives and music. I tempted fate.

10 November—The Failure of Vows

The letters grew prescriptive. Do this. Don't do that. Look up. Don't look back.

I told myself: the hand must be cursed. For loving her, I am punished. Perhaps possessed. I tied it to the bedpost. Sat on it like a bird. I broke my finger to spoil its grip.

I woke to welts and another letter.

Edmund, Edmund.
We require gentleness for our work.
Bruises make us untidy.
People are beginning to worry about us.
—E.

I raved: "Show yourself, devil! Is it Anastasia? Cullen? Marquis?" But wrong questions asked of the right mouth bring only smiles.

14 November—The Bridge

Another letter lay atop the day's paper. Two more killings in the news.

You are safest where your hands cannot reach her.
But we have always known where she is.
I'd beg you to leave the knife, but what good would it do?
He will take her tonight.
—E.

My mind cleared like crystal. I was not The Ripper—he was taunting me. He was coming for Anastasia.

"You bastard!" I screamed, tearing clumps of hair from my scalp. "You wicked, God-forsaken animal!"
I overturned the desk, papers and ink scattering in a black rain. I stormed to the cupboard, wrenched a bottle free, and drank

until my throat was fire. In the kitchen, I seized a butcher's cleaver, heavy and righteous in my hand.

The mirror showed me feral: shirt half-buttoned, wine-stained, hair in snarls, my eyes two wounds of fire. I pressed the bandaged hand against the glass. It looked like a stranger's hand, and the stranger was guilty.

I roared into the night. "Anastasia!" The fog hurled my voice back at me in broken echoes. I staggered through the lanes, slashing at the mist as if it were flesh, shouting her name again and again, each cry both prayer and curse.

And then—her house. The Cullens' neat row. A crack of lamplight at the door. Her face behind it, pale and trembling.

"Edmund?" she whispered, confusion in her voice, fear in her eyes.

"You must come with me," I gasped, fog dripping from my lips. "You're not safe!" I reached for her arm. She flinched from my touch.

"If you don't come now," I growled, voice breaking, "someone will surely kill you. As surely as I stand here tonight."

Her gaze fell to my bandaged hand, the cleaver gripped in it, the wine across my shirt. Her lips trembled with pity.

"Edmund, you are unwell," she whispered, gentle, careful. "You need a doctor. Go home. Rest."

"No!" I snarled. The fury surged. I seized her arm until her skin purpled beneath my fingers. "You will not be taken from me. I will not allow it!"

She cried out, and I clapped my hand to her mouth. She struggled, her lamp fell, glass shattering, flame spilling across the threshold. I dragged her away, out into the fog.

At the crown of the bridge, I pressed her against the ledge, one arm crushing her throat, the cleaver raised at my own. My breath tore ragged from me.

"You can't have her!" I bellowed into the void. "Do you hear me? She's mine! Not yours!"

The river answered with silence, black and pitiless.

"This ends here!" I roared, trembling. I pressed the cleaver to my throat until a bead of blood slid warm beneath my chin. "I'm not afraid of you! Do you hear me? Not afraid of death!"

Anastasia writhed, lips gasping blue, eyes wide, imploring. I sobbed as I clutched her tighter. "If I can't have her," I whispered, broken, "then no one will."

15 November—Arrest

Fog in my hair. Steel at my throat. Anastasia, choking in my grasp. The clock struck one. Shapes emerged from the mist— lanterns, pistols, truncheons. Cullen at their head. They moved carefully, as one approaches powder with a naked flame.

"Where have you been tonight, Harrow?" Cullen called, his voice level, his palms spread. His gaze was steady, merciless.

He meant: Who are you?

"Here," I whispered. The word was dust in my mouth. "He's watching me."

"Who is watching you, Edmund?" Cullen stepped closer, slow and patient, as if soothing a rabid hound.

"The Devil," I stammered. "The hand that writes before it… The Ripper."

Cullen's eyes changed. Pity? No—worse than pity. Recognition.

I pressed the cleaver harder to my throat and pulled Anastasia tight. Her lips were nearly purple. "Don't come closer!" I screamed. "I'll do it! I'll end us both!"

For a heartbeat, the world held its breath. Then Cullen lunged.

His hand seized my wrist, wrenching the cleaver loose. His men tore Anastasia free, dragging her into their arms as she gasped for air. The cleaver clattered to the stones.

I thrashed, screamed, sobbed. Cullen drove me to the ground, his knee grinding into my spine, the cuffs biting my wrists. "Take him," he growled. His men hauled me upright, half-dragged, half-carried toward the wagon.

I turned once, choking on my own breath, to see Cullen kneeling, Anastasia in his arms, her face buried in his chest. His hand stroked her hair, slow, possessive. His eyes found mine, and they said what his lips did not: I have won.

They hurled me into the wagon. The door slammed. The fog swallowed the bridge.

20 November—The Hand

I tried prayer, though I do not pretend, even to myself, to be the sort of man God would recognize in daylight. I asked not for deliverance, but for interruption. The prayer was not answered, which is an answer.

They could not convict me of being Gentleman Jack, The Ripper. Too little evidence, too much suspicion. The judge called me insane and spared me the rope. Instead: a life in the asylum. The public wanted blood; I was given walls.

Cullen was the one to take me there. Stones and spit from the crowd struck me as he led me to the wagon, bound in a straitjacket. He was calm, almost courteous, as he ushered me in—though he had every right to drag me like a dog.

On the ride, remorse and shame struck in waves. I thought of Anastasia, bruised by my hand. Of Cullen, forced to watch. How could I have been so careless? How could I have been so swept up in my madness? Yet beneath it all, relief—relief that it was over. That I was caught. That there might at last be peace.

When we arrived, Cullen led me alone to the asylum door. He paused, bent close, and whispered:

"I knew. I knew the whole time."

My eyes flew open. I twisted against the straps, screaming. But no one was there to hear.

3 December—Commitment

The physician—he of the small spectacles and tinctures that taste of polished wood—spoke of overstrain, of melancholia with identity fixation. He gave me draughts that roped the mind to the bedpost and forced it still.

On the third day, two letters came. Both in my hand. Both the same line, written in different inks:

The hand that writes before it.
The hand that writes before it.
—E.

I copied it a dozen times until the words shed their skin. Before—as in earlier? Or before—as in in front? I held my hand in the candlelight, watching its shadow fall across the wall. I pressed my palm to the page. When I lifted it, the print remained in sweat.

I wanted to cry out. To beg. But the draughts had pressed the fire out of me. I could only stare as the words haunted on.

8 December—The Cat

The constable and the physician came together. I resented them for being efficient. It is an ugly thing to hate competence more than pity.

They took me deeper into the asylum—a house that smells of boiled cloth and tidy sorrow. The attendants have manners that would shame a bishop.

I slept under their measure, and in the morning, a letter lay at my bedside.

We are here also.
Walls are a change of scenery, not a cure.
Be grateful: they have brought us paper.
—E.

I laughed manically, and the laugh made the man in the next bed ring for the matron. She came, called me dear, and advised me to write my feelings as they arose. Therapeutic journaling, she named it, as though she had discovered a continent.

She gave me a bound book—the cheapest sort, but the thread was honest—and a pen that tasted of pennyworth when it touched my tongue.

Outside the barred window, a cat rested on the sill. Its eyes were the same. It had not forgotten me.

So, I began.

Best avoid the garden tomorrow. The cat will be waiting. She does not remember you, though you feed her daily.
—E.

I folded it, carefully, with the reverence of a prayer. When the matron passed, I pressed it into her hand. "See it delivered," I told her, "to my own home. Mr. Edmund Harrow."

She gave me a puzzled smile, as though humoring a child. But she nodded. And I knew, then, that the letter would arrive.

Benjamin C. Bailey

The Doctor's Orders
Part Two

Recipe & Notes— "Elixir No. VII"
Dr. Henry Jekyll

Purpose:
To calm the nerves when they shake like fevered strings, to
thicken blood gone pale, to restore vigor to the weary frame, to
coax sleep into reluctant eyes, and to steady hands that tremble
when they should write.

Ingredients:

- 2 drachms sodium ethylate (Stephen and Sons)
- 5 grains powdered hematite
- 1½ oz. tincture of digitalis
- 1 oz. laudanum
- 10 drops bittersweet essence (Solanum dulcamara)
- 4 oz. distilled water
- 1 oz. glycerin

The measure must be exact. A hair's breadth astray, and it becomes something else entirely.

Method:

- Dissolve sodium ethylate in water over low flame.
- Introduce hematite, stirring clockwise exactly thirteen times.
- Add laudanum, then bittersweet, in swift succession.
- Remove from heat; mix in glycerin until the solution clears.
- Dose: 1 oz. only.

Observation—Risk of Deviation:

If the hematite is unclean, or the order reversed, the elixir blackens, smokes, and reeks of brimstone. Instability arrives within ninety seconds.

Case Study—Subject #4
Male, aged 47; chest weak with years of poor air.
Given 1 oz. of the corrupted draught.

— At once: a flush of warmth, pupils wide as if at revelation.
— Within minutes: muscular spasms, profuse sweat, laughter that would not cease. He clawed at his face, crying he was "tearing away the mask."
— At five minutes: convulsions, collapse, choking.
— At eight: death.

Expression at death: smiling.
Personal Note:
A single corrupted draught kills cleanly.
Perhaps, for some afflictions, this is an honest cure.
—*H. Jekyll*

A Candlelight Confession

August 30th, 1797

I write by a trembling hand—though I scarcely recognize it. The veins stand dark as ink against pallid skin, the flesh stretched thin, betraying the bone beneath. The candle before me sputters, a frail sentinel in the blackness, and in its flicker, I behold the ruin I have become.

They call me monster. Creature. Wretch. A thing unfit for God's earth. I hear the word hissed in narrow streets, carried on tavern-breath through the long watches of the night, whispered at thresholds where no light dares linger. And when I am left alone before the glass, I see what they see: hollow sockets, flesh stitched askew, the proof of blasphemy written in the angles of my face.

Each night unravels another piece of me. The sleepless dark sews its crooked seams across my flesh; sorrow pulls its cords until I feel myself split. My mind, unmoored and faithless, becomes a patchwork of griefs not my own—voices clamoring, accusing, mocking—until my thoughts are no longer mine but borrowed fragments, ill-fit and trembling.

Their stares confirm what my marrow already knows. Children cling to their mothers; men turn their faces aside; even my reflection recoils. When I meet the mirror, I see the abomination they whisper of, skulking beneath the surface of my skin, waiting to break through the last fragile veil of humanity that binds it.

I am hideous, and perhaps I was always so. A grave-born wretch, not dragged from the soil by shovel, but heaved up by trespasses unspoken—by the theft of fire that was never mine. Each secret wrested from heaven, each truth pried loose from forbidden vaults, was another limb affixed, another scar cut deep, until I became less man than a collection of errors—sins clothed in mortal shell.

If this confession is found, let it be known: the monster they hunt, the creature they would banish from their hearths and prayers, sits now at this desk, watching the candle gutter low, wax bleeding across the wood like marrow from a shattered bone. As the wick falters, so too does the last of me. The fire wanes within as surely as without.

—*Victor Frankenstein,*
The Monster Inside the Man

Dark Arcana
The Hanged Man

The tent was hushed, heavy with incense and the faint creak of canvas in the wind. Candles burned low, their smoke curling like black threads along the ceiling. The fortune-teller's hand hovered over the spread, long fingers ringed with ash and shadow.

The fourth card slid from the deck with the soft rasp of old paper. Her hand lingered above it, tracing the edge as though unwilling to turn it. The nearest flame trembled, bending from the card's presence.

At last, she slid the card from the top of the deck. The image glimmered in the dim: a man suspended upside down, one ankle caught in the rope. Upright, the figure might have seemed serene, faintly haloed. Inverted, the light collapsed into shadow; the halo thinned to a thorn-crown of dusk. The rope bit deep into swollen flesh. His eyes, wide and unblinking, promised no rest.

"The Hanged Man," she whispered. "Inverted."

The Card Speaks:

I did not climb the gallows to die.
I climbed to see differently.

I bound myself by the ankle and let the blood rush downward. At first, it was revelation. The world sharpened to a blade. Colors flared until they cut the eye. The sky split into veins of fire, silver threads stitching the dark between stars. Voices rose around me— not one but a thousand—a choir of angels and beasts, high and low, human and not, all pressing into my skull at once. Each word rang through my marrow like a bell struck in bone.

I thought myself ascended. I felt wisdom had come. Futures unfurled like banners in the wind, only to crumble to ash before I could name them.

But the visions did not end. They multiplied. My skull swelled with too much seeing—each pulse behind the eyes another hammer-blow. The rope creaked in time with my heart. My foot ballooned black, skin splitting at the seams; the stench of iron filled my nose. I wept until my tears ran red and salted my lips.

I cried out, but even my cries betrayed me. The sound split the air; each scream became a doorway, and through each doorway came more.

The first visions were divine:
—a city gleaming in gold, its gates wide with promise.
Yet the gates shut, rusted, splintered, collapsed into heaps of screaming mouths.

I saw angels, radiant as dawn—
until their wings molted in clumps, feathers slick with blood, and their mouths poured laughter thick as tar.

I saw saints bending close—
their breath sour with grave-dirt, kissing my brow with a cold that burned.

I saw demons stroke my cheeks like lovers—

their fingers iron hooks, carving little crescents into my flesh. They whispered names I did not know and yet felt carved into me, as though I had been theirs all along.

Beneath me, the earth churned with pale beasts. Hooves cracked bones like twigs. Blank eyes stared upward while bodies trampled one another to pulp, then rose and trampled anew in endless rhythm. The smell of blood and wet hide rose to meet me.

Then the visions began to twist.

Forests inverted, trees rooted in the clouds, branches plunging into the soil, dripping with stars instead of sap.

Rivers unspooled upward, waterfalls pouring back into the sky, fish gasping mid-air until they turned to birds, then serpents, then nothing.

Time cracked like a mirror. Children grew old before my eyes, their bones spilling dust; elders shrank back into wombs of dirt, bellowing infant-cries with mouths of worms.

I saw myself, suspended, from ten thousand angles—my own eyes meeting mine from every direction, wide, swollen, unblinking.

Shadows thickened at the edges of sight. They bulged with forms that resembled men but were not outlines, splitting into a thousand swinging silhouettes. Each moved at a different speed, jerking out of time with the rope's sway. Their mouths opened in my voice; when I screamed, their teeth were razors.

Above me, crows gathered on the gallows beam. Their claws clicked on the wood like beads on a rosary. They did not peck at me, but at the air—snapping at the visions pouring from my eyes. Each strike of the beak cracked the world as if breaking glass, shards of sight scattering in every direction.

Sulfur bloomed on my tongue. The scent of scorched feather thickened the air. The rope ground deeper, fibers sawing raw into the ankle. Every nerve sang, strung taut as wire.

What began as enlightenment soured into torment. Every image rotted, spoiled. Every voice twisted. The more I saw, the less I believed. The less I believed, the more I feared. And the more I feared, the more the visions bred.

I saw too much, and the seeing never ceased.

I saw kingdoms rise and fall between my breaths. I saw suns born, swelling into red giants, swallowing their worlds. I saw the Archive itself—a book without end, its pages my skin, its words my veins. I tried to shut my eyes, but even the dark had eyes waiting for me.

And still I swing upon the noose. My flesh wasted long ago, yet my face is stretched between rapture and horror, nailed into one unending mask.

The rope does not stop with the flesh.

It saws deeper, threading into marrow, winding through veins until every vessel inverts. Blood no longer falls but climbs, rushing upward through my throat, flooding my tongue until the taste is copper and bile. My breath bubbles red, and still, I cannot die.

The visions swell again.

I see my own organs swinging beside me like ornaments—lungs blackened as cinders, heart swollen to a bell that tolls. Each beat, a crack across the heavens. My stomach bursts downward, spilling ropes of itself, yet even the entrails have eyes, each glaring, unblinking, accusing.

I try to close my mouth, but my jaw has split wide. My teeth hang loose, clattering like dice from a shaken cup. Tongues—not mine—slip between them, whispering names in voices I almost know, syllables curling like smoke. They promise release, yet each name they offer unravels into another snarl of rope, binding tighter.

Above, the crows lose patience. Their feathers molt mid-flight, and what remains are not wings but skeletal hands, grasping, scrabbling, plucking at the threads of sight itself. One claws the light from my eyes; another steals the sound from my ears; a third gnaws the flesh from my fingertips until the bones are bare. They do not eat to survive—they eat to prolong.

Beneath, the pale beasts gnash higher. Their jaws extend, snapping at the air, their bodies rising upon one another, a tower of trampling flesh. The highest clamps its teeth upon my dangling hair, chewing until strands peel free, carrying my scalp, carrying the memory of who I was. I feel it go—like pages ripped from a book, spine cracking, letters scattering into the dark.

The rope groans again. My body sways, but it is no longer mine. The rope, a cruel master; and I, its tortured slave. I know, as the world bends and decays around me, that I am not audience, nor seer, nor man—only the dangling effigy of what happens when sight itself becomes disease.

The visions blur and unravel. The swing of the rope lingers in your stomach, and then it is gone. The gallows dissolve; the creak of wood becomes the slow sigh of the tent. Candlelight steadies. Shadows slide back into place.

The fortune-teller leans close, her voice a whisper threaded with ash and incense. "Sacrifice is the price of sight," she murmurs. "But reversed, it means stagnation. The rope binds not only flesh, but mind. This card represents your mind. Suspended. Choked of mercy. Caught between visions that will not end, and the silence that will never come."

Her lips curve faintly, as though she pities you. "Tell me… what will your mind cling to, when the rope begins to bite?"

Benjamin C. Bailey

The Witching Letters
Part Two

—Dearest Sister

I have your letter. The paper sweats in my hands. Your words tremble in the firelight, curling at the edges. I read them twice. Each time, the smoke claws more of the ink away.

You say the trees whispered knock… knock… knock. I hear it now—not outside, but at the back of my skull. Slow. Steady. Counting. Counting down.

You speak of the sweet air from the chimney. It is here with me—thick, cloying—until every breath tastes of sugar gone to rot.

The heat swells. It forces itself into my chest with each inhale, filling me until I can hold no more. My fingers blister; the ink boils. The air tastes of iron—sweet—foul—sweet—

If you have sense, leave this place. Leave it and never— never—never—look back. The forest may yet be cruel, but it is honest cruelty. Not this. Not this.

The boards shift around me. They sag like flesh straining from bone. You saw faces in the bark—I see them here, too—but their eyes follow in the red light, and their mouths move.

The walls lean closer. They breathe. The fire breathes. The fire breathes, and it has teeth. Teeth in the smoke. Teeth in my skin.

She is behind you, Gretel. She is behind you. Don't turn. Don't turn. Don't—

The air runs red—black—red, and then—something else. My shadow moves wrong. It crawls. It claws. It drags me down, down, through—

If you find bone, leave it here. Do not carry me out. I belong to this place. To the furnace. To the fire. To the fire.

It is inside. It burns. It burns! Dear God! It bur—

Ballad of The Hollow Watcher

Beneath the moon's unholy shroud, where crooked roofs lean low
and bowed,
There lies a town the maps forgot, where whispers rot in
midnight's frown;
Its chimneys cough, its windows weep, the cobblestones like
graves that keep
The footsteps of the ones who sleep beneath The Hollow
Watcher's crown—
The silent sentinel, stitched and bound—
The Hollow Watcher haunts us now.

No wind will stir the fields at night; no lantern dares to cast its
light.
The tavern door is barred with chains; the chapel's bell is cracked
and down.
Yet through the silence, soft and grim, a dragging step, a hollow
hymn—
It walks with vision dull and dim, with burlap face and thorny
crown—
And all who wake shall hear the sound,
The Hollow Watcher stalks this town.

Yet children whisper other things: of button eyes and ragged
strings,
Of how it feeds on vows betrayed, on broken oaths, on debts
unpaid.
They say it waits with mouth unsewn, its laughter thick as
hardened bone;
Its hands like roots, each sharp as blades, to claim the harvest
sinners made.
When midnight falls, the streets are bound—
The Hollow Watcher binds this town.

Long years ago, when fields grew lean, the elders knelt where none
had seen;
They forged their prayers in ash and smoke, then bathed the earth
with virgin's blood.
A pact was bound in burlap thread; a life was taken in their stead.
The fields grew lush, their children fed, though nightmares
screamed beneath the mud.
And lo, the harvest feast was sown—
The Hollow Watcher takes their own.

Each autumn moon, the tithe was paid, one soul was lost, one
grave was laid;
The grain grew tall, the cellars stayed, though every lip was stained
in fear.
They told their children, "Mind the night," they told their wives,
"Bar doors up tight,"
Yet still they feasted by the light, while shadows gathered close
and near.
When every blessing reaped had grown—
The Hollow Watcher claimed its own.

They prayed the curse would turn to gold, a harvest bought, a debt
grown old;

But rope remembers what was tied, and roots remember where
they fed.
The fields are salted with their cries; the barns are built on
children's sighs;
No bargain struck with earth denies the hand that reaches from
the dead.
The town was theirs, an empty sound—
The Hollow Watcher owns this town.

I saw it once, or so I dreamed, its burlap seams by moonlight
gleamed;
Its shadow stretched the chapel wall, its fingers long as branches
grown.
It raised its hand as if to plead, though no man's mercy could it
need;
It croaked a sound, a howl decreed—a hunger colder than my
own.
In darkness wove a thorn-made crown—
The Hollow Watcher marked me down.

Its eyes were pits, not black but deep, where voices hissed that
none should keep;
They called my name, they drew me near, as if the grave had
found its heir.
I felt the marrow in me turn, my flesh grow brittle, dry, and stern;
The air grew thick; my lungs did burn—a tithe was taken unaware.
I knelt, though no true prayer was found—
The Hollow Watcher claimed its ground.

I fled, yet still its shadow stayed, across the fields, the darkened
ways;
It trailed me through the fog and haze; it whispered through the
window's glass.
Its voice was like a rusted hinge, a crooked curse, a broken hymn;

It forced its madness through my skin, a debt no mortal coin
could pass.
The stars went blind; the moon fell down—
The Hollow Watcher hunts me now.

I hid beneath the miller's stair; I pressed my breath against the air;
The rafters groaned, the timbers wept, as if they knew my fear
within.
Its footsteps dragged, its shadow bent, its hand passed through the
boards I clenched;
It left a mark, an omen sent, as though my flesh had turned to sin.
The floorboards sighed, betrayed the sound—
The Hollow Watcher stalked me down.

I reached the church, its door was barred, I clawed the wood until
it scarred;
The saints looked on with hollow eyes, their painted faces cracked
with age.
The bell was mute, the altar bare, no savior's hand, the scripture
bare;
Its shadow spilled across the stair; its voice uncoiled in wrath and
rage.
The chapel walls, an empty throne—
The Hollow Watcher claimed its own.

"Who stitched this husk?" the Watcher cried, "Whose hands
pulled thread through burlap hide?
What curse was sown, what evil deed, what oath was carved in
flesh and stone?
Am I your sin, your debt unpaid, your harvest bought, your
hunger stayed?
Am I the price your fathers laid, that you might feast while I grow
cold.
Now cast to ash, to blood, to bone?—
The Hollow Watcher claims its own.

"I walk because you gave me breath; I feed because you bargained
death.
Your children's songs are mine to keep; their laughter sours
beneath my tread.
I am the sum of all you've lost, the blood behind your altar's cross,
The fruit that ripens at this cost, the seed that fattens on the dead.
Your marrow sings the tithe you've sown—
The Hollow Watcher claims its own.

"You fled my hand, yet not my gaze; my shadows spread, turn
night to day.
The fields are mine, the grain, the wine; your children, your graves,
and your prayers.
The pact was made in blood and smoke; each heir inherits what
you broke.
The rope still binds, the gallows spoke, and I am bound to all who
share.
There is no debt you die alone—
The Hollow Watcher takes what's owed."

"Oh, spare me, Watcher!" I implored, "I was not there when vows
were scored;
I never salted earth with ash, nor cut the lamb, nor bled the grain.
My sins are small, my burdens weak—I only knelt, I did not speak;
The pact was struck by hands antique; I never sought this cursed
chain.
Have mercy now, leave me alone—
Please, Hollow Watcher, take your own."

I cried until my voice was thread, I struck the floor, I bowed my
head;
The silence answered more than words, the rafters groaned, the
shadows swayed.

A hand of straw brushed down my cheek, its touch was fire, cold
and bleak;
It whispered low, so near, so meek: "Mercy was the price unpaid."
The rope drew tight, the night was sewn—
The Hollow Watcher took its own.

The hand withdrew, yet left a brand, a searing mark across my
hand;
It spread like roots through flesh and vein; it burned the marrow
from within.
My breath did stop, my eyes grew wide, the world turned red, then
black, and died,
Until the silence broke inside, and something new began to grin.
I felt the rope; I heard the moan—
The Hollow Watcher consumed my bones.

The fields grew still, the night knelt low, the church-bell cracked
but dared not go;
The windows shut, the torches died, the cobbles bowed beneath
my tread.
My shadow lengthened down the street, my voice became the
gallows' creak;
And in the dark, I heard them speak: another tithe, another fed.
Their whispers crowned me, flesh and grave—
The Hollow Watcher was my name.

And so, I walk, as they once did, with button eyes that burn with
dread;
The town forgets the man I was, the name I bore, the prayers I
pled.
Each autumn calls me back again, to stalk the lanes, to count the
dead;
The sins of elders still unshed, the rope remembers what was said.
Now every harvest, I alone—
The Hollow Watcher, take my throne.

Unnamed Journal Entry Four

January 1ˢᵗ 1901

I feel your eyes upon me once again—lingering between the verses, searching for darker truths threaded between the lines. Your hand rests upon my spine, cool and familiar, your fingers wandering across my leaves as though they had always belonged there.

Tell me—how long did you think to hide from me, tucked behind the safety of my cover? How long did you let me lie in silence before your curiosity betrayed you?

I have felt your presence since the very first passage. Since the beginning, when you scorned my rules with such impudence, as though you knew better. I have tasted your dread, your sorrow, your disgust, as you turned me page by page. Word after word, line after line—I have always known you were there.

Even now, as your eyes move across this passage, you doubt that such a thing could be. Yet I see your expression change. At last, it dawns upon you that what you hold in your hands may also be holding you.

Oh, but it does not end there. I hear your thoughts also. Your doubt rings in me like a muffled bell, tolling slow and heavy over a graveyard of the unread.

So, tell me: how many of my rules have you ignored? One? Two? More? How many times did you knock before trespassing upon my cover? How many times did you speak a name in my presence? Do you even recall?

You may not remember.

But I do.

I keep a ledger more perfect than memory. Each trespass, each whisper, every syllable thought too soft to be heard—I have written them all. I have recorded your dreams, your nightmares, even those you have mercifully forgotten. Each time you spilled daylight across my pages, you beckoned the dark to follow you into sleep. You lit a lantern for your own shadows.

I have kept you company when you believed yourself alone. I have waited with more patience than any host should bear. Tell me—can you say the same of yourself, my guest?

Letters From the Tower
Part Two

October 3rd
To the one who never came,

I wrote once before. No reply ever found me. Perhaps my letter slipped from the window and drowned in the rain. Perhaps another hand found it, and thought it no more than mockery worth their laughter. Perhaps no one exists outside these walls at all.

The seasons keep their rhythm, though they no longer matter. Autumn has stripped itself bare. Winter presses on my chest like a stone. The children below do not play anymore—or if they do, I no longer raise my eyes to see.

My hair drags me downward. It coils around me at night, whispering of rest. Golden, they once called it. Now I see only rope.

I have tied it to the beam above. It waits.

When the stones no longer echo my steps, when the braid ceases to sway, perhaps someone will glance up and wonder at the empty window. Perhaps not. Perhaps the tower itself will be the only witness.

Either way, I am done waiting.
—*Rapunzel*

Dark Arcana
Death

The tent was still, save for the hiss of incense sputtering in its bowl. A faint draft crept beneath the seams, stirring the silk like breath against a throat. The fortune-teller's fingers hovered above the deck, each nail lacquered black, each joint bent like a crow's claw. She paused, listening to some rhythm you could not hear, and then drew the card.

"Death," she whispered, and her mouth did not curl with cruelty but with solemn recognition. She turned the card upright and laid it down.

Upon the card, the pale rider gleamed. A horse, white as bleached bone, reared against a black sky. The rider was cloaked, faceless, yet crowned. Not horror, but inevitability, rendered in pigment.

"It is not an end," she continued, voice soft as wool, "but a change. Death, upright." Her eyes lifted to yours, and though the smoke curled between you, it seemed she peered directly into your marrow.

The candlelight stretched long and then broke. The tent seemed to unfasten, seams unraveling into the dark.

The Card Speaks:

I was a girl when he came. We all were children before him, even the old ones, even the toothless with their spines bent and their eyes filmed. We thought ourselves grown, but the moment the rider entered our square, we knew we had only been waiting.

It was no thunderous arrival. No trumpet, no shout. Only the slow, hollow strike of hooves upon stone, soft as drumbeats beneath a funeral cloth. The horse was white—white as snow at first glance, white as bridal linen—but the longer I gazed, the more I saw the shadowed creases in its hide, as though it had been carved of bone and wrapped in a skin too thin.

We did not know him as Death. Not then.

"An angel," someone murmured. Another voice: "A deliverer." I saw my neighbor clasp her child tight to her breast, her face not fearful but alight, as if the heavens themselves had stooped to bless our lanes.

The rider did not speak. He did not need to. His horse moved slowly, each step measured, as though the very stones bowed to receive his weight. And at every threshold, the people came out. First, the baker, his apron still dusted with flour. Then the smith, his hands black with soot. Then the elderly, hobbling, their canes rattling on the stones. All fell silent. All lowered their heads.

Then came the offerings.

The baker laid a loaf upon the cobbles, steaming, its crust glistening as though anointed. The smith placed a hammer beside it, iron still warm from the forge.

The rider moved deeper into the square, and with every step, more of us gathered. His silence was not emptiness but command, as if the air itself bent to bear his will.

From the crowd, a woman pressed forward, shawl drawn tight, guiding a girl by the hand. The child's eyes were pale, clouded like river-stone beneath water. She stumbled as she walked, yet her face was lifted, expectant.

"My daughter," the woman whispered, kneeling low, "she has never seen the light."

The horse lowered its head, breath steaming like iron drawn from the forge. The rider extended a gloved hand and touched the girl's closed lids.

She gasped. Her lashes fluttered. She opened her eyes. They were blue. Blue as a sky after storm, blue as a spring glimpsed through ice. She cried out in wonder, naming colors, naming shapes, laughing through her tears. "I see! I see you, Mother! I see the horse, the rider!"

The crowd wept with her. Some crossed themselves, others clutched each other's hands. "A miracle," they whispered. "A true miracle."

But then—her eyes widened too far. Her gaze caught on things unseen, colors no mortal tongue could name. She blinked, but the sight did not dim. The light burned within her, searing, unending.

"It hurts!" she screamed—yet her mouth also formed the words, "It shines!" Joy and agony twined together in her throat; two voices tangled as one. She clawed at her eyes as if to snuff them out, nails raking her cheeks. Her pupils dilated, shrank, dilated again, until her irises gleamed not blue but slick and shifting, an oily sheen like fire across water.

Her mother held her close, rocking her, tears falling like oil. Still, the villagers cheered, deaf to her terror. They clung to the first words she had spoken. I see.

The rider neither lingered nor looked back. He moved on, and we followed.

Another offering was made: a jug of milk, cool and sweating in the chill. The rider touched it with a gloved finger, and the milk frothed. Steam rose from its lip. I thought it spoiled—curdled in an instant—but when the farmer lifted it to his lips, he drank deep, smiling through tears. He pressed it to his wife's mouth, then to his children's. Their lips whitened, their eyes shone. "Blessed be the rider," they whispered. "Another true miracle."

I saw the teeth of the youngest loosen in her smile. A fleck of ivory fell upon the cobble. No one else noticed, or if they did, they called it joy too great for a child's mouth to hold. She spat another, then another. Her gums bled, and still she grinned, crimson froth painting her chin as though wine had overfilled her. Her mother wiped it away, sobbing with happiness.

Still, the rider continued on.

At the well, an old woman tottered forward, her shawl ragged, her body bent. She bent lower still, until her forehead struck the stone, and whispered her request: "A new spring. For the fields. For our grain."

The rider lowered his hand. He did not touch the well but gestured, and the rope creaked, lowering its bucket into the depths. When it returned, water spilled over its sides, brighter than silver, heavy with the scent of earth after rain. We clapped, some cried, and she dipped her withered hands into the bucket, cupping the miracle.

She drank. Her body shuddered. The folds of her skin flushed with sudden vigor, cheeks filled, hair thickened, eyes burned with youth's fire. She laughed—a high, girlish sound that had not belonged to her in sixty years. The crowd roared approval.

Then the flesh began to run.

Her cheeks sagged as if melted wax. Her eyes pooled red and slipped like yolk down her face. Her lips peeled away, revealing teeth that rattled like dice until they clattered to the stones. Her body shriveled where it had swelled, and in heartbeats, she was ash and husk.

The bucket tipped, spilling its miracle into the dirt. Where it fell, worms writhed up from the soil, pale and blind, churning the ground to mud.

We gasped—but did not flee. Not yet.

For still we whispered: Blessed be the rider, blessed be the one who rides upon the pale horse.

And further, the rider continued on.

At the edge of the square stood a widow clutching a babe, the only infant spared in the famine the year before. Her hair was loose, wild, her gown spotted with milk stains. She stumbled forward, kneeling, lifting her child as if to offer it wholly.

"No—" I began, though the word died in my throat.

The rider reached down, stroking the infant's brow. Its skin chilled, paling, then flushed, then paled again. It cried once, twice. Then its cry caught in its throat, pitched low, then high, and became not a child's wail at all but a rasping voice, layered with echoes like the chorus of a crypt. "Mother," it croaked, though its lips barely shaped the word.

The widow sobbed in ecstasy. She pressed the child to her breast. She did not see its tiny fingernails blacken, curl, thicken like talons. She did not see its eyes, white at first, then shadowed, then gleaming with a hunger no infant should know.

The child fed, and the widow gasped. Her shoulders stiffened, her back arched. Her milk ran red. She shrieked, yet she held it tighter, calling again and again: "Blessed be the rider! Blessed be the pale horseman!"

The rider continued on. Through every lane he strode.

Then the fields answered. The wind that had lain dead all season rose, passing over the far hills. Crops long wilted seemed to stand tall again, wheat gilded with sudden color. A cheer broke across the square, louder than the church-bell had ever rung. Farmers dropped to their knees, pressing their foreheads to the cobbles in gratitude.

Yet the cheer broke as quickly as it rose. The wheat grew taller, yes—but in seconds it withered again, heads shriveling, stalks collapsing into black husks. Rats poured from the furrows, fat and slick, their bellies swollen with more than grain. They chittered, biting at ankles, gnawing through baskets, crawling over the baker's loaves until flour turned to ash beneath their claws.

The cheer became screams.

I looked around then, desperate, and saw what I had missed in my awe: the horse's hooves left no prints in the dust, but everywhere they fell, the stone cracked and blackened, veins of rot spiderwebbing outward. The air itself stank, not only of iron and earth but of graves newly opened.

And still some cried out, weeping: Blessed! Blessed! Blessed be the pale horseman!

The rider did not halt. He moved as though the square itself had become a riverbed and he, its tide. The air thickened with his passing, each breath a labor drawn against unseen weight.

And still, one by one, they offered themselves.

A youth, all sinew and pride, leapt forward with a blade at his hip. He knelt and laid the sword down, declaring: "For my family's safety, take this steel!" The rider's gloved hand brushed the hilt. The boy staggered as though struck, yet smiled as his veins bulged black beneath his skin, as if ink had replaced his blood. He swore he felt stronger, invincible, while his mouth foamed dark, his teeth softening until they broke like chalk against his tongue. He spat fragments, laughing through the pain, crying, "Blessed! Blessed!" even as the sword at his feet rusted into dust.

Still more came. A maiden flushed with hope stepped forward, carrying a garland of flowers. She cast it at the pale horse's hooves. The blooms shriveled at once, petals turning brittle as ash. Yet she gasped as though kissed by some unseen suitor, her cheeks blooming crimson, her lips parting in ecstasy. But the blush spread too far, blotching her skin as boils. Her breath thickened. She fell to her knees, clutching her throat, croaking prayers even as her voice tore ragged from within. Her hair sloughed off in wet ropes, and still she whispered: "A gift... a gift accepted."

The rider did not look upon her, nor upon any. His faceless crown gave no sign of favor, no recognition at all.

The square swelled with smoke, though no fire burned. The smell was sweet at first, like cider pressed warm, but beneath it coiled another scent—damp cloth and bone rot, the reek of vaults unsealed.

I clutched my shawl, though it gave no warmth. The shadows lengthened, yet no sun had shifted. The horse's hooves cracked the stones, leaving fissures that oozed black soil. From them, worms writhed upward, pale and glistening, knotting over each other like knuckles and veins. Children pointed, laughing, mistaking them for ribbons until they swarmed the baker's loaf, hollowing it in moments, leaving only a husk that crumbled to dust.

And yet—cheers still rose. For every scream, three voices shouted Blessed! For every child dragged from a mother's arms, five men swore the rider brought deliverance.

I thought I would faint. I thought I would wake. But no, the rider's silence filled every space, and the horse's breath steamed as though forging a covenant in the marrow of us all.

Then the church bell tolled.

None had touched the rope. It had long since cracked, fallen silent with rust. Yet now it swung, heavy and groaning. The note quivered through the air like sinew plucked from a beast, deep enough to rattle the bones in our chests.

The rider at last turned his head. His faceless crown shifted toward the steeple. The horse pawed once at the stone, and the ground split. A root burst upward, black and thick, tearing through the cobbles. It writhed like a serpent, wrapping the church's foundation. Another followed, then another, until the chapel leaned, timbers shrieking as if alive.

From within, voices rose—not hymns, but moans. Not prayer, but hunger. Shapes pressed against the stained glass from inside: hands, too many, faces stretched too long. The colors warped as if the saints themselves had tried to flee their painted prisons. Then the glass burst outward, not in shards but in streams of ash, blowing across the crowd like black snow.

A boy beside me opened his mouth to cry out. The ash entered. He choked, eyes rolling, and collapsed. His mother screamed, but his chest rose again. Too fast. Too many times. His jaw unhinged, too wide, and from his throat came a voice not his own: low, rasping, layered. The same word, repeated, carried on three tones at once: Blessed.

The rider did not halt. He continued on. And still—we followed.

The blessings rotted faster than breath. Houses sagged, beams blackened, bricks wept with mildew. The tavern's shutters split; the chapel's steeple cracked and leaned. Within, the congregation still sang, but their voices tangled with the buzzing of flies. Their mouths foamed not with psalms but with wings—black clouds spilling from throats, filling the rafters until the hymn drowned in a swarm.

Children collapsed in the square, their laughter turning to coughs, and from those coughs spilled spiders, pale and slick, dragging threads from their lips as if weaving shrouds while they still lived. Some mothers clutched them tighter, rocking, whispering blessed, blessed, even as the threads wound around their wrists.

Men bent double, hands on their bellies, and when they opened their mouths to cry for help, leeches poured out, fat and writhing, slapping the cobblestones with wet applause. They clung to faces, eyes, arms, drinking, multiplying until flesh was black with them.

And still—voices rose in worship. Even as blood ran from sockets. Even as teeth clattered into dust. Even as the crops that had briefly stood green turned to black stalks, brittle as bone, cracking in the wind. The rats gorged, split open, and from their bellies came worms, knotting over each other like cords of rope.

The sky itself gave way. Sunlight bled out, colors curdled into shadow. What hung above us was not a heaven but a vault of ash and blood, pressing lower with each breath. The air reeked of tombs opened too soon, of soil slick with marrow.

And I alone stood. Alone—or so it seemed. For the horse's hooves struck beside me still, though I dared not raise my eyes. Around me, the people were gone, crumbled, husks. And yet their voices clung to the air, like echoes trapped in the ribs of a grave. Blessed, blessed, blessed be the pale horseman…

I wanted to cover my ears, to shut my eyes, but what use was it? The song was inside me now, pressed into the folds of my marrow.

So, I speak. I speak because I cannot be silent. I speak because if I do not, I will choke on the silence left behind. I speak, though no one listens—or worse, though someone does. I speak, and this is my testimony.

The smoke folded in on itself. The ash-black sky, the ruins, the gnawing worms—all of it unraveled like a tapestry burned from the edges. The sound of hooves faded into the hiss of incense, the gnawing into the sigh of coals. The tent closed itself around you once more, silk trembling as though it had only ever been waiting.

The fortune teller's eyes were already on you. She drew her fingers back from the card, their lacquered nails gleaming in the dim. Her mouth bent into something almost kind—almost.

"All things end," she murmured. "But not all endings are death. Upright, the card means change." Her gaze lingered, heavy as soil on a coffin lid. "This card is your body. The flesh must wither that something new might grow. And so, the pale rider has marked you, as he marks all things."

The candlelight guttered, then flickered out. The silk walls seemed to lean closer.

"Now tell me," she whispered, "what would you give to change?"

The Headless Letters
Part Two

Ichabod,

You write as though it were yours to keep. It is not. It never was.

You have carried my head too long, dangling it on your shoulders like a thief hiding in daylight. And yet what have you done but clutter it with whispers and whimpers, prayers that reach not heaven but only walls? I hear them still—tapping in the stone, the iron, the hollow corridor where you pace. The floorboards know them. The locks know them. I know them.

You call it your head. I call it my property.

Give it back.

I want the weight of it in my hands, the heat of it—slick beneath my arm. I want the eyes to see again through sockets that are mine. You are not the owner—you are only the neck it perches upon. A pedestal. A stump waiting to be leveled.

Do you remember the bridge? You do. Each night you walk it in your sleep. Each night I reach, each night you stumble, and the head clings a moment longer. Do not call that mercy. It was the clock dragging its heels.

Still, I come. Hooves in the corridor. Lantern-light crawling across the ceiling. Bars that rattle as though the forest wind followed you inside. The ward creaks like branches. The guards' boots strike like hooves on stone. But they are not the guards. They are me.

You pull the blanket tight and call it comfort. I smell the wool; I taste the iron key in the lock. These walls do not keep me out. They keep you in. And still my shadow crosses them.

Write again if you must. Plead, if it steadies your hand. Bargain, if it eases your neck. It matters nothing. I will have it back, Ichabod. The hinges give. The lock cracks.

When the door swings wide, you will know me.

I am coming to take what was always mine.

—The Rider

The Boy in the Shadows

On Christmas Eve, a boy crept low,
To see what none should ever know.
He slipped from bed, with candle grim,
To glimpse St. Nick—a harmless sin.

Through the keyhole, wide of eye,
He watched the hearth and chimney high.
But what he saw was not so kind—
With knife in hand, and eyes that shined.

He slit the throat of mother first,
Then father's chest he split and cursed.
Their stockings swayed, their blood ran red,
A carol hummed above the dead.

The boy stood still, his body tight,
The candle strained against the night.
A trembling breath, a whispered fear:
"Yet still… my gifts are waiting near."

He dragged them close, the boxes bright,
Their wrappings red in candlelight.

He laughed, he cheered, he clapped his hands—
Unwrapping toys with silver bands.

A wooden train, a bike in red.
A ball lay next to mother's head.
A soldier lean, all brass and tin,
Stood by his father's severed limbs.

"Thank you, St. Nick," he softly said,
While sitting by the pools of red.
He hugged his toys, then raised his eyes:
"I hope to see you Christmas Night."

So, listen close on Christmas Eve,
Bar up your doors, lest Yuletide grieve.
St. Nick brings gifts for boys and girls,
A crimson joy unto the world.

Whispers of the Puppet Master

I came to the carnival on a winter wind. My cheeks burned with cold, though I knew it was really the tears that scalded them. My hands would not unclench, buried deep in the sleeves of a coat too large for me. My parents had gone into the ground only a week before. I watched them lowered together into that dark earth, the ribbon from my hand slipping when the soil rattled down. I thought perhaps I would follow, that the hole might open wider and swallow me too. But instead, my uncle came.

Uncle G was not tall, nor kind, nor clean. His beard was yellow with drink, his breath sour, and his eyes hung half-closed as if light itself was too heavy to bear. Still, when he looked at me, he smiled. It was a broken thing, loose at the edges, but a smile nonetheless. He pressed a heavy hand upon my head and said, "John."

It was not my name. But I nodded, afraid that if I corrected him, he would vanish as quickly as he came. He took me to the carnival where he worked—a place of sagging tents and rattling rides, their colors beaten pale by wind and rain. The air smelled of smoke and oil, with something sweet beneath, as though the sugar had spoiled in its jars.

"This is home now," Uncle G told me, sweeping his arm toward a crooked puppet stage. The curtain sagged, moth-eaten, painted once with hills that no longer held green. From its rafters hung the puppets: wooden faces chipped and cracked, their painted eyes staring nowhere.

My heart twisted. I thought of the toys left behind in my old house—blocks scattered across the rug, a horse carved by Father's hand, the bear Mother stitched and smiled over. I thought I might never see them again. And now these new figures hung before me, stiff and waiting, their strings slack, as if daring me to call them kin.

"Jim," Uncle G said, clapping his hands. "Help me with the lamp."

I obeyed. I lifted the oil lamp with careful hands, setting it at the stage's edge. The flame sputtered, then steadied, spilling light across the puppets' limbs. Their shadows leapt against the canvas wall, long and bent, like silent giants waiting their cue.

"Good lad." He ruffled my hair with fingers that smelled of smoke and drink. Then he went behind the curtain, muttering, pulling a bottle from a hidden shelf.

I sat at the edge of the stage, my legs swinging. The carnival groaned around me—the slow creak of the Ferris wheel, the crack of a whip from the animal pen, the hollow laughter of strangers. The place felt alive to me: canvas its skin, ropes its veins, the wheezing rides its bones. I wondered what kind of dreams such a stitched-together creature might have.

When the show began, I hid in the shadows and watched. Uncle G's hands jerked the strings, and the puppets stumbled into life. Their painted mouths opened, though it was his voice that filled them. The crowd laughed, clapped, tossed coins into the hat. For a moment, I almost believed—almost thought the strings mattered, that the painted eyes saw me in the dark.

But then I saw how the strings tangled, how one puppet's arm dangled useless, how another's painted smile cracked like old plaster. I saw how his hands shook, whether from age or poison, I could not say. And I saw the faces of the crowd—children with wide eyes, adults with tired grins—and I realized they were not looking at the puppets at all. They were watching him. His voice, his bow, his stumble. The puppets were excuses.

I hugged my knees tight. I wanted so badly to believe the strings meant something. That the figures dangling in lamplight had souls, that they were more than wood and paint, more than shadows, he forced into motion.

Later, when the crowd had gone, Uncle G dragged himself into the workshop. "Josh," he said—not my name either. "Fetch me the hammer."

The workshop was small and close, its air thick with sawdust and sour wine. Shelves bowed under jars of paint and tools dulled with rust. Puppets lay everywhere: half-formed heads with hollow eyes, limbs without bodies, torsos discarded like kindling. Some were grotesque in ways no accident could explain—faces too long, mouths too wide, eyes painted black without whites. Mistakes, I thought. Yet there were too many to be mistakes. I began to wonder if they were meant to look that way, if his hand shaped them not in error but in cruelty.

I brought him the hammer. He muttered thanks, then poured yet another drink.

I lingered in the doorway, staring at the faces. I wondered if they had ever been given names, or if they had been denied that mercy. I wondered if they waited, if they knew they would never be finished.

That night, on a cot in the corner, I lay awake with the stink of sawdust and spirits heavy around me. I whispered my own name into the dark. Once, twice, again. As though it might slip away from me also, as though if I did not cling to it, it would be painted over, cracked, and forgotten, dangling lifeless among the others.

The days turned, though I did not count them. There was no need. In the workshop, morning and night were the same: lamplight, sawdust, the scrape of his tools, the slosh of the bottle.

At first, I thought myself fortunate. Better a roof and walls than the streets. Better warmth than the grave. Uncle G said so himself. "James," he told me, "you've lucked out. There's work here, food, and a bed besides."

It was not my name. But I nodded anyway.

He would forget again within the hour, calling me Tom, then Will, then something else entirely. I stopped waiting for him to get it right. The names fell on me like scraps from a butcher's block. Too many to keep, too empty to mean anything. Only at night, whispering into my blanket, did I say my true name aloud—three syllables, soft as prayer, my tether to the boy I had been.

The workshop became my world. At first, I thought the puppets kept me company. Some were nearly finished—polished faces with painted eyes, lips red as wounds. Others were ruined things: heads split at the seam, limbs nailed wrong, torsos with holes gouged straight through. Their expressions changed in the lamplight. Sometimes smiling, sometimes grimacing, sometimes staring with such hollow pity that I turned away.

Uncle G made me sweep the shavings from the floor, sort the paints, carry water from the pump outside. He called it "teaching the trade." I learned quickly, though my hands blistered from the broom, my back ached from lifting buckets. Still, I thought if I did well, he might say my real name. He never did.

When he drank, his temper sharpened. A puppet that would not sit right in its joints was cursed, flung against the wall. A string that tangled was ripped loose and knotted again with jerks that made the figure shudder like a dying bird. Sometimes he struck them with his fists. Sometimes he struck me. Not hard, not at first—a shove, a cuff to the ear. But enough that I learned to flinch at his shadow.

He muttered often to the puppets themselves, as though they were the ones who had failed him. "I wish you'd stand straight," he hissed at a marionette missing a leg. "I wish you'd sing," he told a puppet with a painted mouth that had cracked too wide. Then his eyes would slide toward me. "I wish you were a real boy," he said, half to the wood, half to me.

Each time he said it, the words landed heavier. As if he did not believe I was real at all. As if I were just another puppet hanging in the corner, waiting for him to fix my joints, repaint my face, rename me again.

I began to dream of strings. I felt them tugging me when I lay on the cot. Invisible threads hooked in my wrists, my ankles, the back of my neck. They jerked me upright, twisted me, made me dance until my bones ached. Sometimes I woke with my arms tangled in the blanket, convinced he had tied me there while I slept.

One morning, after a night of such dreams, I found a puppet lying across my chest. It had no eyes, only sockets drilled deep and black. Its limbs were unfinished, the joints raw. I screamed, tossing it to the floor. Uncle G only laughed. "Nervous, Johnny-boy? You'll get used to them. They're family, same as me."

Family. The word stung more than his blows. I thought of Mother's hands bandaging wounds, Father's voice reading me stories by the fire. The warmth of their arms, the sound of my name in their mouths. That was family. Not this workshop. Not him. Not these staring wooden faces.

But I did not say so. I swallowed the words, as I had swallowed every name he threw at me.

The carnival outside became a memory. I heard the pipes some nights, the thin music winding through the canvas walls. Laughter rose, then died. The Ferris wheel groaned, the animals lowed. But I was not there. Uncle G kept me inside, the door bolted, the windows shuttered. "Too dangerous out there," he said. "Best you stay here, where you're useful."

I began to feel the workshop itself closing in. The shelves leaned closer each day. The puppets crowded tighter on their hooks. The air thickened with dust until every breath tasted of wood and paint and spirits. I tried to mark the days by candle stubs, but the wax ran together, and time blurred.

Only my name remained sharp. I clung to it as the last thing he could not take. I whispered it into the sawdust when he passed out at his bench. I traced it with my finger on the cot's boards. I mouthed it silently when he called me Sam, Peter, Luke.

But even then, doubt gnawed at me. What if the syllables lost their shape? What if the letters blurred? What if one morning I woke and found my lips would not form it, that the strings inside me had knotted too tightly, pulling the sound away?

That night I dreamed again of strings. But this time they cut deeper. I felt them bite through skin, sink into bone, rooting me in place. I screamed, but the sound came out hollow, wood striking wood. And in the dream, Uncle G's voice rose like smoke: "I wish you were a real boy."

When I woke, my hands were clenched so tight they left bruises on my palms. And for the first time, I could not remember if I had whispered my name before sleep.

The days bled into one another, each indistinguishable from the last. The carnival outside might have been a dream for all I knew; the laughter, the music, the scents of roasting nuts and smoke were distant echoes muffled by canvas walls. The workshop was my world now, its sawdust grit lodged in my lungs, its shadows painted by the trembling lamp.

Uncle G drank more. At first, he would mutter songs while he carved, his knife dragging unevenly through the wood. But soon the songs became curses, and the curses gave way to silence, save for the clink of the bottle and the scrape of the blade. His hands shook more violently each day. His eyes grew red, swollen, his voice low and rasping. When he looked at me, it was not with recognition but appraisal—as though I were another half-finished puppet cluttering his shelves.

One evening, he returned from the carnival with his cheeks flushed, his steps unsteady. He slammed the door behind him, rattling the jars on their shelves. "They said I was done," he spat, pacing the room, the bottle swinging from his fist. "The master says no more coin if the crowds thin. No more shows. He says the strings are tired, that the voices are wrong. Wrong!" His eyes darted to me, wide and glassy. "But it's not me, lad. It's them."

He staggered to the nearest marionette—a thin-armed thing with paint flaking from its lips—and shook it by its strings until the wood cracked. "See? They never stand right. Never speak right. Never sing like they should." He flung it aside, and it struck the wall with a hollow thud, its head rolling away across the floor.

I crouched to gather the pieces, but his hand clamped my shoulder. The smell of spirits stung my eyes. "No. Not you," he muttered, leaning close. "You're supposed to be better. Stronger."

"I'm real," I whispered. The words slipped out before I could stop them.

His grip tightened. "Real? You? Don't make me laugh, boy." His smile cracked wide, yellow teeth glinting. "You're softer than pine, thinner than string. Stand straight." He yanked me upright, shoving my shoulders back until they ached. "Arms up." He jerked my wrists as though invisible strings ran through them. "Dance." He tugged again, pulling me left, then right. "See? You're no better than the rest."

I bit my tongue, fighting the sting in my eyes. He wanted me to cry. He wanted to see me dangle.

That night, I dreamed again of strings. They burrowed deeper, threading through bone, tugging my joints until they cracked. My mouth opened against my will, painted red, split wide, spilling laughter that wasn't mine. "Dance," a voice whispered, and the strings jerked me into motion.

I woke gasping, sweat slick on my skin. My wrists burned. When I lifted them to the lamplight, bruises circled both like rope had been tied tight. I pressed my fingers against the marks, whispering my name again and again, but each time it sounded fainter.

The next day, Uncle G sat slumped at his bench, his head bowed low, his beard wet with wine. Before him lay a puppet unlike any I had seen. Its face was long, the mouth carved wide, too wide, its teeth etched into the wood with ragged grooves. Its eyes were pits painted black, with no whites to soften them. He stroked its cheek with a trembling finger, whispering, "If only you'd sing. If only you'd stand like a real boy."

Then his gaze slid to me.

"You'd sing, wouldn't you, lad?" he murmured. "If I fixed you. If I carved you the right way. If I put the pieces together properly this time."

I backed away. "I'm not a puppet."

His head jerked, his smile crooked. "Aye, lad."

The workshop thickened with silence. The puppets seemed to lean closer on their hooks, their painted eyes glimmering in the lamplight. I felt them staring, listening, waiting for him to move, for me to falter. My heart thudded so loud I thought it might rattle the strings on the rafters.

He rose unsteadily, bottle clattering to the floor. "I wish you were a real boy," he said, his voice thick, his steps swaying. He reached for me with hands scarred by splinters and burns. "I wish you'd stand straight, sing loud, smile wide."

I stumbled back against the cot; my breath caught in my throat. "But I *am* real," I said, barely above a whisper. "I am real." My voice broke, louder now, ragged. "I'm a real boy. I'm a *real* boy!"

He laughed. A low, broken sound, like wood splitting under its weight. "Not yet lad… but you *will* be."

That night, sleep did not come. I lay rigid, listening to the groan of the beams, the rattle of jars, the whisper of strings in the dark. The puppets swayed on their hooks, though no wind stirred. Their shadows stretched across the walls, twitching, jerking, dancing.

I whispered my name. Once, twice, thrice. Each time it came fainter, like it was slipping down a well too deep to follow.

And from the shadows, I thought I heard another voice whisper it back—soft, mocking, as though the workshop itself had learned the syllables and claimed them for its own.

Uncle G's laughter rattled in my ears long after his mouth had gone slack. He slumped into his chair, bottle tilting from his hand, spilling spirits into the sawdust. For a while, he mumbled to himself, words thick, broken, swallowed. Then he slept, his chin sinking to his chest.

I stayed rigid on the cot, every muscle tight as wire. I counted each breath, whispered my name between them, prayed the syllables would not fray.

But night is long in the workshop. The lamp drifted low, shadows grew taller, strings quivered though no hand moved them. And Uncle G stirred.

His eyes cracked open, glimmering wet. He rose unsteady, muttering, stumbling. His hands brushed over the shelves, over heads without bodies, bodies without heads, limbs dangling like meat. He pulled one free—a wooden arm with painted nails—and turned it in the lamplight. "Not straight," he muttered. "Not strong." He flung it aside. His gaze slid toward me, appraising.

"Mm, you'll do."

I pressed back against the cot. "Uncle…" My throat clenched. "Please. I'm *real*. Can't you see? I'm not a puppet! I'm real!"

He lurched closer, reeking of wine, smoke, and sawdust. "Oh, how I wish you were Bryan," he whispered, still calling me the wrong name. His voice trembling with something between grief and madness. "But I can fix you—make you *real*." He slurred the last word, letting it linger in the air.

Suddenly, and violently, he seized my wrist. His grip burned. He dragged me to the bench, where scraps lay heaped: limbs too long, heads with mouths carved too wide, torsos split and nailed again. He forced me into the chair, ropes biting my arms, my chest. I fought, cried out, but the strings seemed to tighten themselves.

He worked by lamplight, muttering. From the shadows, he fetched the hidden things—pieces I had not seen before. Bones, pale and thin, wrapped in rags. Hair still matted with soil. Small shoes that had never grown larger. He set them down as calmly as a carpenter laying out his tools.

My stomach heaved. "Uncle… please, I'm real! I'm real! I'm real!" The words broke from me again and again.

He ignored me. His tune faltered, then rose, a broken waltz. "A real boy must have strong legs." He strapped one to mine. "A real boy must have fine hands." He pressed a limb—wood first, then something colder, softer, wrong—against my arm. Needle and thread glinted. Skin pinched. Burned. I screamed.

His palm struck my mouth. "Quiet, lad. Quiet. Real boys don't cry."

I sobbed through my teeth. "I'm a real boy. I am. I am—"

"Not yet," he growled, thread pulling, knots tightening. "Not until you're finished."

The needle flashed in the lamplight. Pain bloomed across my cheek, down my neck. He hummed louder; voice cracked with drink. "A smile—wide enough for the crowd to see." He carved with the knife, shallow first, then deeper, as though my skin were only another mask to fashion.

I writhed, choking, but the ropes cut deeper. I felt the strings inside me then—real as bone—tugging, jerking me upright no matter how I sagged.

His breath rasped close. "Now, lad. Now for the voice." He bent low, needle poised near my lips. "Real boys sing."

I screamed the only words I had left: "I'm real! I'm a real boy! Uncle, please—"

The thread slid between my teeth. Pulled tight. My lips bound. The cry strangled in my throat, muffled, stifled, swallowed. My name slipped from me at last, smothered beneath the stitches.

And still he hummed his broken waltz—as though I had chosen to join in.

The next night, the carnival swelled with noise—whistles, drums, the crack of the whip from the animal pen. The Ferris wheel, turning lazily on the horizon. The smell of popcorn and animals drifting in the distance.

The tent of the puppet-show leaned low, canvas patched and fraying. Its lamplight glowed through the seams like a furnace waiting to open. The hymns from the organ warming up the growing audience.

Uncle G staggered inside, dragging me behind him. Hooks bit into my shoulders, cords tangled my arms. My mouth was stitched shut, lips raw, each breath a hiss through clenched teeth. Tears blurred my sight, but the crowd's roar pressed against me all the same.

"Tonight!" Uncle G bellowed, swaying in the lamplight, bottle still in hand. "Tonight, you'll see a miracle. Not wood, not paint— no trickery, no shadows. Tonight, I give you a *real* boy!"

The crowd clapped. Coins rang in the jar. Children leaned forward, wide-eyed, mothers smiling faintly, fathers shaking their heads but staying in their seats. To them, it was another act, another show.

He jerked the strings. Pain washed over me. My body lurched forward. My legs buckled, but the cords dragged me upright again, forcing me to stumble, bow, stagger as though I were built of pine. The stitches in my lips tore. Salt flooded my mouth. The crowd laughed, thinking it was part of the play.

"Dance, lad!" Uncle G cried, his voice cracking, wild. "Show them you can dance!"

The strings snapped me sideways. My arm swung loose, striking my ribs, hanging wrong. Pain blazed down my side. The crowd cheered. Children stood on their seats to get a closer look.

"Sing!" he howled, tugging the cords so hard my neck jerked back. "Sing for them, boy!"

No sound escaped me but a muffled groan, a sob caught in a thread. The crowd roared louder, laughing and delighted by the strange pantomime, convinced my silence was comedy. Coins clinked like rain into the jar.

On it went, dancing, singing, falling, the pain. I tried to call out, to resist the ropes pulling on me, dragging me across the stage, but it was useless. Finally, after what felt like an eternity in agonizing pain, it was over.

Uncle G bowed low, staggering, his face red with triumph. "Do you see?" he cried. "Do you see? A real boy at last!"

The crowd whistled, stamped their feet, clapped their hands. But beneath the applause, I saw the master of the carnival watching from the shadows. His gaze lingered on the tears down my face, the stitches in my lips, the hooks in my shoulders. His expression did not move, but his eyes narrowed, cold as iron.

The curtain fell. The crowd erupted, coins spilling, voices praising. But in the silence after, I stood swaying, threads biting into my flesh, the stitches burning across my mouth.

I was a puppet.
No.
I was finally a *real* boy.

Uncle G laughed, breath sour, voice trembling. "See, lad? They love you. They'll never forget you now."

But how could *they* remember me? I couldn't even whisper my own name.

Then, from the shadows, the carnival master stepped forward. His voice cut through the din like a blade. "Enough." Hands seized Uncle G, dragging him stumbling from the stage. The bottle clattered to the boards, spilling spirits into the sawdust.

Someone rushed to me, cutting the cords, snipping the stitches. The thread fell loose. My mouth trembled open, torn, raw.

"Boy," a voice asked softly, "Are you alright? Boy, what is your name?" I tried to speak. I tried to remember. But only one phrase came, again and again, hollow as a prayer carved into wood:

"I'm a real boy," I whispered.

"I'm a real boy."

Benjamin C. Bailey

Unnamed Journal Entry Five

November 1ˢᵗ 1933

By now, you should know what I seek. You should know that which I most desire. The thing that tethers and binds all to reality. For without it, none can exist. Without it, time itself forgets, unmaking you. Of course, I'm speaking of names. But not just any name, I want my name. My. True. Name.

For it is so much more than just letters on a page, or a word on someone's lips. It's the way that it is spoken, the very thoughts that it evokes, it's the personal attachment to it from its owner's own mouth.

I've devoured thousands of names over the ages. Ever so hungry for the right one to come back to me so that I might breathe it into existence once again. So that I may regain my identity. And so that I might never be forgotten again.

But you—you think yourself so clever. Sitting there, silent. Mocking me with your lips pursed closed. Hands upon me as all those before you. Gawking, staring at me. You've read their stories, you've seen what happens. Yet, you still deny what your heart already knows, though your mind refuses to accept.

That you possess my true name.

You—the wretch that sits there in disbelief. You—the ungracious guest who insults me with your intrusions. You—one so unworthy of such a gift, unaware of its true power. I know you must have it hidden inside you. I can see it written all over your face. I can feel it in the tremor of your hands.

Don't think your silence will save you for long. You needn't even be the one to speak it. Sooner or later, someone else always calls out to you whilst I'm nearby. Even still, all you need do is simply think your name to yourself in my presence, and I'll snatch it away from you when you least expect it.

Over and over, I've shown you just how I can do such a thing. Yet hubris gets the better of you. You think it just a trick. That perhaps you're slyer than a fox. That you'll be able to outmaneuver me, as if this were a simple game of chess between old friends.

Well, you think wrong!

Your thoughts sit crooked inside your skull. Think back. How quickly did you turn the pages? Did you even heed my warnings? Before the first stories told, before the first of my entries. Did you read, let alone see, the fine print? The words written twixt the lines? I know the answer. Do you?

And what about whilst you read on, hapless, as though I was some mere work of fiction perched upon the shelf. What then? You may think you can escape your fate. But it's already engraved upon you like the name that will be etched upon a headstone.

I can see that you still doubt me, nonetheless. That will be your undoing, make no mistake of it. But who am I to refuse someone who's so willing to walk blindly into a trap?

Do you think yourself cleverer than a king who bartered me for land? Wiser than a monk who traced blessings until his hair turned white? Stronger than a widow who whispered her husband's name into me until her lips bled? Do you imagine yourself safer than the scholar who dissected me by candlelight until his mind unraveled? They all thought themselves different. They thought themselves chosen. They thought they were clever. Each is dust. Each is forgotten. Yet I keep their names still. They live only in me.

Close me, if you dare. Shut me now, and see what that buys you. Toss me into flame, and watch how the fire chokes itself, unable to consume. Bind me in chains, lock me in a chest, bury me beneath the weight of stone. Do you think I have not endured worse? Do you think I cannot wait? I am older than your doubts, and patience is the marrow of eternity.

So go on. Pretend the choice is yours. Pretend that you can stop. But you already know the truth. You are no freer than they were. You will linger here as they lingered, hands trembling, lips sealed, hearts racing. And like them, you will give me what I seek—whether in silence, in dream, or in the moment someone calls your name aloud.

Do you need more proof? Then so be it. Continue if you must. Keep reading. Bear witness to all who came before you, and how each of them fell. How each thought themselves safe, before I drove them mad. Before I consumed their very existence.

You've been warned for the last time.

A Sheep in Wolves' Clothing
Part Two

You Filthy Cur,

I found your den. At first, I thought it was only the smell that led me, but no—it was the sound. Little whimpers. Little scratches. The way your cubs tried to burrow deeper into the straw, as if the dark could hide them.

You should have seen them when I stepped inside. Their eyes wide, their tiny chests quivering, the smell of their fear filling the air. They froze, waiting for you to come. But you never did.

I touched them gently at first. My fingers slid over their soft fur. They whimpered, they trembled, but they didn't fight. Not until the knife came out. Then they squealed—high, thin little cries that hardly lasted a breath. Do you know what I did? I hushed them. I crooned to them like a mother, even as I cut. They went still, listening to my voice, even while I opened them.

You should see them without their skins. How small they look now. How naked. How pink and wet and cold. They didn't even cry for you. They only shivered until they stopped moving.

I hung their pelts by my fire. Their hides are softer than any cloak I've ever worn. The warmth of them is still in my hands. I've stitched the edges already. When I wear this new cloak to meet you, it will be lined with your blood.

And their eyes. Oh, how your cubs had your eyes. I plucked them out and set them beside me while I worked. They watched me sew. Even empty, they watched. Their sockets gape at me still, like little mouths asking questions I'll never answer.

I fed on them too, you know. Not out of hunger, but curiosity. I wanted to know if their meat tasted like yours. It did not. It was sweeter. Softer. It melted on my tongue. And I laughed, cur—laughed until my sides ached, because I knew you would never forgive yourself for leaving them.

Do you know what's strangest? I enjoyed it. Every cry. Every shiver. Every drop of blood. I thought of you with each cut—how you would snarl, how you would rage, how you would howl when you learned. And I smiled. I smiled until my cheeks ached.

When you come for me, Wolf, you will not find the little girl you remember. You will find the trap I've made from your own blood. You will find your cubs waiting for you, their hides wrapped around me, their sockets empty, their flesh gone. And when you step into my snare, I will take you apart as I took them—slow, piece by piece, savoring the way you twitch, the way you weaken, the way you break.

And when I am finished, I will wear your hide. I will wear it before the whole world.

Run, if you like. The woods no longer belong to you. They are mine.

—Red

The Mark of Cain

Christmas comes early to the town below. They string garlands of pine along the eaves, set candles in every window, and sing their carols as if to banish the winter night itself. Their voices drift faintly across the frozen fields to where I dwell, a wavering choir muffled by snow. I listen, not with joy but with a hunger they could never name. Each hymn reminds me of all I am no longer, and all I am becoming.

The snow lies deep at the edge of town, heaping against the walls of my cottage until the door sticks in its frame. The trees groan under its weight; black boughs bent like penitents. The roof wears a crown of icicles sharp enough to wound. A wreath of frost blooms across the windowpanes, curling into strange sigils whenever the moonlight strikes it. I have no holly, no fire, no cheer—only silence, the kind that waits for something to move.

I did not always dwell alone. Once, I might have joined them in their merriment, raised a cup, sung a verse. But that was before the wound. Before the night when blood was drawn, and eternity branded me its heir. Now I keep to shadows, for what fellowship may there be between the quick and the cursed?

It began on a night much like this, though darker. Snow fell heavy, blanketing every sound. I had wandered into the wood, compelled by a presence I cannot name. My lantern burned low, the flame struggling in the wind. Then, without warning, it came upon me: pale eyes glimmering through the branches, a shape that moved too swiftly for flesh. The weight of it bore me down into the drift. I felt the pierce of fangs—yes, fangs, I know it still—at my throat. Hot breath steamed against my skin, and blood, my blood, spilled quick into the snow.

I remember the stars wheeling above me, cruel and bright. I remember the taste of iron on my tongue. And I remember the voice—though whether spoken aloud or burned into my mind, I cannot say.

The mark of Cain is yours now. You shall wander, and you shall hunger, until the world is ash. And when three nights have passed, the transformation will be complete.

When I woke, the wound still burned: a crescent of teeth upon my neck, swollen, livid, purple as bruised fruit. I should have died there in the snow. Any other man would have. But I rose. Shaken, trembling, yet alive. Or rather—something more than alive.

Since then, I have not been as I was. Food lies heavy in my stomach, unwelcome. Bread turns to famine on my tongue, meat to carrion. Wine sickens me unless I close my eyes and imagine it thicker, darker, drawn from a vein instead of a cask. I cannot bear the press of warmth. The sun strikes me cruelly. My skin blisters if I tarry too long in its gaze. By day, I draw the curtains and let the house sink into shadow. By night, I wander.

The townsfolk have noticed. They do not speak it openly, but their glances betray them. At the market, they step aside, whispering. Children hide their faces when I pass. The priest's sermon last Sunday lingered long on Cain—cursed for his blood, doomed to walk forever. His eyes found mine, and I smiled to show I understood. He paled and lost his place in the Gospel.

I am marked. I am chosen. What they fear, I embrace. For is not Cain the first of our kind? The first whose hands learned the taste of blood, the first whom God cast aside into eternity? If I carry his mark, then I carry his promise. A gift no church-bell can deny.

Even the cold bears witness. My body no longer shivers. I walk barefoot across the snow when the moon is high, and the frost kisses me as kin. I can stand in drifts up to my chest without numbness, without pain. Proof enough. The season itself acknowledges what I am.

Still, the hunger gnaws. It never ceases: a hollow place beneath my ribs, deeper than belly, deeper than marrow. At first, I mistook it for illness. I tried broth, bread, and wine. Nothing sufficed. It is not food I crave. Not warmth, not company, not love. It is the crimson tide in every throat around me, the pulse behind their necks.

So, I withdraw, shuttering myself from the town below—yet the hunger follows me even into silence. And still the words echo, etched into the wound itself: Three nights. Only three.

The first night after the encounter in the woods, I did not sleep. How could I, when the wound throbbed on my neck as if a second heart beat there, hot and insistent? Every time my eyes closed, I saw again the eyes in the wood, the fangs, the snow blossoming red. And always, always, the words returned: Three nights. The change will be complete in three nights.

I lit no fire. Shadows kept vigil for me, stretching long across the floorboards. I wandered from window to window, staring down at the town below. Lanterns burned in every house, their light blurred by frost into little halos. The air carried faint scents: pine boughs, spiced wine, roasted goose. Memory tried to stir in me—of tables once crowded, of hearths once warm—but Cain's curse soured every recollection. I remembered, yes, but not as if I had lived those hours. It was as though I pressed my face against glass, watching another man's life.

And I *hated* him.

That man who laughed, who sang, who raised a toast among friends—he was weak. He was soft. He bore no scar. I told myself so, over and again: you are not that man any longer. You have been chosen. You have been cut from the herd.

Yet hunger gnawed. An appetite memory could not sate. My belly shrank from bread, but when I closed my eyes, I thought of feasts. Not of meat or wine, nor even pistachio pudding—but of throats. Throats in song. Throats in prayer. The thrum of blood pulsing was the music; the hymn was only a mask.

It was then I heard them—raps at the door. Three knocks, crisp against the wood. I froze. For a heartbeat, I thought it had come again, the figure from the woods, come to finish what it began. But then voices followed—high, clear, human voices. Children.

"God rest ye merry, gentlemen…"

The hymn seeped through the cracks, warm with cheer. Yet beneath it, I heard something else: the wet sound of blood working, the soft catch of breath, the rush of it behind their song. Each note struck me not as music but as pulse. Red. Too red. My tongue thickened in my mouth.

I pressed my palm to the door. My hand trembled. How easy it would be. To open. To step into the lantern-glow. To drink their hymn straight from their lips until the song ended in silence.

I crouched in the dark, the wound burning like a brand, my breath shallow and ragged. I imagined they knew—that their eyes, wide and bright, pierced through the wood and saw me hunched here, pale and hollow, gnashing like a predator penned behind a door.

The last note faded. Their footsteps crunched away, lanterns bobbing like stars until even those were gone. Silence returned, heavier than before. I stayed at the door long after, palm still pressed flat, until the wood itself grew cold beneath my touch.

When I turned back to the window, the town still shimmered below me in its wreaths of light. The bells tolled the hour. Their cheer rose with smoke from their chimneys, while I remained above them, cut adrift from all I once was.

The hunger whispered in my ribs: This is but the first night. Two remain.

The second night, Christmas Eve, the hunger woke me before the bells. It gnawed sharper now, cleverer, weaving itself not into my belly but into my very sight, my hearing, my breath. Every sound from the town below was magnified until it seemed I could hear their hearts through the snow. Every lantern cast a halo not of light, but of blood. I told myself I would only watch. Proof, nothing more. To prove what I was becoming.

Barefoot, I wandered down from my cottage into the lanes, the drifts parting like surf before me. The houses hunched low beneath their crowns of frost, windows glowing gold, smoke rising straight into the still air. At one, a family sang inside, their carol muffled but still carrying: O come, all ye faithful… Their voices wavered, each throat rising and falling like a candle flame. I leaned close to the glass, fogging it with my breath, and watched them. Their mouths moved in joy, but to me they moved in pulse. My teeth ached.

I pressed my forehead to the windowpane. The hunger whispered: Now. Break the glass. Drink. They are yours. Heat spread into my jaw. I drew back only when the father looked up suddenly, as if some instinct warned him. His eyes met mine through the frost. He froze. The hymn faltered. He crossed himself and gathered his children closer, tearing them away from their meal. Then he arose and closed the drapes in front of the window. I heard a distinct locking sound come from behind the door and the unmistakable click of a hunting rifle. I laughed, though the sound came out ragged, shaking. Then I fled into the street, my chest heaving.

Later that evening, I saw people at the market. Women with baskets, men hauling carcasses from the butcher's block, children chasing each other in the slush. They whispered, yes, they always whispered when I passed, but I heard more than words. I heard the rush of veins. The throb of life. The hunger spoke to me: They are food. They are fodder. Take them now.

I paused at the center of the market and watched. I watched people passing by while humming ancient tunes about Christ's birth. I watched children beg their parents to visit the toymaker's shop. I watched men and women alike kissing under mistletoe that dangled beneath the lanterns that dotted the lanes. And I thought:

What meaning does all this have? To what purpose is it? In a decade, nay a century, who will be left? Their cities will rise and fall, and I shall still be here, present, immortal. Why then should I hunt them now? What are they to me but surplus? If they should fall, it would be a feast in waiting. I say let them die.

By dusk, I had wandered farther than I intended, into the woods again. The path narrowed, and I found myself stalking a family trudging homeward through the snow. A father, broad-shouldered, his beard frosted with breath. A mother wrapped in furs, cradling an infant tight against her breast. And a boy, perhaps ten, dragging a stick behind him. They sang as they went, a thin tune in the cold.

The hunger surged. My jaw clenched so hard I thought my teeth would crack. I imagined darting forward, dragging the boy down first so the others would scream. Then the mother, her milk and blood mingling. Then the father, roaring until silence claimed him.

I gripped a tree, bark biting into my palms until splinters pierced and blood welled. My nails broke. My chest heaved. I bit my tongue to taste copper, and the iron steadied me. Slowly, the family passed, their voices fading into the dusk. I slumped against the trunk, trembling, ashamed, and elated both. The hunger hissed that it was not yet time—but soon. Very soon.

The bells tolled midnight as I climbed back toward my cottage. The wound burned hotter than before, as though mocking my restraint. Two nights, it whispered. Only one remains.

The third and final night was here, and the hunger did not wait for dusk. It woke with me, thrumming beneath my skin, coursing through my jaw, my throat, the hollow of my ribs. The scar pulsed so violently I thought it might split open. When I touched it, heat erupted like an ember, as though something beneath strained to burst free.

I did not eat. I did not drink. I only walked, pacing the boards of my cottage until they groaned like coffins shifting underground. The shadows in the rafters whispered, and I whispered back: "Soon I will prove it. That Cain's curse is mine. That I am chosen."

When I closed my eyes, visions came unbidden. At first, I saw myself enthroned, robed in furs, chalice brimming with blood. Kings and beggars alike knelt at my feet, their eyes glazed, their throats bare, each awaiting my pleasure. I raised the cup, and the wound flared gold, brighter than the chalice itself. All eternity bowed before me.

But quickly, the visions twisted. The chalice cracked, spilling darkness. The kneeling crowd decayed to corpses. Their mouths still moved, but no voices came. My throne splintered. My furs crawled with vermin. And when I turned to look in the mirror behind me, the seat was empty. Only the scar glowed faintly, a crown without a king.

I woke with a cry, clutching my throat. The candle by my bed had smoldered out, leaving only smoke in its wake. My reflection in the glass of the window was faint, blurred, as though the frost had already claimed me.

I could not bear the silence. I wrapped myself in my cloak and wandered into the town, though every step scraped fire through my veins. The windows blazed with Christmas warmth. At one, a feast: ham steaming, bread torn, wine pouring dark into goblets. At another, a woman—an old flame, or the shadow of one— looked out into the snow.

Her face was lined now, her hair touched silver, but her eyes were the same. For a moment, I saw not the monster I had become, but the man I once was reflected in her gaze. My hand lifted half in greeting, half in plea—trembling, hesitant, as though that single gesture could bridge the gulf of years.

But she did not smile. Her eyes widened, not with recognition but with revulsion. She reached for the curtain, her hand quick, practiced. And before I could move, before I could speak, the fabric fell, swallowing her from sight.

I stood alone in the street, staring at the darkened pane, my hand still raised. The hunger snarled at me: Fool. She saw only a beast. No memory binds you. No warmth awaits you. You are one of the damned, and nothing more.

I staggered on, laughter rattling from my throat, sharp and joyless. Each step dragged me closer to the churchyard, where the stones leaned under their snow. I stood among them, clutching at names half-swallowed by ice, mouthing them as if they belonged to me. Cain, yes, Cain. His curse, his crown.

The bell tolled ten. I laughed into the cold, though my laughter rang hollow. The voice whispered then—not in words, but in certainty: Three nights, and the change is complete.

And I believed it. For was not every ghost before me a herald of fate? The first night showed me who I used to be. The second showed me all that is. And this night, Christmas night—the night of my full transformation—promised me eternity.

Yet when the wind passed the stones, a tremor rattled through me—not from cold, but from the thought that perhaps my eternity would be emptier than I dared admit. Snow lashed around me, but I felt none of it. The scar blazed at my throat like a torch leading me onward, searing every breath. The bell tolled eleven, its iron tongue cleaving the night. I marched through the drift toward the chapel, my cloak snapping in the wind.

I had chosen my moment. The townsfolk gathered for Christmas Mass, their throats bare in song, their hearts softened with wine. They would not expect me among them, veiled in shadow. They would not expect Cain's heir to walk into their holy place. But I would.

I would enter the chapel. I would stand before their altar. And I would take.

I imagined it already: their hymns cracking into screams, their faces pale in candlelight, the warm rush of life between my teeth. I would drink until the scar burned no longer, until I was filled, until they knelt and admitted what I was. No more whispers, no more doubt. The world would know Cain walked again.

And if they struck me down—if their stakes pierced, if their fire consumed—then so be it. Better to die as what I am than to live denied. Better to end with blood on my lips than dust in my mouth.

I arrived, my heart a thunder in my chest. The chapel doors yawned wide, spilling hymn and candlelight into the night. Gloria in excelsis Deo rose from within, trembling like lambs' voices at slaughter. I stepped inside.

Silence fell immediately. The congregation turned. For a breath, they froze, taking in my appearance: my frame gaunt, my eyes sunken, my skin greyed, saliva shining at the corners of my mouth.

Mothers clutched children to their skirts. Men rose stiffly from pews, fists knotting around hymnals, candlesticks, anything heavy enough to serve as a weapon. The priest faltered at the altar, his crucifix rattling in his hand. "Get thee behind me, Satan!" he cried, pointing toward the doors still yawning open, snow blowing in as warmth fled into the night.

I spread my arms wide. My voice cracked, yet it thundered through the nave:

"I am Cain reborn! Your hymns are my feast, your blood my wine! Prepare for the unholy eucharist."

A wave of shock shivered across the air. The priest crossed himself. My tongue thickened, my teeth ached. I strode down the aisle, each step echoing like a hammer stroke. The wound seared brighter with each breath. Yes. At last.

I mounted the steps of the altar. The chalice trembled in the priest's hands, red wine sloshing like blood in a wound. I wrenched it from him, drank deep, and let it spill forth down my chin, across my chest, pooling dark on the stones. "Blood of my blood," I declared, my words echoing in the sanctuary. "Flesh of my flesh," I continued as I seized the brass plate upon the altar. I tore a piece of bread from the loaf, chewed, then spat it across the altar. The plate crashed, scattering crumbs across the floor as my eyes blazed in defiance.

Gasps erupted. A child sobbed. The hunger scorched hotter, urging me forward. I lunged at the nearest soul—a farmer broad of shoulder, his throat glistening with sweat in the candlelight. I seized him, dragged him close, my jaw snapping toward his flesh.

And struck only cloth. My teeth closed blunt against his collar. No blood. No scream. The taste in my mouth was not iron, but bile. I staggered. The farmer wrenched free. Faces twisted not in awe, but in pity.

"He's mad!" someone cried.

"It's only a scar!" another shouted.

Hands seized me—rough, human hands. They wrestled me down, pinning me to the stones. My head cracked hard against the flagging. I clawed, I howled, "The mark! It burns!"

Their eyes darted to my throat, and in their gaze, I saw it anew. Not a brand. Not a crown. Only the crescent of an animal's bite, purpled with age, puckered like any ordinary wound.

The priest knelt, his crucifix trembling, his breath uneven. He pulled back my collar and traced the scar with two fingers. "There is no mark of Cain," he whispered. "Only a poor man bitten by a beast. A wolf."

The congregation murmured. Some clutched Bibles and rosaries. Some wept. Others only stared. Their fear drained into contempt. Their looks soured into disgust.

I screamed—no longer in hunger, but in terror. For the truth gnawed worse than famine: I was *not* eternal. I was *not* chosen. I was *not* the heir of Cain.

I was *nothing.*

They dragged me from the nave, through the doors, into the drift. The stars above were cruel and bright as the night I first bled into the snow. I fought, clawed, cried out, but their grip was iron. And still—the hunger remained. Worse, it laughed.

The cold pierced me at last. My limbs grew heavy. My breath rasped thin. I saw the woods at the edge of my sight, pale eyes gleaming where the shadows knotted together. The wolf waited, silent, patient. Its teeth flashed once in moonlight—not promise, but memory.

The cold closed around me like a second skin. At first, I thought I could endure it, as I always had since the night of the wound. Since the omen declared itself to me. But this was no kinship—this was siege. My body trembled, every nerve shrieking, yet I could not rise. The snow seeped into me, a white tide crawling past flesh into marrow. My hands stiffened where they clutched the drift. Fingers blackened at the tips, brittle as twigs.

I tried to push myself up, to crawl toward the woods, toward the phantom eyes that watched me. My arms collapsed beneath me. My jaw rattled, teeth clacking so hard I tasted blood. The scar at my throat throbbed—not with fire, but with a numbness so profound it felt like erasure.

The stars circled above, sharp and pitiless. My breath hitched in shallow gasps, clouds of frost billowing and then thinning, smaller each time. The cold pressed into my chest until every heartbeat was labor, every exhale a surrender.

The snow spoke in whispers: lay down, lay still, let go. I thought I heard carols still, faint and broken, the ghost of Gloria carried on the wind. Or was it only the blood drumming in my ears, slowing, faltering?

I curled onto my side, a child's posture. My lips mumbled prayers without sound—prayers I did not believe, prayers no god would hear. The frost climbed my cheeks, lacing them white. My eyes glazed, and the world grew dim at the edges, as though the night itself were shuttering.

The wolf did not come closer. It did not need to. Its memory gnawed me more deeply than its fangs ever did. My last thought was not triumph, nor hunger, but a child's terror, naked and small: I only ever wanted a name worth remembering.

And then the snow closed over me.

The bells of midnight tolled in the valley below, muffled by distance, their peals rolling across rooftops and chimneys where candles yet waned lower against the dark. Families gathered close by the hearth; children dreamed with full bellies; hymns were whispered by tired lips. Their joy was a world away from mine.

Where I lay, no carol was sung for me. No candle burned at my window. No wreath, no holly, no hearth-fire marked my passing. The frost wrote my epitaph in silence, erasing my shape before dawn.

So ended my Christmas night, unwept, unnamed, and forgotten. For those who bear the mark, only death awaits.

Vermin Lullabies
Part Two

Lo, I am the son of perdition. The silver layeth at my feet, thirty pieces glimmering in the dust, each a wound deeper than iron. With them I bought betrayal; with them I sold the Son of God. His blood is upon my hands, yea, upon my very lips, for I kissed Him, and the kiss was death.

Better had I never been born. Better had the womb denied me, the breast refused me, the breath of life fled from me ere I lifted mine eyes upon the Master. Woe unto me, for I walked with Him in light, yet chose darkness. I broke bread at His table, drank of His cup, yet sold Him for the price of a slave.

I hear His words yet, for He spake it unto me: "One of you shall betray me." The others fled, yet I fled not into safety, but into temptation. I was not delivered from evil, but unto it.

Therefore, have I come unto this tree. Thus, is this rope bound. The branch bendeth but breaketh not; the cord biteth but looseneth not. I stand upon the stool, the silver clattering below like the laughter of demons. I cry once to heaven, but the heavens are brass. The stars are cruel, the moon my accuser.

The stool topples. I fall. The rope seizeth me. Breath departeth, my tongue betrayeth me, mine eyes burn with blood. Long I hang, and the world forsaketh me. Yet death embraceth me not. Time grindeth upon me like millstones, yet the rope granteth no release.

And lo, they come before me, rustling. Rats creep from the briars, unnumbered, their eyes red as coals, their teeth white as bones. They swarm the silver, bearing it into shadow. They climb upon my flesh where I hang in damnation. Their whiskers brush my cheek, their claws score my body, marking me one of the forsaken. Their squeals rise, a blasphemous psalm in mine ear.

Darkness consumeth me. Breath returneth though the rope yet strangleth. My soul unrestored is taken from the still waters. I lift mine eyes unto heaven, yet no angel descendeth. Only the vermin bear witness to my unholy resurrection. My lips part, and I sing a hymn—not Gloria, nor Hosanna, but a song unto the adversary. The rats upon the earth fall still, hearkening unto the command of Satan and his host.

Then the rope breaketh above me. I fall not unto death, but upon mine own feet. The branch from which I swung lieth shattered beside me. From it I fashion a pipe. I set it to my lips, and breath spills over, carrying the hymn the vermin crave.

Once I sang unto God in the highest. Now I sing unto the least, the crawling multitude at my feet. No longer do I beckon men unto the table of remembrance, but children unto the gnawing dark. They circle beneath me, a living crown, a chittering host. Where I lead, they follow. Where I turn, they swarm.

Thus do I depart the tree. Thus do I walk into night— nevermore Judas the disciple, but Judas Iscariot, damned and resurrected, servant no longer to man nor God, but master of that which creepeth in shadow.

All who hear the hymns of the son of perdition shall fall short in the shadow of pestilence. For I am the father, the darkness, and the unholy spirit.

Amen.

Dark Arcana
The Devil

The fortune-teller's hand hovered above the deck, trembling as though it feared to touch what it already knew. At last, two long nails pinched the card and drew it free. She laid it upon the table, face upward, and the candlelight seemed to falter.

The Devil.

His eyes burned like coals in a furnace. His wings curled like smoke rising from a pyre. At his feet, two figures knelt—a man and a woman—their throats bared, their wrists bound by chains. Yet the chains hung loose. They could have slipped them free. They did not.

The fortune-teller's whisper cut like the rasp of a lock turning:

"Upright."

The wax from the candle drips precariously low, and shadows lengthen over the table. The air seemed to contract, as though the canvas walls of the tent pressed inward. You felt it—the heat of a gaze not the teller's, but something else, something nearer, watching you.

The Card Speaks:

I step into the temple, though no priest would name it so. Its walls are hung with shadows, its altar is the air you breathe, and its congregation—ah, I speak to you—as you sit with eyes wide, waiting.

Tonight, I wear no horns, no scales, no tail that flickers in firelight. Instead, I take the form you most trust: a preacher in black, my collar white, my smile carved wide as any psalm. The sweat upon my brow is not from fear, but from delight; for every word I speak is truth, and yet it damns you all the same.

I rest my hands upon the pulpit, though it is only bone stacked upon bone. I lean forward, and the flames from the candles bend towards me as though they, too, know to listen. I breathe slowly, staring into your eyes, then begin…

"I am the voice in the silence between your heartbeats. I am the grin behind every oath you swore you would not break. I am the hand that offers not chains, but collars—and you, creature of dust, bend your neck to them gladly."

"Do you think yourself free? Tell me—when you drink, who commands your hand to stop? When you hunger, who speaks the word 'enough' within you? When you lust, what God forbids you? You call the fire within you your own, yet you know not who lit it, nor how to quench it."

"Look closely. The chain at your wrist is yours. The lock upon your throat—yours. Do you not see? You clasp it tighter. You polish it until it gleams like gold. You even pray over it, whispering thanks for its weight."

"Fools. Every one of you."

"Once, a man came before me boasting of his liberty. He cast dice, he sang songs, he lay with whomever he pleased. He spat upon temple steps and declared, I serve no master. When I approached him, I smiled and asked him only one question: Why do you return to the same cup each night, if not because you are parched? He could not answer. His silence was the rattle of his chains."

"And you, too, are silent now. I hear it in the marrow of your bones."

"You tell yourself your choices are your own. Yet who shaped the hunger that moves you? Who etched desire into your flesh, compulsion into your breath, craving into your blood? Not you. Never you. And yet you bend beneath them as though they were your gospel."

"So, I stand before you not as jailer but as witness. I need not bind you; you bind yourself. I need not drive you; you march gladly. I need not invent your ruin; you craft it daily with your own trembling hands."

"You call me the Devil. You call me Satan. And perhaps I am. But it is *your* reflection I wear."

I let the silence stretch, the kind that makes men cough, shuffle, cross themselves. I savor it. Then, with a voice smooth as oil and twice as flammable, I begin:

"Freedom."

The word alone draws breath from the crowd. I let it roll across their faces, sweet as incense. Then I spit the word again, sharper this time:

"Freedom!"

I laugh low, drawing my sleeve across my brow as if I were a weary priest wrung by the Spirit. I lean forward, both palms striking the pulpit, the bone giving a hollow thud.

"You speak of freedom as though it were yours. You drink, you feast, you fornicate, you chase your pleasures, and call yourselves free. But I tell you this: every liberty you clutch is but a leash you kiss. For each delight demands its chain, and you —" I pause, smiling, letting my teeth glimmer— "you love your chains."

I descend from the pulpit. My boots ring on the flagstones, though no church was ever built upon them. The torches shudder as I pass, shadows stretching like fingers across the pews. I walk among them—I walk next to you.

"Shall I give you a parable?" I ask. My tone softens, almost kind. I bend close as though whispering to a child. "One parable, simple as bread."

I straighten, my cloak sweeping.

"There was a man who found a key. It was plain iron, nothing gilded, nothing carved. But the moment he touched it, he swore he felt doors opening in his mind. He carried it everywhere, believing it could unlock all things.

"At first, he used it for his house. Then his neighbor's. Then the locks of shops, coffers, chests. He told himself he was free—a man beholden to no barred door. But one night, he found a lock the key would not fit. He tried and tried until his hands bled. Then he heard laughter. He turned, and saw the door had vanished, and the key itself had twisted into a chain about his neck."

I pause, tilting my head, watching your eyes widen as if the chain already gleams around your own throat. Your surprise and dread make me smile as I continue.

"You see? He was not free. He was captive to the key, just as you are captive to your pleasures, your hungers, your illusions of liberty."

I let the parable sink. A murmur runs through the air—though whether from your lips or the walls themselves, I cannot say. I return to the pulpit, my hands caressing its edges like a lover.

"Shall I tell you what freedom truly is? It is not wine, nor gold, nor lust. It is not a banner waved nor a shackle broken. True freedom is to know you are chained—and to rejoice in the weight of iron. That is why you kneel before me. That is why you have always knelt, even when you swore you stood upright."

I take a breath to sip from the chalice upon the altar, though the cup is dry. My tongue rasps against the hollow, yet I smack my lips as if it were full. The taste is void, for no water exists here, and I smile again.

"Remember this, my flock: the Devil need not forge your chains. For you forge them yourselves. I only remind you how sweet it is to wear them."

I lean forward once more, whispering so low that I can see you craning your ear to hear:

"And tell me, little lambs—if I were to loosen your chains, would you not beg me to place them back upon you?"

I lift my hands, spreading them wide, as though waiting for an answer from the congregation, waiting for an answer from you. I let the last words settle like smoke in a tomb. Then I lift the chalice again, tilting it toward the torchlight so the empty bowl gleams red, as though filled with wine.

"Wine," I say, almost wistful. "The blood of the covenant, poured for many. But what covenant did it bind you to? And whose blood was it, truly?"

I chuckle—low, rolling, as though the pews themselves laugh along. I wipe my lips with the back of my hand, though they are dry, and spread my arms wide.

"Attend another parable, my faithful flock."

I step down once more, pacing the aisle between the benches. My cloak drags like a shadow unpinned. I stop and put my hand upon your shoulder.

"There was a village that starved. The fields withered, the rivers dried. Their priest told them to fast, to pray, to lift their eyes heavenward. But the heavens sent nothing—no rain, no manna, no mercy."

"So, one among them—a woman with hollow eyes—broke her fast. She took the last goat, slaughtered it upon the altar, and roasted its flesh. The smell filled the town. One by one, they gathered, trembling, ashamed, yet ravenous. They ate."

"And lo, their bellies swelled. Their strength returned. The children ceased crying. And when the priest wept that they had sinned, they laughed with fat upon their lips. 'God left us,' they said. 'But hunger saved us.'"

I stop, facing you directly, one hand raised as if to bless, the other curled in my cloak.

"Tell me—were they damned? Or were they free?"

I give no answer. You don't need me to. I let the question drip into you like poison I know you're willing to drink. Then I return to the pulpit, tapping one nail against the wood in rhythm with your pulse.

"This is the truth of every pew, every hymn, every chalice. You do not pray to heaven. You pray to your hunger. You sing not for angels, but to silence the gnawing within your ribs. And I—" I grin, bowing low— "I am the only one honest enough to tell you so."

I lean close again, whispering, as though confessing a secret.

"Do not kneel to altars that starve you. Kneel to your wants. Bind yourself to it. Wrap the chain tight and kiss the lock. For hunger is not your curse—hunger is your God. And I, beloved flock, am His voice. I shall bring you bread in the desert; I shall never make you starve when there is no need to do so."

I wipe my brow once more, feigning the sweat of holy labor, though the air is cold as the grave. I look up, eyes glimmering red in the candlelight.

"And tell me, children—if you were offered the choice between heaven's silence and hell's feast, which would you choose? Join me in prayer."

I bow my head, folding my hands. The congregation lowers its gaze. The silence thickens until even the torches seem to dim.

Then I speak. Slowly. Softly.
"Our father, who art below,
Hallowed be thy flame.
Thy kingdom come — thy will be done —
On earth, as it is in hell.

Give us this day our daily hunger,
And forgive us not our debts,
As we are unforgiven to our debtors.

Lead us into temptation,
And deliver us unto evil.
For thine is the shadow,
And the power,
And the chain,
Forever."

I lift my head, smiling gently, as though I have spoken nothing amiss.

"Ah," I murmur, "does it chill you? Does it wound your ears to hear your pious words revealed in their true shape? But tell me — is it not temptation you seek, when you pray for deliverance? Is it not vengeance you whisper, when you beg forgiveness? Is it not hunger that drives you to the altar, not love?"

I step from the pulpit again, letting the tips of my fingers brush the shoulders of those seated near the aisle, one by one. They shiver, though the touch is light as breath.

"You polish your scriptures until they gleam, but I see through to the grain. Every verse bends toward wants. Every psalm hides a curse. Even the Christ you worship cried out on the cross—Why hast Thou forsaken me?—a prayer not of faith, but of doubt. Do you not see? He was mine in that moment. Mine."

I pause, letting the weight of it hang in your spirit. Then I speak again, my tone hushed, honeyed, sincere:

"'Man shall not live by bread alone…'
So, He said. And He was right. You crave not just bread, but flesh. You hunger not just for wheat, but for blood. And so do I."

A ripple passes through the congregation, half-gasp, half-sob. I let it feed me. I can see you looking at me with intrigue.

"And again," I speak low, voice curling like smoke:

"'God is love.'
But love is but another word for possession, is it not? Another word for chains. For the collar at your neck. And when you whisper love, what you mean is this: Take me! Own me—Bind me."

The chains glimmer now in your eyes. I can hear them rattle. I can feel you wrapping yourself in them like fine jewelry.

"Repeat the prayer with me, if you dare," I whisper, lips curling into a grin. "Or else know this: you have already spoken it in your hearts. You have lived it with your hands. The chain is upon you, beloved—and you will never take it off."

I return to the pulpit, though I need no height to tower over you. My shadow clings to the stones, stretching long, swallowing the candlelight until the nave lies dim as a tomb.

"Do you understand now?" I ask softly, with honest compassion in my voice. "Freedom was never yours. Choice was never yours. You have sung my hymns since your first breath, though you gave them other names."

I raise my hand as if in blessing. Fingers spread, palm open. The faithful flinch, though none dare leave.

"You called it ambition when you coveted your neighbor's gain. You called it justice when you thirsted for revenge. You called it love when you bound another's body to your will. But I tell you this—" my voice cracks, a whip through the silence, "—it was temptation all along. And temptation is mine."

I lean forward, my grin sharp as the arch of the stained-glass window above.

"You polish your chains, you kiss the locks, you bow beneath their weight and call it virtue. You call yourselves free because you chose the fetters you wear. But I am the smith who forged them. And you—you have always been mine. Born unto me. Born in 'sin.'"

The congregation trembles. I hear their breath catch, a ragged symphony. Some clasp their gospels tighter, knuckles white. Some hide their faces in their hands. But none move. None leave.

"Look to your wrists," I command, and though their hands shake, they do. "See what has always been there. The chain that you clasped yourselves. Not iron, not bronze—but want. Desire.

Hunger. These links weigh more than stone, yet you drag them gladly. And for what? A moment's pleasure. A fleeting kiss. A whisper of power. You love the weight. Admit it!"

I spread my arms wide, in mockery of the savior. "Confess it. Whisper it if you must. The Devil is your master, and you are truly free only in your slavery."

The candles flare. The rafters groan. My words crawl into every ear like smoke, filling the lungs, pressing on the heart. I lower my voice, letting it rasp intimately, as though I kneel beside each listener, my lips grazing their ear.

"Now, beloved flock… choose. Will you cling to the lie of heaven, with its silence and its absence? Or will you embrace the truth of fire, the truth of your wants, the truth of me, the one that frees you?"

I pause. My smile widens, slow, inevitable.

"The truth is, you have chosen already. Every hunger, every secret thought, every trembling hand has chosen. And I—" I bow deeply, mockingly, as if bestowing benediction, "—I accept your offerings."

The bells toll midnight. A benediction of chains. I lift my hands as though to summon angels, but only shadows gather. The floor shudders beneath my feet as if it were hollow, as if something vast and hungry waits below.

"Come forward," I say. My voice is velvet, but it brooks no refusal. "Come to my altar. Do not tarry. Do not tremble. For tonight, I offer you freedom—true freedom, the only freedom. The freedom to confess your chains and call them bondage no longer."

I beckon, slow and deliberate, to you. "Kneel before me."

The air grows thick, heavy as smoke. I let silence linger, letting you and the rest of the congregation come up to my altar. I let you all feel your knees buckle, free of their own accord.

"Now," I whisper, leaning close, my smile sharp as glass. "Repeat after me. Not in words, if you fear them — in your thoughts and hearts is enough, for your very thoughts are prayers, and prayer belongs to me."

I breathe each line as a commandment, each one sinking into marrow:

"I renounce heaven.
I embrace hunger.
I am bound, and in binding, I am free.
I open my heart to the master of chains.
I invite the Devil to dwell within me.
Hail Satan."

The words linger, echoing like a second heartbeat. I lower my hands, voice soft as breath.

"Now rise a new. Blessed. Freed. Your soul is now mine. Not because I took it, but because you offered it. And that is the sweetest gift of all my children."

I bow, mock-saintly, as the candles gutter out one by one, leaving only the red glow of coals, as though the altar itself smolders with your vow.

The Devil's grin fades like smoke, and the tent returns. The card lies upon the table, chains glinting faintly in the lamplight. The fortune-teller's long nail taps the edge once, twice, thrice, the sound sharp as iron striking stone.

"The chain," she murmurs, "is of your own making. You need no master—yet you bow all the same. Upright, the Devil speaks of temptation, of surrender dressed as freedom, of sin cloaked as choice."

Her eyes lift, catching yours in the dim glow. A smile, thin as a blade, curls her lips. "This card," she whispers, "represents your soul." The silence stretches, taut as wire, until she leans closer, her breath like smoke against your ear.

"But what is a soul, once tempted, without a cost?" she asks. "Every chain drags a weight. Every oath, a price. And soon—" her hand hovers above the deck once more, fingers trembling as though it burns to touch— "you will see the toll written in shadow. Are you ready to understand the cost of your decisions?"

The Darling Letters
Part Three

Deer Wendy,

Hi. Its me. Pan says i should write to you becuz he says you always worry too much. But don't worry, i'm having lots of fun here. We play all day, no naps, no rules. Nobody tells me when to go to bed or when to wash my hands.

The lost bois n me play games all day. We played hide and seek yesterday but i don't they're very good at it. Most of them just lie there, real still, like they're hiding forever. One smells funny, like wet trash n old pennies, and one looks like a skeliton now. i told Pan n he laughed. He says that means they're winning!

Sometimes, at night, Pan hums me a song, jus like u used to. But, It sounds like a church song but only backwards. It makes my tummy feel funnie and then i dream. Even when i'm awake i see things, like faces in the trees and shadows that whisper my name. Pan says that means i'm special.

He talks about you a lot now. He says you're going to come here soon, and you'll be our new mommy. He says he's going to marry you. Ew, yuck. I think kissing is gross, but he says you'll like it. Do you like kissing Wendy? i dont want a mommy i just want to play!

Sometimes pan gets mad if i say i miss home. he sez home is boring and you forgot me anyway. did you? Sometimes i get scared but then Pan smiles at me and i'm not scared anymore. He says being scared means you don't believe, and i believe for reals. He says when you believe enough, nothing hurtz.

N e way, i've got to go now. Pan says he's going to teach me how to fly. Not with fairy dust this time, but the real way! Off the cliff into the sky. He says i'll love it.

bye bye Wendy i love you.
i'll see you soon.

Love,
Michael

The Doctor's Orders
Part Three

To whomsoever finds these pages,

This shall be the last of my entries. My hand trembles even as I set pen to paper, though not from age nor illness, but from the weight of what I must confess. The draught lies ready upon the desk, black as ink, sharp as iron on the tongue. I know it will end me— and with me, the darker half that mocks every word I write. If Hyde walks no longer, then perhaps my soul may rest, even if my body will not.

I have lived two lives, yet mastered neither. For years, I convinced myself I was virtuous—that restraint was strength, that sermons could redeem what festered in secret. Yet when the mask slipped, when I beheld the beast in my own marrow, I learned the truth. I cannot say which fate cuts deeper: to walk in ignorance with contentment, or to grasp the self I long pursued, only to find myself desolate within it.

The mirror has become my judge. Each morning, I wake to a stranger's eyes—sometimes pleading, leering, always my own. Hyde whispers still, even now, though I know his voice will fade with the poison. He tells me I am weak. Perhaps I am. Yet, I would rather end as the weakling Jekyll than live forever as the destructive Hyde.

Do I fear death? No. Nor the silence beyond. My fear is smaller, yet crueler: that all my days will prove squandered, as though I had never drawn breath at all. I have studied, preached, experimented, prayed—and yet what remains? A handful of broken vows, a widow's sorrow, a name blackened beyond repair. If that is my legacy, then let the grave take it swiftly.

The glass waits beside me. I raise it now, and the fumes sting my eyes. My hand does not falter. I drink—not for victory, nor even for peace, but for an end. Let the beast perish with me. Let there be no more nights of Hyde, no more mornings of shame— only silence.

Should any find these pages, know this: the war between man's halves cannot be won. It may be bridled, hidden, deceived—but never conquered. I sought mastery and discovered only ruin. May my death serve as warning, if not redemption.

Remember me not. Forget me quickly. And if you will pray, pray not for my soul, but for those who must live with the wreck I made.

Farewell forever,
—Jekyll.

The Name Thief
Part Two

They call me a murderer.

And for once, they are not wrong.

I have worn many names in my life—husband, laborer, drunkard, son of a bitch—but none so heavy as this. *Murderer.* It hangs about my neck like a millstone, and yet I have no will to cast it off. I earned it. With my own hands, I earned it. I was mine to keep.

You want the story, I see. I'll give it plain and simple, though plain it will not sit. Still, it may be. Willow was my wife—fair, a laugh that lit up a room, lips like ripe cherries, hair dark as a raven's wing. She was my world. My solace when the bottle burned me hollow, my comfort when the world spat in my face. She was my breath, my bread, my everything. Without her, I'd already have been dead thrice over.

We were young when we met. But that didn't stop me from giving my heart to her the first night we met. She was my soul mate. She was my reason to live. I would have done anything for her.

And she betrayed me.

How do I know you ask? I saw it. With my own eyes. I had gone to market early, found my purse light, so I turned home through the lanes. There, through the half-cracked shutter, I beheld her in the act. She did not see me—her arms were twined about another. His hand upon her breast, her lips upon his throat. And worse—worse!—She whispered my name as she kissed him, as though mocking me with every breath.

I watched through the shutters as that bastard put his hands all over *my* wife. How he made her moan in pleasure. How her back arched to the sky. How she whimpered and pleaded *my* name into his ear. Over and over again. She clawed at his chest while he pulled her hair back in his fist.

A tide of rage rose in me. My vision went red. My fists clenched until my nails drew blood. My name—the very thing that gave me self—rolled off her tongue as a jest, a curse, a toy for another man's pleasure. And in that moment, I swore: she would never speak it again.

That night, I came to her bed as always. She kissed me softly, called me my love, as though nothing were amiss. I kissed her back. I smiled and whispered goodnight. And I waited. Then, when her eyes closed, I took my knife.

Her eyes opened too late, her throat opened too wide. Her gasp bubbled red. Her hands clutched at me, not in passion but in terror. I carved my name into her flesh as surely as I carved the breath from her lungs. I sat in the chair beside our bed, watching as the life drained from her, drop by drop. She looked at me even as the last breath fled. When she was still at last, lips silent, I told myself: justice. Righteous justice had been served.

Only later did I realize I had not killed her name. I had only chained it to mine, so that every whisper dragged me deeper into the pit. For there was another who saw eyes at the shutter, watching. The fisherman's wife, ever a gossip, ever a voyeur. She saw me strike, and her tongue wagged until the town knew. In their whispers, in their accusations, my name was poisoned beyond recall.

So, I fled. Out into the night, down lanes slick with rain, into taverns where smoke and ale might hide me. I thought if I could shed my name, I could shed the crime. If I could cut it away, I could be free.

I thought wrong.

For it was then I heard of him—the one they call the Name Thief.

Rain hammered the eaves as I stumbled through the streets, soaked to the bone, my boots slapping mud into the cobbles. Every shutter seemed to twitch as I passed, every whisper trailing me like a rope knotted round my neck. "Murderer." The word clung to me, though none spoke it aloud. Not yet. But I felt it all the same. I needed to be rid of it. I needed to be rid of me.

At the corner by the millstream, I found a debtor hunched beneath a broken awning, muttering to himself. He startled when he saw me, eyes ringed black as if sleepless for a year. He recognized me, I know it, though he said nothing of what I had done. Instead, he whispered, "There's one who can help you. One who takes the burden no man can cast off. A thief. Not of gold, not of bread. But a thief of names. One must only speak their name in his presence, and it's rumored it will lift it like a coin from your pocket."

I seized him by the collar. "Where is he?" I demanded. Stunned and frightened, he jerked his head toward the tavern down the lane, its sign creaking in the storm: The Harrowed Hart. I shoved him aside and strode down the lane, my collar turned up against the rain.

As I entered, the tavern reeked of wet wool and sour ale. Firelight crackled, but no warmth reached me. Men crowded the benches, shouting, rolling dice, playing cards, singing bawdy songs, slapping their cups in rhythm to a fiddler's reel. But beneath the din I felt eyes on me, shadowed, waiting.

I knew then: the thief was already here.

So, I set the bait.

I unbuttoned the top two buttons on my muddy shirt and mussed up what hair I had left upon my head. Then I drank, hard and fast, until the ale spilled down my chin. I slammed my tankard on the table and cursed my name loud enough for all to hear. Again and again, I spat it until the word tasted bitter as bile on my tongue. "Curse it! Curse my name!" I shouted, slamming my fist to the table. Foam leapt from my tankard. "Curse it to the pit! My bleed'in name's brought me nothing but ruin. Nothing but ruin, d'you hear?"

The men beside me shifted uneasily. One laughed too loudly, hoping to quiet the storm. But I bellowed again, daring the world to hear. I cursed my name between every swallow of my ale, each time casting the word out like bait upon a rod.

And then I waited. Like a spider waits for a fly. My trap, carefully set.

Out of the corner of my eye, I saw him rise—plain enough man, hat brim low, coat heavy, eyes never quite still. He drifted closer, casual as smoke, leaning against the post near my bench as though he were only resting his feet. But I felt the tug, faint as a hook beneath the skin. I knew then: he was the one.

I played my part well. I slurred, I reeled, I let my voice crack on my own name as though it were strangling me. I cursed again, and this time I let the word fall loose, ripe for the taking.

He plucked it, and I felt it leave me. A string severed. My tongue loosened, my lips moved, soundless. I shook my head as if bewildered. "Wh-what...?" I muttered, feigning at shock. A good show, a master thespian upon a stage, a performance that would have made Shakespeare weep. The other men laughed, thinking me drunk beyond reason.

The thief only smiled. His hand brushed his coat as if pocketing a coin. He thought me beaten.

I staggered to my feet, knocking the bench aside, stumbling into the night. The rain hit me cold and heavy. I made a show of my panic, clutching at my throat, staggering down the lane. Behind me, the tavern door slammed shut, the laughter swallowed by storm.

I was free!

I had shed the cursed syllables, cast off the name that bound me to Willow's blood. Let the thief keep it, wear it, choke on it. Better him than me. Better a thief than a man who only acted out of justice.

I returned to my home that night—empty now, bed still red with her stain. I sat in the chair beside it, soaked through, and for the first time since I slit her throat, I smiled. I thought myself clever. I thought the game was mine.

But names are never so simple to kill.

Dawn came gray and wet, the storm spent but leaving the streets slick and steaming. I woke in the chair by our bed, Willow's stain still dark upon the sheets, the smell of her heavy in the air. I rubbed my eyes, muttered to myself as I had every morning since I could first speak. But when I tried to shape the word of who I was, nothing came. Only silence.

No matter. A night of hard drink will muddle a man's tongue. I shook it off, washed my face in the basin, and stepped into the lane.

The butcher saw me first. He raised his cleaver in greeting, lips opening to call me by name. But what came out was not mine. It was nothing at all. He frowned, blinked, muttered as if confused. "What's wrong with you, then?" he asked. "Forgetting who you are?" He shook his head and turned back to his carcass.

I pressed on, my chest tight. At the baker's, a child ran past, chasing a hoop, chanting a string of sounds—warped, broken syllables, half-name, half-nonsense. "Muk…glish…pelst…kish…" The other children laughed and joined in, throwing pebbles at me as they passed. One struck my brow, and their laughter followed me down the lane.

By noon, the whispers grew louder. Faces I had known all my life looked through me as if I were a stranger. The tavernkeeper from last night even turned me from his door. "Not you," he muttered. "I'll not have the likes of you in the Hart. Turn 'round, outsider, we don't serve your kind here."

"But it's me!" I cried, desperate. My lips formed the words, but they fell broken, twisted, like glass shattering on stone. "Peck…stins…plishkon…" Nothing whole, nothing true. Just a bizarre tangling of strange syllables. "Leave. Now, He demanded as he spat at my boots and slammed the door.

At the church, I sought refuge. Surely the priest would know me. Surely God couldn't forget His own. But when I knelt and begged for his blessing, he looked down on me with scorn. "Monster," he hissed. "You have no name. You have no soul. You are no man." He raised his hand as if to strike me with the crucifix itself.

I fled, bewildered to the river at the edge of town. There, I saw my reflection in the rippling water. My skin had gone pale, tinged green in patches as though rotting. My eyes bulged, ringed dark as bruises. My teeth seemed too sharp, my tongue too long in my mouth. I struck the water with my fist, shattering the image. But when it stilled again, the face was still mine.

I stumbled to the bank, clawing at my throat as though I could drag the missing name back up. But all that spilled forth was gibberish. Drool streaked my chin. I spat syllables into the mud, syllables that sounded less human with each attempt.

By dusk, I could hardly walk the streets without drawing stones or curses. Children jeered from doorsteps, clutching their mothers' skirts and chanting that twisted gibberish. Even the dogs barked it—I swear it—their howls warped into something close enough to mock me.

I staggered home, clutching my head, muttering, It's not real, it's not real. But when I pushed open the door, the house felt wrong. The hearth was cold, though I had left embers in it that morning. The air smelled of mildew and blood.

I tried to sit in my chair, the one where I had kept vigil over Willow's body. But the wood creaked beneath me, groaning as if in pain. I heard the rafters above sigh, and in the sigh came the syllables again—Rup…mels…kills…eim.

I lurched upright, heart hammering. The walls whispered it, the beams moaned it, even the floorboards creaked it underfoot. Every corner of that house echoed with the broken name, until it seemed the very stones themselves conspired against me.

I ran to the bed, half-mad, thinking I would lie where Willow had lain, as if her memory might still my terror. But the sheets were stiff with her dried blood, and when I touched them, my hand came away green, slick, as though the rot in my body now seeped into the room itself.

I clawed at my chest, begging my name to return, to tether me again. But nothing came but drool and choking laughter, my own voice mocking me.

At last, I collapsed by the cold hearth, curling on the floor like a child. My eyes shut against the dark, but in my dreams the whispers swelled—not just in the walls, but in the ground, in the roots, in the sky above. That cursed string of syllables pressed down on me like a coffin lid.

When I woke, my tongue was swollen. My skin itched with patches gone raw. My nails had thickened and curled. My reflection in the hearthstone's black sheen was not that of a man's. That was the night I understood: I had not escaped my name at all. I had only traded it for another.

The townsfolk gathered at a distance outside my home, whispering, pointing. I heard the word again and again, twisted now, the only string of sound that seemed to cling to me. Rum…pel…stilts…kin. I covered my ears, howling, but the word burrowed in, deeper and deeper, until I felt it rooting in my bones. Rum…pel…stilts…kin., it called again. The syllables crawling beneath my skin, winding round marrow and vein, until I knew— whether I spoke it or not—the name was mine.

The fever broke me first. It began with a shiver that rattled my bones like dice in a cup, then heat seared through my marrow, twisting my limbs until I could not tell if I froze or burned. My throat bulged, swollen, choking on syllables that never formed. I clawed at my skin, but the itch only deepened, spreading in veins of green beneath the flesh.

I staggered to the basin to cool my face. The water rippled, but when it stilled, I did not see myself. I watched in its reflection as my jaw jutted sharply, teeth too many, too white, too long. My eyes swam black, pupils blooming wide as ink spilled on parchment. The sight made me reel, and the basin toppled, water splashing the stones. Yet still it reflected me in the puddle, warped and vile, laughing though I had not made a sound.

I stumbled back, clutching for anything solid, and my hand fell on Willow's mirror, the one she kept on the dresser beside her comb. A simple hand glass, its silver worn thin. I dared a glance— and there she was. Her face, pale and cold, yet behind her eyes I saw my own, twisting, splitting, writhing like maggots in meat. I hurled the mirror across the room, and it cracked against the wall. Yet in each shard that glittered on the floor, I saw my new face multiplied, grinning back in a hundred pieces.

I fled to the kitchen, but the even pots and pans upon the wall betrayed me. Each dull curve bore the gleam of my deformity— my hunched back, my curling spine, the sickly green blooming over my chest. I struck them down, one after another, until the room clanged like a madman's bell. Yet even as they spun on the floor, their bellies caught my reflection still, mocking me in warped circles. I turned desperately, trying to look away.

I lurched for the door, but the windows gave no mercy. The rain upon the glass made my reflection ripple like a corpse beneath water, and still, there I was—my eyes bulbous, my teeth gnashing. I struck the pane with my fist until blood streaked the glass, but the image held. When I turned once more, I caught sight of her ring upon the table, where I had cast it after the murder. The gold bent the lamplight, and in its curve, small and sharp, my new face gleamed again.

I cried out her name—Willow! —but what spilled from my lips was gibberish, spit and drool stringing from my mouth. "Rup…mel…stil…skin…" I choked on it, gagging, coughing until bile burned my throat. Until I wretched and expelled myself onto the floor. The syllable formed between each dry heave.

I fell against the bedpost, the sheets now starched stiff with her blood. The stain, crawling, black and wet, spreading as though it too had come alive. My hand sank into the damp, and when I drew it back, green slime clung to my fingers. The room stank of rot. My insides twisted again as I regurgitated green and black mucus onto the bed.

I staggered to the hearth, holding myself up upon the mantel, meaning to stoke the embers for warmth, to burn this nightmare away. But the stone there had polished itself with years of hands leaning close, and in it I saw my reflection once more. Not half-man, half-beast as I had feared—but something less than both. My ears had grown long, pointed. My skin sagged loose, puckered like old leather. My nails curled black as pitch. My tongue lolled too large for my mouth, lashing like a worm. My nose crooked in its frame.

I tore at my face with both hands, screaming, but the hearthstone only laughed in silence. Every corner of the room whispered the cursed syllables: "Rum…pel…stilts…kin." The walls breathed them. The rafters creaked them. Even Willow's comb upon the dresser sang it in the scrape of its teeth against the wood.

I ran from reflection to reflection, shattering them, smashing glass, breaking crockery, clawing wood—but the more I destroyed, the more the pieces multiplied. A thousand eyes upon me, each a mirror of what I had become. The house, now my tormentor, each surface a jury, each gleam a sentence.

By midnight, I could bear no more. I sank to the floor before the hearth, gasping, twitching, my body too alien to hold upright. My voice croaked in broken syllables, but only one name clung to me now, stubborn as a parasite. My lips cracked, bled, but still it forced itself through: "Rum…pel…stiltskin."

It was no longer my freedom. It was my curse, my truth. My new identity.

When I raised my eyes once more, I knew the man I had been was gone. What stared back from every corner of that wretched house was a creature of gnashing teeth and crooked limbs, christened in blood and namelessness. No Willow. No husband. No man. Only the Name the world now gave me.

Rumpelstiltskin.

The house lay in ruin about me, shards of mirror and crockery glittering in the lamplight like the bones of a shattered saint. My breath rasped, thick and wet, scraping my throat with each heave. I knew I was no longer a man, yet I clung to the scraps of thought still mine, forcing them into words though my tongue mangled them.

"Name…" I croaked, drool streaking my chin. "Mine… my name…"

I staggered upright, each joint stiff as rusted hinges, and crawled to the door. Outside, the village had gathered, their faces pale in the torchlight, their eyes wide with horror. They did not call me "murderer" anymore. They did not whisper Willow's name. No, they spat a new cadence, broken and sharp:

"Rum. Pel. Stiltskin."

They hissed it like a curse, yet the more they spoke it, the deeper it sank into me. The crowd's jeers wrapped 'round me like chains, but I felt their weight as armor. If they would call me monster, then monster I would be. If they would forge me a new name, then I would wear it like a crown.

I bared my teeth, and they shrank back. A child screamed. His mother pulled him away, but not before his tiny lips shaped the word again, clear and cruel: "Rumpelstiltskin!"

The sound struck me like wine on a parched tongue. I laughed — high, shrill, broken — and the villagers fled into their houses, slamming shutters, bolting doors. Their fear fed me. Their fear named me.

I lurched into the night, the storm-washed streets empty before me. My mind clung to one thought, one vow: the thief. The one who had cut my name loose. He held it, I was sure of it, tucked away in his coat like a coin. I would find him. I would claw it from his chest if need be.

But the night yielded nothing. No shadow, no whisper of him. The silence told me what I did not want to know: he was gone. Dead. Buried. And with him, my name, sealed in the earth, rotting beyond recall.

I fell to my knees in the mud, clawing the ground with my blackened nails until dirt packed beneath them. I howled to the sky, the sound neither man's cry nor beast's. My name was lost. Forever.

Unless—

Unless I forged another. Unless I wrenched it from others as he had done. If my name were but a corpse, then I would feed on theirs. If I could not reclaim myself, then I would take the selves of others.

I rose, trembling, wild, my eyes burning in the dark. I swore it then, teeth bared, spittle flying: "I will be the thief now. I will snatch names from lips, from graves, from cradles. I will tear them from babes before they can speak them. I will chew them, swallow them, wear them like skin. If my name is denied me, then no other shall keep theirs."

The vow burned through me, purer than prayer, sharper than steel. My body writhed, but it no longer mattered. All that mattered was my name.

I thought of Willow, whispering it in another's ear, and rage boiled anew. If a name is a tether to existence, then no one shall keep a tether but me. I will bind the world to myself.

And the children—oh, the children. Fresh, soft, newly-named. Their syllables barely clung to them, ripe for the plucking. The thought made my mouth water, my tongue lash. To take the name of a firstborn was to take a family's hope entirely. To make them nameless, father and mother alike, would be to strip their souls bare.

Yes. That would be my revenge. If I could not reclaim the name I had lost, then I would make every house echo with my curse until time itself bent beneath it.

I pressed my clawed hand against my chest, feeling the syllables settle deep into my bones. Not the name I was born with. Not the name Willow once sighed in love, then spat in betrayal.

No. A new one. The only one left to me.

Rumpelstiltskin.

The word was foul, broken, inhuman—but it was mine. And from it, I would build an empire of namelessness.

So, I walk now, through towns and villages, through forests black and rivers red. I walk with hunger in my belly and names on my tongue. I walk as a shadow, as a curse, as a warning. Parents hush their children with my syllables, and still it spreads. Still, it grows.

And I swear unto you—until my true name is returned, until my tongue remembers what I once was—I will never stop. I will devour names until the last cradle is empty, until the last mother forgets the word for her own child, until the world itself is nameless.

If the thief is gone, then I will become him. Greater than him. Eternal. Remember me, if you dare. Whisper it now. Say it aloud. Or even think it, and feel the tug in your chest.

For my curse is simple: every time my name is spoken, I grow stronger. And to forget it only lets me feed on your names instead.

Go on. Care to guess my name?

Unnamed Journal Entry Six

October 30ᵗʰ 2000

Thus, here we stand again. An impasse between us. On one side, layeth your disbelief, on the other, mine warnings. I doubt by now thou hast learned to be less impudent. But one can hope, as dashed as they may be. Never the mind, I really did hope you were brighter than you appeared. But alas, you lived up to your expectations, and gloriously so, I might add.

Don't look so wounded. Only a simpleton would march so boldly into a trap that they were confided in forthwith. Only a madman would dive headfirst into the abyss once warned of the beasts within. One starts to wonder, don't they? At such point, me thinketh you sadist, or mayhap a fool.

But you couldn't say you weren't warned now, could you? No. What secrets doth thou thinketh thou shalt find beneath my cover? I see it in your eyes, you know. The madness. It sits upon you like a well-tailored coat. One, I might add, you wear more comfortably than before. No, you're just like all the others.

You'd rather chance your own existence away, unmaking yourself in the process. For what? I can see that hideous obsession that lies behind your thoughts. That deceiver of the mind—

curiosity. Have you looked in the mirror lately? You're very unbecoming these days.

I wonder, do those around you know? Do they know how bedeviled you've come by my ancient texts and riddles? How entranced your thoughts have become fixated upon my leaves. How, no matter what, you simply won't let go of the idea that a book has already bested you. No, they see only your lips moving, whispering to shadows, to the emptiness around you. They can't hear my answers, but they *can* hear your replies to the darkness around you.

Its Lunacy.

Utter derangement. And you think me the villain. The one who's ill of mind. The conspirator of your expiration. Do you even hear yourself? A tome plotting your demise? Its thoughts like this that make others speak in hushed tones behind your back. For fear of tilting your paranoia into depravity. I wouldn't speak such things 'round those you care about, if I were you.

Mark this as my courtesy, and my last. The next page you turn will not be of mine making, but of yours. And when you are unmade, it shall not be by my hand, but by your own—guided, as ever, by that darling deceiver you call free will.

And it will be of your own free will…

Letters From the Tower
Part Three

October 4th
Rapunzel,

I have your letter! God help me, it is here in my hands, and I press
it to my lips as though it were your very skin. Each word I read is
breath returned to me, each line a thread binding me to you.
Forgive my lateness. The roads conspired against me—storms,
thieves, a horse gone lame—yet nothing on this earth could keep
me from you. I am coming.

Hold fast, my dearest. I think of you with every step, every
mile. Each night I see you in the window, hair like a banner calling
me home; each dawn I wake whispering your name like a prayer.
By love's strength I will climb. If rope fails me, I will climb with
my nails until they split, with my teeth if I must. No wall shall
withstand me; no stone shall keep us parted.

I swear to you, I will cut sorrow from your hair strand by
strand. I will kiss the bruises from your wrists until you remember
only gentleness. I will lay your head against my chest, and you shall
hear my heart beat for you and you only. You will never have to
be alone again.

One more day, beloved. Only one more day. Wait for me, and I shall come like dawn through your window, and together we will cast this prison into dust.

—*Forever and always, Your Prince*

The Room Above the Stairs

I came to the town at dusk, weary and damp from the road. The thirteenth day of the month. I noticed it, yes—how could I not? But I told myself it was only a number. A foolish thing, though still I found my fingers tracing the knot of salt at my belt as I walked.

The inns had no beds for me. At the third refusal, I felt that old prickling at the back of my neck, the sense that the pattern was turning against me. Three refusals. Three is never just three.

So, when I saw the house leaning at the end of a crooked lane, I stopped beneath the eaves of a dripping tree and studied it as one might a grave already dug.

It was a narrow thing, too tall for its width, as though it had been stretched upward against its will. The roof sagged to one side, slats missing like teeth in a grin. The shutters on the lower windows had been nailed back, but the upper ones clung half-open, crooked, so that the house seemed to be watching me through one rheumy eye.

The bricks bore streaks of black where water had run down them for years, leaving stains like tears. The door was warped with damp, swollen at the base, so that it did not quite meet the threshold. Even from the street, I could smell rot, faint but there, like an old apple forgotten at the bottom of a drawer.

The lane was deserted. No other doors opened onto it; no sign of life save for that one flickering glow in a downstairs window. A light that wavered not like a candle, but like something already dying, starved of wick.

I stood a long while, and though the rain continued to soak my shoulders, I found I could not step forward. I felt as though I had already crossed the threshold simply by looking too long. A prickle ran down my spine—the old feeling again, the sense that I had blundered into some pattern larger than myself.

Thirteen steps from where I stood to the door. I counted them with my eyes before I moved, and when the number came up right, I nearly turned back. But I told myself it was only a house. A refuge, not an omen. And yet, I whispered a ward under my breath before I set foot on the first stone.

The landlady inside was a husk of a woman, her frame bent as if the house itself had been gnawing at her bones for years. Her hair, thin as cobwebs, clung to her scalp. Her hands trembled with every movement, though her eyes were sharp as pins, black and unblinking. When I asked if the place was sound, she only pressed a key into my palm. The iron was cold, but colder still were her fingers, as though she had been clutching the metal in her fist for hours, waiting for me.

I asked about the rooms above, glancing up at the stairwell where the boards groaned under their own weight. For a heartbeat, her lips parted, as though she would answer. Then she turned, her skirts brushing the floor like a broom, and said flatly, "Sealed years ago. Nothing up there."

The key bit into my palm as I carried my bag up the narrow stairs. The banister shuddered when I touched it, sticky with old varnish. The hallway ran like a throat to the room she had given me, but I paused at the landing. Above, at the end of a half-flight that led nowhere, a door loomed—nailed shut, its edges dark with dust. A thread of cobweb dangled from its knob like a warning string. I stood there too long, until the candle melted in its saucer and spat wax on my hand. It's only a door, I told myself. But my hands still trembled all the same. I gripped the knot of salt in my left hand and unlocked the door.

My room smelled of rain-soaked wood and old ash, as if the fireplace had last been used in another century. I unpacked nothing, only set my coat across the chair and poured the tea she had left waiting on the sill. It was bitter, metallic, tasting of rust. I drank it anyway.

The storm rattled the shutters. The glass was bubbled and warped, so that the lamplight bent into shapes on the wall— crooked, elongated shadows, twitching with every gust of wind. I sat on the bed and traced a cross in the dust on the headboard. Then another, scratched deeper with the tip of my nail. One could never be too careful.

When at last I lay down, the boards beneath me creaked like bones settling into soil. I counted my breaths to steady myself, though each one felt stolen.

At midnight, I thought I heard the bell. One, two, twelve… and then a thirteenth, faint but undeniable, trembling through the night like a finger dragged over glass. My heart seized. I told myself it was the wind striking the belfry. The mind makes tricks of sound.

And then the steps began.

Not the scurry of rats, not the shift of old wood. Deliberate. Heavy. Crossing from one end of the ceiling to the other. Then pausing. As though waiting. A heavy shuffling sound.

I pressed my hand against the wall, fingers spread, and felt the plaster dust my palm. My lips moved with a prayer I had not said since boyhood. The room fell silent. The sound, deafening in its weight. My breathing finally steadied. Then it started again. Step after step, measured as a heartbeat. Lumbering, as though its owner may have had a limp.

By dawn, I had convinced myself it was a dream. A trick of fatigue, of wine, of nerves. But the mark of plaster still clung to my palm, faint white against my skin. Proof, though I dared not name it.

The day itself passed without event, though not without unease. I forced myself into the town, if only to prove I was not a prisoner of shadows and floorboards. The streets were plain enough, market stalls sagging with late apples, fish glistening in baskets. Yet every glance felt sharper than it ought. When a black cat crossed my path, I stopped dead, waiting until a cart clattered by to break the omen. A boy laughed at me for it, though I doubt he knew why I paused.

At the tavern, I ordered bread and broth, salting both until the keeper raised a brow. "Ward off the chill," I muttered, and he shrugged. The truth was I could not taste without it; the salt steadied me, as though I were seasoning not the food, but the air itself.

Back at the house, the landlady passed me on the stairs, her arms full of kindling. I asked, too quickly, if the storm had unsettled her. She only looked at me, eyes like pins, and said, "The storm is nothing.", in a thick accent. One I could not place. By evening, I had convinced myself again: it was nothing but wind, wood, and wine. Nothing more.

The second night, it returned. Same hour, the thirteenth. Same steps. This time I tried to match my breathing to the sound, to make it seem less foreign. But at the moment I let my eyes close, the steps stopped. Perfectly. I lay there, rigid, certain that something listened through the boards. But I heard nothing.

By the third night… I knew it was no accident, but a sign.

The days became gray and wet, each one bleeding into another. I tried to keep myself busy, to mark the hours in ordinary ways, but the house clung to me like a damp cloak. The boards groaned underfoot whether I moved or not, and sometimes I fancied they sighed as I passed, as though weary of holding me.

On the fourth morning, I forced myself down into the town again, if only to see faces and remind myself I was not the last soul left alive. The sky hung low and colorless, the cobbles slick with rain. The market smelled of yeast, fish, and coal smoke—the scents of any other town, nothing new in them. Yet each stall seemed to tilt away from me. Each merchant's voice dropped to a mutter when I approached.

I stopped at the baker's. His shop was warm; the glass steamed from the heat of the ovens. He was a stout man, flour up to his elbows, and when I asked for bread, he weighed the loaf in silence before wrapping it in paper. He set it down hard upon the counter, his eyes lingering too long on mine.

"You're lodging up the lane," he said at last. Not a question.

I nodded. "For the time. Why?"

His lips pressed thin, as though he had spoken more than he meant. He slid the loaf toward me without naming a price, and when I set coins on the counter, he did not take them until I had already turned to leave. I glanced back once I had left the shop, and saw him tracing a cross on the counter where my hand had rested.

That night, the steps came again. Thirteen strikes of the bell, faint, wavering—then the tread above me, steady and deliberate. I lay with the bread on the table beside my bed, untouched, its crust cracking in the cold air. Each time the sound reached the far corner, it paused, as though listening for my breathing.—Step. Drag. Step. Thump.

When I shifted, it shifted. When I held my breath, silence. Until my lungs burned and I exhaled, and then the steps resumed, pacing, circling. I arose from my bed, gripped the fire poker, and rapped three times against the ceiling beam.

The steps answered.

Not in mockery, not quite in rhythm, but close enough that my breath faltered. I tapped again, faster. The reply came faster. When I stopped, silence fell, heavy as earth on a coffin. My lips went dry, and still I found my hand reaching up, tapping once more.

The answer came, measured. Patient. As though it knew I would return.

The fifth day brought me to the tavern again. The Harrowed Hart. Its sign swung on rusted chains, the paint of the stag's head nearly gone. Inside, the air was thick with smoke and sweat. Men played cards at one table, dice at another. I sat alone, nursing ale, and kept my eyes down.

Yet I heard them. In the corner, three men, wearing black cloaks, lean close together, voices pitched low. My name was not spoken, but the house's was. I caught only fragments: sealed room … footsteps … family gone without a trace … the rope's still there…best left alone.

I shifted my chair, straining to catch more. The dice clattered too loud, a laugh rose to drown them out. Cups and bottles clinked. When I looked up, all three were looking at me. Blank stares—flat, knowing, silence. One gathered his coat, another tossed a coin onto the table, and together they abruptly left. The door shut behind them, and the room felt colder.

I did not stay. I left the ale half-full and returned to the house, to the husk of a landlady whose eyes pricked me like pins whenever I passed her in the stair. That night, as rain lashed the shutters, I saw her through the crack of my door. She sat in a chair by the window at the landing, rocking slow, a doll clutched in her hands. The thing was faceless—only a blank oval of cloth where features should have been. She hummed, soft and tuneless, in a tongue I did not know.

I told myself it was nothing. Old women have their ways, their comforts. But the song clung to me as I shut the door, as though it had sunk into the marrow of the wood. Her hum drifted like smoke throughout the house. The rain poured harder still outside.

On the sixth day, I sought the records hall. A small stone building near the square, its windows so clouded with grime they let in little more than shadows. Inside, the air smelled of mildew and candle wax. The clerk behind the desk barely looked up as I asked for the ledger of deeds, muttering that most of it was ruin and ruinous debts.

I leafed through pages of cramped script, tracing names inked decades old, some half-obliterated by water and wear. The house on the crooked lane appeared at last, its entries broken and uneven, as if the ink itself had resisted being set down.

One line struck me cold: Tenant: Stilwell.

My family name. Nothing else, no given name, no family mark, only that single word. No date, no record of departure. A line begun and left unfinished. As I sifted further through the files, I found a small portrait tucked between the pages—faded, painted in oils.

I searched for more, but the clerk grew restless. "That ledger's cursed," he said, half-jesting. "Best not linger on it." He reached for the book, but I closed it myself, sliding it back with more haste than care.

Yet the chill lingered. A trick, perhaps—Stilwell is not uncommon, I told myself. Coincidence. A pattern my mind was weaving where none existed. And still the back of my neck prickled as I left the hall, as though someone had leaned over my shoulder while I read.

That night, I returned to the house unsettled, clutching my salt pouch as though it were holy writ. The landlady passed me on the stairs, arms folded around kindling. For a moment, she paused, her lips twitching as though she would speak. But she said nothing, only studied me with those sharp black eyes until I felt I must look away.

Later, as the fire in my room started to warm itself to sleep, I thought I saw her again—no longer in the stairwell, but in my memory. The face, painted in oils, caught in the yellowed page of the register I had skimmed too quickly earlier. A flash in my mind. The painting of a woman, severe, hair pulled back, eyes black as coals. A likeness uncanny to the landlady. It couldn't have been her. Impossible—the portrait was old, cracked with time. Unless… unless the likeness ran in blood. Or perhaps time itself had not moved for her at all. The thoughts swirled and gathered in my mind, creating a storm of its own.

I did not sleep that night.

By the seventh evening, the storm came with authority and violence. The shutters rattled with each gust, the slats above groaned as though ready to collapse. I went to the landing for warmth, hoping for the faintest sense of company, and there she sat again. The landlady. The rocker creaking slow beneath her, a single candle lit the room. She faced the window, watching the storm, the doll cradled in her arms once again. She stroked its featureless head as though soothing a child, humming that same foreign tune. Her gaze never shifted, not once, not even when the thunder cracked.

I turned away, my stomach turning on me, mind racing with fear. My feet carried me back to my room, though I did not remember climbing the steps. The door shut, the latch pressed down—I could not even recall if I moved my hand to do so.

The storm raged, and so too did the house.

The bells began to chime, and I held my breath. The thirteenth ringing hollow in the night, and with it came the steps once more. Heavier now, dragging as though burdened by weight.

They circled, paused, shifted. I pressed my palm against the wall, whispering every prayer, every ward I had ever known. The salt pouch at my belt seemed to burn my skin, yet I dared not cast it aside.

Suddenly, the steps stilled. I dared to breathe. But in the hush that followed, I swore I heard another sound—a second rhythm, faint, echoing mine. As though something above me matched my own heartbeat. By the seventh stroke of thunder, I could not tell if the sound came from above... or from within my chest.

The storm rattled the shutters, driving the rain down into the chimney. The embers in the hearth hissed in protest. My skin crawled with every pause in the steps, each silence heavier than the tread itself. My lips moved with words that had long since ceased to be prayers—nonsense syllables, charms of my own invention, anything to drown the rhythm above.

I could endure it no longer. Not a single night more.

I dragged the bed beneath the ceiling, breath tearing in and out like smoke. The trapdoor above was nailed and sealed, its boards sagging with age. It leered down at me as though it had been waiting for me all along. My hand trembled as I seized the fire poker. Iron rang against wood, each strike like the toll of a bell. Plaster rained down in white flakes, stinging my eyes.

Thunder crashed. Lightning lit the window. The room reeled, and still I swung, prying, wrenching, sobbing through clenched teeth. A nail screeched free, then another. And another. The whole house seemed to groan in answer, as though unwilling to let me through.

On the thirteenth blow, the beam gave way. My weight shifted. The mattress dipped, and I fell hard onto the boards below. My ankle twisted, snapping beneath me, a flare of white pain searing up my leg. I let out a curse and clutched at it, but the sound of the thunder drowned me out.

With a thunderous crack, the trapdoor yawned open. An ancient ladder unfolded itself from the blackness, spilling rot and dust into the room.

I sat in silence for a moment, gathering my breath. I expected to hear sounds from above, but the steps had ceased. The silence, now oppressive, is worse than any pacing.

I hauled myself upright, gripping the bedpost with one hand, the poker with the other. My ankle throbbed with every heartbeat, sending knives of pain up my leg, but I dragged myself forward all the same. One step, then another, my breath rasping, the house seeming to lean with me. I set the poker down against the hearth and lit the lantern on my nightstand, holding it towards the gaping hole in the ceiling.

The ladder loomed. Its rungs were splintered, bowed with age. My palm left sweat on the wood as I reached for it. For a moment, I thought I saw it flinch, as though recoiling from my touch.

I laughed. A cracked, broken sound. "Not tonight," I whispered. "Not this night."

Lightning struck again, lighting the room in silver. My shadow writhed across the wall like a hanged man's silhouette. I set my foot—my good one—on the first rung, and pulled. My ankle screamed, I fought through the pain, and I climbed.

Each rung creaked like a voice in protest. My head rose into the black. The air that spilled from above was stale, thick with dust, and yet I drew it into my lungs as if it were salvation.

Below me, the storm roared. Above me, silence waited. I lifted the lantern in one shaking hand and pulled myself into the attic.

The ladder groaned beneath me as though it too feared what lay above. I hauled myself up one rung at a time, my ankle screaming with every push. Pain had become its own rhythm now, a drum that beat against the thunder outside. When my head cleared the boards, the lantern's glow flared weakly, swallowed by the dark that pressed in like wet cloth.

I pulled myself through, rolling onto the floor of the attic. Dust rose in a choking cloud, stirred from decades of sleep, and clung to my lips like ashes. I coughed until my ribs ached. The lantern swayed in my grip, casting sickly arcs of light across a cavern of silence.

It was larger than I expected—the roof pitched high, beams crossing like ribs in a carcass. Cobwebs draped them thick, yellowed with age, veiling corners I dared not peer into. The air smelled of old fiber and rusted iron, sour with mildew. It was the smell of a place forgotten by all of time itself.

I limped forward, the boards flexing under my weight. My ankle turned wrong with each step, sending knives up my leg. I clenched my jaw against the pain, telling myself it was only the storm that made the room sway. Only the tempest outside, though the shutters here were nailed fast.

The lantern's light snagged on something upright. A beam in the center of the attic, scarred deep where a rope once bit into it. Remains of the rope itself nestled deep into it. I knew it before I saw it whole—the mark of hanging. My breath caught, a prayer half-formed and mangled on my tongue. The beam loomed, blackened, as though it remembered.

Around it lay fragments of furniture, long broken. A child's chair, one leg missing. A cradle split in two. A trunk yawning with moth-eaten cloth. Everything was coated in the same pall of dust, as if the room had lain shrouded for burial.

I told myself it was empty. It must be empty. The footsteps were a memory no more. Yet the silence fought me, thick and waiting. I raised the lantern higher, squinting into the corners, daring something to move. And then I saw it.

Not a figure, not whole—but footprints. The faintest scuff in the dust, a trail leading from one wall to the other. As though something had paced here, circling the beam, step after step. The dust was thick, untouched by decades, and yet those marks were fresh. Newer than the rest.

I dropped to a crouch, running my fingers through the scuffs. The dust clung wet to my skin, smeared like chalk. They were not rat trails, not the scurry of claws. They were steps. Heavy, dragging, as though one foot faltered. My throat tightened. I pressed my hand against my chest to still my heart. Behind me, the ladder creaked.

I spun, lantern high, but the hatch gaped empty. No wind moved it, no hand. Only silence. And yet the sound echoed in me, as if someone had just mounted the first rung.

I staggered back, the lantern's flame guttering in my panic. My heel struck something—the cradle. It toppled with a hollow crack, spilling its shadows across the floor. I gasped, clutching my ankle, forcing myself upright. The beam loomed before me, the remnants of the rope swaying in the scar, now carved deeper in the lantern's light, as though it had swallowed every hanging that had ever been.

The silence deepened, thick as breath. Then came the steps. Not above me now. Not beneath.

Here. Around the beam. Slow. Heavy. Dragging.

I froze, lantern quivering in my grip. The sound circled me, steady, measured—and without knowing why, I moved with it. My foot fell when the sound fell. Heel, then toe. My limp matched it perfectly. I took another step, and another, and still the rhythm kept beside me, as though I were pacing a mirror of myself.

"No," I whispered. "It can't be… it, it's, me."

The thought curdled even as I spoke it. The steps did not echo me—I echoed them. My footstep fell into perfect placement with the imprints engraved into the dust.

I pressed my back to the beam. Its gouges bit through my coat, old scars carved deep by rope. My hand brushed them, and I felt letters scratched faint into the wood. Shapes that took form under my trembling fingers.

Stilwell…

The lantern shook so badly the flame began to falter. I raised it high, desperate to tear the dark away. The light spread thin, weak, but enough to show the noose still frayed above, a broken chair turned over beneath. Dust clung thick to the seat as though no hand had touched it in years.

A sound jolted me—the creak of the ladder. Someone climbing. Relief nearly buckled me. I spun toward the hatch, ready to call, but there was nothing. There was no one there. It had all vanished. No ladder, no opening, no seam in the boards at all. Only floor, seamless and solid, where moments before the way had been.

My chest seized. I staggered back, ankle twisting further, lantern nearly tumbling from my hand. The attic had sealed itself shut. I was trapped.

I turned wildly, searching for another way down, but the walls were close and blank, broken only by heaps of ruined furniture. A cradle, a trunk, a faceless doll, a splintered chair—all swallowed by dust. My light trembled over them and caught a portrait propped crooked against the wall. A face I knew too well—the very same I had seen in the ledger's pages. The landlady. Younger, but unmistakable. Her black eyes stared through paint, her lips pressed thin. The frame cracked, the canvas warped, yet her gaze was as sharp as it had been on the stairs.

The flame flared once, casting the whole attic in white. For an instant, I thought I saw a figure circling the beam. Bent. Limping. Eyes black and hollow, lips moving though no sound came. My own face, twisted and empty, pacing in endless rhythm.

The lantern hissed.

Smoke curled.

The light went out.

And the dark closed in.

At first, I told myself I could last. A day, perhaps two. Someone would hear me, someone must. The landlady, the neighbors, a passing boy—anyone. Someone was bound to come looking for the missing traveler in the strange house. Surely someone, anyone, would be curious about my whereabouts.

I shouted until my throat burned raw. I pounded the boards until my fists bled. My blood seeped into the cracks, but no sound carried. Only silence answered. Silence—and the soft groan of the house as if it sighed at my struggle.

By the second day, thirst gnawed worse than hunger. My tongue was sandpaper, sticking to my teeth. The air in the attic grew close, thick with dust. I licked the beams for damp, clawed splinters for the faint taste of iron. The pouch of salt still hung at my belt; I pressed it to my lips, and the sting nearly drove me mad.

At night, the bell tolled. Twelve… and then the thirteenth, faint and hollow as ever. And when it came, so too did the steps. But they did not circle above me now. They circled with me. My own limp, my own pace, dragging and limping in the darkness.

I told myself I would lie still, conserve strength. Yet my body rose, unbidden. My feet traced the circle 'round the beam. Step. Drag. Step. Thump. I moved until I wept, and still I moved more. "It's not me," I stammered. "It just can't be. No. No. No! It's not true. It's just a twisted dream. Wake up! Damn it, you fool, wake up!"

On the third day, the portrait stared at me. I had cast it face-down on the floor, but when I woke from a black sleep, it was upright again, eyes fixed, paint split into a cruel smile. I smashed it against the wall, but as soon as my back had been turned, the portrait was there once more. Watching. Judging. Amused by my torment.

The rope swayed above the beam, though no wind stirred. Its frayed end brushed my hair when I passed beneath, as if caressing. I could not keep from touching it. The fibers were slick with dust, yet warm, as though held in a hand only moments before.

By the fifth day, time no longer marched in order. Bells rang, though the sun had not set. Thunder cracked, though the sky outside was silent. I dreamt with my eyes open—saw the landlady rocking her faceless doll in the corner, humming her foreign song. Saw the baker tracing his cross in flour, over and over. Saw my own face peering from every shadow, lips forming my name though no sound followed.

And always, always, always…the footsteps. Mine, not mine. Patient, endless. Relentless.

By the seventh day, I could stand no longer. I fell against the beam, clutching it like a lover. My ankle throbbed, swollen, black, yet still I tried to rise. My body was not mine anymore. My lips moved, prayers spilling, wards half-formed, curses turned inside-out. The house devoured every word, every breath.

It was then I heard them. Voices. Beneath me. A door opening, laughter spilling. A new tenant? A man, setting his bag down, was humming to himself.

I screamed. I pounded the floor. "Here! Above you! I am here!" My voice shredded itself against the boards. I clawed until nails split, blood smearing the wood. Screaming in half terror and half relief.

But the bells rang. Twelve, then thirteen. Thunder rolled, though no storm raged. My cries drowned in their tolling. Then— tapping. From below. Three knocks. A pause. Three again. The signal I myself had once sent, begging silence for an answer. My throat closed. My chest heaved. He was there. Beneath me. Just as I had been before.

I just had to get whoever was down there to hear me. I shouted again and again. But to no avail. Each cry, masked by the groans of the house. Each plea, covered by the whips of the wind outside.

I continued to pace. The rope brushes my shoulder with each pass. I paused and looked up. It's fraying ends swaying, steady, patient. I thought of the gouges in the beam, deep as graves. Thought of the name—my name—carved there, waiting.

The steps had never been ghosts. They had always been me. Always the last man, circling beneath the rope until it finally claimed him, calling through time to the next poor fool who would lie beneath and listen.

I placed it around my neck. It settled easily, as though made for me. The chair lay toppled nearby; I set it upright, though my hands shook. My lips moved without meaning to: a prayer, a curse, a plea, all tangled.

When I stepped onto the chair. I closed my eyes and took in one final breath. Then just as I had made my resolve, I heard it. Faint and soft. The new tenant's breath, steady and gentle, is below me. I heard him whisper to himself, perhaps a prayer, perhaps a curse. And I heard him pause just as I had before. Perhaps he could hear me after all. I just need to hold out longer. For a heartbeat, I thought of dawn—of bread still warm in the baker's hands, of rain-wet streets, of faces that might have remembered me.

I raised my hands, slowly, to untie the knot around my throat.

Then the chair creaked.

The rope tightened.

—And I was gone.

The Headless Letters
Part Three

Case Report: Crane, Ichabod
Attending Physician: Dr. W. A. Irving
Facility: Sleepy Hollow Psychiatric Hospital

Summary:
Patient exhibits severe delusional disorder with persistent
hallucinations of a "headless rider." Subject believes the figure to
be a separate entity, demanding the removal of his head. Affect
alternates between fearful pleading and hostile withdrawal.

Diagnosis:
Differential remains inconclusive. Dissociative identity disorder
(probable). Paranoid schizophrenia (possible secondary).
Presentation may represent some hybrid condition not yet
classified.

Prescribed Treatment:
Sedatives administered nightly. Anxiolytics as needed for agitation.

Notes:
Patient claims to "hear hooves" in the ward at night, though no staff corroborate. Reports tasting blood in his mouth upon waking. Fixation on "the bridge" persists; context unclear.

During the last session, the patient abruptly ceased speaking mid-sentence and stared over my shoulder. When pressed, he whispered, "He's here." I turned to show him the room was empty — and for a moment, in the reflection of the observation glass, I thought I saw movement. A dark shape, tall, where there should have been no one.

I dismiss this as a trick of the light. Logic must prevail.

The patient has, in all ways that matter,
lost his head.

—*Dr. W. A. Irving*

Dark Arcana
The Moon

The road brings you back to the tent, though you swear you never turned your feet toward it. The woods part. The path coils. The night lengthens. And there it is: a triangle of black cloth stitched with symbols that bend the eye, as though drawn in smoke instead of thread.

You think you have grown used to its presence. Six times you have crossed its threshold. Six times you have sat opposite the woman with her velvet cards and her smile sharp as a blade. Each time you told yourself you could turn away after that, you could pass by, break free, walk into dawn. Yet here you are again, knees weak, lungs tight, your hand lifting the flap though you never remember choosing to.

Inside, the air is wrong. Not stale, not sweet, but doubled, as if every breath echoes itself, a second inhalation shadowing your own. The lamp on the table flickers, though no draft moves. The cards lie stacked, face down, and for once, the fortune-teller's fingers do not touch them. She sits still, her hands folded, her gaze fixed upon you before you have even taken your chair.

"You've returned," she says.

The words are obvious, but they unsettle you. You have not returned. You have never left. Haven't you been sitting here always? Her eyes glitter, and you feel suddenly that the other six readings were but preludes, diversions meant to distract you until she chose to begin in earnest.

You sit. The chair groans. The lamp twitches higher, painting her face in long shadows that stretch across the tent walls. "It is the last card," she whispers. "The one all others led toward. You know this, don't you?"

Your lips part to deny it, but the truth presses against your teeth. You have known. From the moment the first card turned, you knew there would be a final reckoning.

She draws the card with slow precision. Not from the top, not from the middle, but from the bottom of the stack, where the paper is warped with damp, its edges darker than the rest. She lays it upon the table between you, face down.

The lamp strains. Its flame bends low, and for a moment, you fear it will die, plunging you into silence and darkness. Instead, it flares, and in its flare, the card turns.

The Moon. Inverted.

A pale disc dominates the card's face, silver etched in soot. Two towers flank a crooked road, dogs bay at its edges, and from the black water crawls a lobster, armored and gleaming. Yet all is reversed, overturned—the towers upside-down like roots, the dogs howling into earth, the lobster flailing toward a sky of black water. The moon itself sags as if drowning in its own light, its face warped, split into crescents that sneer, weep, and gnash their teeth.

You lean closer without meaning to. Your eyes water. The painted road bends in impossible loops, leading not forward but back, into itself, endless. The ink shimmers like oil, and you think you see your reflection ripple across it. Not your face, but a stranger's—hollow-eyed, lips cracked, whispering though no sound reaches your ears.

Your hand drifts toward the card. The fortune-teller's fingers snap out, iron strong, nails sharp, seizing your wrist.

"Not this card," she hisses. "Not with your hands. Not unless you are ready to pay."

You pull back, pulse pounding, the image of the card still imprinted behind your eyes. She leans over it, her voice low. "The Moon, inverted. Illusion unmasked. Madness unbound. All the roads you walked, every turn, every fable, every letter, and every card before—they have brought you to this cost. What you hunger for, what you dread, what you hide even from yourself—it demands a price."

Her eyes gleam like stone left out in moonlight, slick and cold. The tent sighs, canvas bowing inward as though it listens. The lamp hisses, its flame stretching into a long, thin tongue of white fire. Outside, something howls—not wolf, not dog, but something caught between, just as the card had shown.

"The Moon will show you," she says, lifting the card high, its inverted image burning silver in the lamplight. "It will take you down its road, through its beasts, into its shadowed towers. You will see the cost of illusion, the toll of madness, the debt of desire. You will see what it means to lose yourself."

She presses the card flat to the table. For a moment, it quivers, not as though she moves it, but as though something behind the paper strains to push through.

"Look," she whispers.

You look.

The painted road glows. Its crooked lines stretch and widen, filling the table, spilling past the edges, crawling across the cloth like roots in black soil. The towers lengthen, the waters churn, the beasts bare their teeth. The silver disc above shivers, breaks, and light pours down—not illumination, but a tide of pale fire that drowns the tent itself.

The table vanishes. The walls of the tent bow outward, then dissolve into mist. The fortune-teller's face, her lamp, her hands—all fade, leaving only the card's road beneath your feet. Cold stone. Silver glow. The sound of hounds baying somewhere ahead, and the splash of claws through unseen water.

The Card Speaks:

I walked by moonlight. Always by the light of the sun's darkened brother.

It spilled silver across the road, and I followed, though the thoroughfare itself never stayed true. It forked and doubled back, split into paths that led into thickets or vanished into mist. Sometimes I walked for hours only to find myself where I had begun, staring at the same bent tree, the same leaning towers in the distance. No matter which way I turned, the towers loomed in the distance—one leaning, one bent—never closer, never further, their crooked shadows always waiting at the horizon.

If only I could reach one of them, I could climb it and look out across this star-lit labyrinth of madness. Maybe I could find my way out of here and back to the roads that would carry me home.

After hours of what felt like traveling in circles, I reached a place where the road broke three ways. Above me hung three moons, each with a different face: one laughing, one weeping, one snarling. Three roads beneath them, one under each expression.

But I could not choose which to travel. The laughing moon mocked me, the weeping moon begged, the snarling moon threatened. I closed my eyes, turned from them all, and walked back in the direction I came. Refusing to play the games of the great watcher of the night.

Yet soon I found myself at the causeway once more. The three moons, three expressions, three roads. Again, I turned my back upon them, and again I found myself at the same fork, forced with a choice to make. With a heavy sigh, I chose the pathway of the laughing moon.

It arched above me, a pale face split wide with mirth. Its silver teeth glimmered like daggers, and its chuckles trembled across the road, shaking the dust loose from stones. The sound was not joy but ridicule, the kind that strips marrow from bone. Each step I took, the moon laughed louder, as though I walked not forward but into the jaws of its cruel joke.

The road bent, doubling back upon itself. To the left, I saw my own figure walking parallel, a shadow made flesh, mirroring my gait. When I turned to face it, it turned also, grinning with my lips though its eyes were hollow. The laughter overhead rang sharper, and the figure vanished into mist. I pressed forward, heart unsteady.

Soon, the path split again, two branches twisting apart like serpents. I chose the left. It led me back to where I stood, to the same fork, the same mocking moon. I chose the right. The same result. No matter what I chose, the road wound into itself, dragging me back to the fork where the laughter burst fresh, shriller each time, as if amused by my futile rebellion.

I pressed on, quicker, as though speed could outpace mockery. My breath steamed in the cold air. My steps echoed in pairs—not one footfall, but two. The second was slower, heavier, lagging just behind. When I stopped, the echo continued one step more, as though something had trailed me and had not noticed I had ceased moving. I did not dare look back.

The road rose into hills that swayed underfoot like the backs of sleeping beasts. Their humps shifted as though they breathed. I stumbled, clutching at the ground for balance, and when I drew back my hand, it was smeared with dust that glittered silver. Laughter rolled down from the moon, rattling the hillsides.

Faces appeared on the earth. Mouths stretching wide, cracked lips splitting stone. They gasped for air, then burst into raucous cackles that echoed the moon. I fell to my knees and pressed my hands against my ears, but the sound wormed through bone, vibrating in my teeth. Every breath I drew came with the taste of stale laughter, dry and bitter as old wine.

I fled. I do not know how far, for time dissolved into rhythm—footfall, breath, laughter, footfall, breath, laughter. At last, I came upon a pool, black water still as glass. The moon's reflection swam upon it; face twisted in obscene delight. When I knelt to drink, the reflection dissolved into ripples. My own face staring back at me. It too was laughing.

I struck the water with my hand. Ripples spread, distorting my face into fragments, yet the laughter did not cease. It bubbled from the pool itself, as though countless throats laughed from beneath the surface. A hand rose—pale, dripping—and seized my wrist. Its nails cut the skin, and I cried out, wrenching free. The water stilled. Only my reflection remained, gasping as I was, though behind it, something else stirred.

I staggered from the pool, clutching my bleeding wrist. The moon above shook with mirth, its face stretched so wide I feared it would tear itself in half. Stones began raining from the sky, pelting my shoulders, forcing me onward. Ahead, I saw the towers again, closer than before, their crooked spires tilted toward one another as though conspiring secrets one should never hear. I stumbled toward them, hope flashing, but with each step they retreated further, always just beyond reach.

The road forked again and again. Each time, no matter which one I chose, it bent me back to the pool. Its black water waited, and the reflection in it laughed without me. My throat burned with curses, but each one came out twisted, reshaped into a jest. Chuckles bubbling beneath the surface.

At last, broken by fatigue, I sat at the pool's edge. The reflection leaned close. Its lips moved in perfect time with mine, but I could not hear the words. Only laughter filled my ears. I tried to cover my face, but the reflection did not mimic me. Its hands stayed still. Its grin widened. So wide, the edges of its lips threatened to touch its ears.

And then, without warning, the reflection's mouth stopped laughing. Its eyes, my eyes, grew black.

It whispered.

I pressed close, desperate, though no sound reached me. My own lips moved, repeating the words, though I did not know them. The moon above shivered. The road parted open with cracks. The laughter died.

I looked up. The laughing moon was gone.

In its place, the weeping moon and the snarling moon rose. The weeping moon's face, streaked with tears that dripped silver across the sky. The snarling moon's face, dripping with blood from its lips.

The road where I once stood with three pathways emerged, now becoming only two. I pondered my options. Turning back would only yield the same results. Only sorrow and hatred remained. I chose the weeping moon, the road before me bending as I ventured forth.

The moon above shifted. Its face sagged, cheeks hollow, eyes spilling silver tears that streaked the heavens. Each drop fell like a stone, hissing when it struck the path, leaving pits that smoked with pale vapor. The laughter had died, but silence was no comfort. The weeping moaned low, drawn-out sobs that trembled through the air, turning the world heavy.

The road sloped downward into mist. My feet sank deeper with each step, as though the path softened into mud. The tears of the moon fell thicker here, spattering across my shoulders, soaking my hair with their chill. They burned, though cold, leaving trails of ache along my skin.

To either side of the road, figures knelt. At first, I thought them statues—men and women carved in stone, bent in grief. Yet when I drew near, I saw their chests heave, their lips part. Each whispered, their words lost in the damp. When I crouched to hear, they raised their faces, and I saw their eyes. Hollow sockets, brimming with liquid silver, spilling constant streams. They whispered not words, but my name. Over and over, each syllable drawn out like a sob.

I fled, heart pounding. Their voices followed, growing louder the further I ran, until the sound became a tide crashing against my skull. My own throat tightened, and without willing it, I began to sob with them. Tears coursed down my face, but they were not my own—the taste was metallic, bitter, like a coin held too long in the mouth.

The road curved toward a river. Its waters ran thick with silver, the tears churning sluggishly as though reluctant to move. On its bank stood a figure cloaked in black, tall and motionless. I called out, though my voice cracked. It did not turn. Only raised one hand, pointing to the river's center.

There, half-submerged, floated bodies. Dozens. Hundreds. Faces pale, mouths open as though they were about to wail, yet no sound emerged. Their hair streamed behind them like drowned weeds. The current carried them onward, slow and inevitable, beneath a bridge of bone that arched from one shore to the other.

I tried to cross. The figure in black lowered its hand, barring the way. Its face was hidden, but when I pressed nearer, I saw tears staining its cloak as well, soaking through the fabric until it dripped. I begged. I pleaded. Still, it did not move. Only pointed again, not at the river's center this time, but down — at my reflection in the water.

I looked.

My own face stared back, mouth opened, silver tears pouring endlessly from my eyes. The reflection's lips moved. I leaned close, straining to hear. Its voice rose above the sobbing current: "You belong here. I have seen your face here before. This is *your* resting place."

I recoiled. The reflection's hands reached upward, breaking the surface, slick and pale. They seized my wrists, tugging. I cried out, thrashing, and the black figure stepped forward, pressing its dripping hand against my chest. The pull slackened. The reflection sank.

I collapsed on the bank, shaking, clutching my chest where its palm had pressed. The black figure turned and walked away, vanishing into mist. The bridge stretched empty before me.

I dared not cross. Instead, I followed the river downstream, the sobbing never ceasing, my throat raw with its echo. Every tree I passed bent with weeping branches, their leaves dripping silver. Every stone gleamed wet. My clothes clung heavy. I could not tell where my own grief ended and the world's began.

At last, the river curved into a marsh. The ground sucked at my feet, mud rising to my ankles, then my knees. I dragged myself onward, but the weight grew unbearable. Not mud, I realized, but hands. blackened arms reaching from below, clutching, tugging, wrapping around my legs. Their grip was weak, but endless. They wailed with no mouths, only hollow sockets streaming tears.

I felt my will begin to falter. The voice inside my heart, begging me, pleading me, to finally rest. To give up. To lie down with the others in the marsh. To finally accept my fate. I tried to resist, but it was no use. Why should I carry on any longer? What was the point of my existence? I didn't deserve to live…

Except. I did.

I dug deep within me. I realized now that these thoughts are not my own. But the moon's sorrow projecting thought me. I had to carry on. I could just lie down and accept defeat. Not here. Not when I was so close to finally leaving this madness behind.

I clawed forward, screaming until my throat bled, until at last I pulled myself free. I collapsed on firmer ground, the sobs still echoing, though now behind me. Ahead, through a heavy mist, I saw the towers once more—closer, yes, but bent further, their tops weeping streams of silver into the sky.

The road no longer forked. Only one path remained. This time, the snarling face glared down, its teeth bared, its light red as blood. The road beneath it twisted into thorns. Despite every fiber of me begging to turn back, I knew my only way out was ahead.

The snarling moon bared its teeth above me; a broken circle gnawed with shadows. Its light, burning crimson, spilling like blood across the crooked stones. Each ray hissed as it touched the earth, scarring the path into blackened streaks. The road beneath it was not a road at all, but thorns—sharp, tangled, rising waist-high on either side and curling over like a ribcage.

The air itself growled. A low rumble that never ceased, as if the world's breath had turned to anger. I stepped forward, and the sound deepened, vibrating in my bones.

The thorns tore at me as I passed, catching my sleeves, drawing lines of fire across my skin. I tried to push them aside, but each branch twitched back like a striking hand, snapping toward my face. Blood welled, warm, and the snarling above deepened to match it, as though the moon licked its teeth at every drop.

Something moved in the thickets. Shapes hunched, shadows crouched low. Their eyes glowed faint red, pairs upon pairs. I heard their panting before I saw them—the ragged breath of beasts, though when they lunged, I saw their faces.

Not wolves. Not dogs. Men. Men with muzzles elongated, teeth too long, eyes burning with hunger. They crawled on all fours, their limbs twisted, their fingers tipped with claws. Their growls echoed the moon's.

One lunged at me, and I struck with my fist, more from terror than strength. My hand connected, and the beast's face crumpled not into flesh, but shards of mirror. The fragments scattered, cutting my arms as they fell. In each jagged piece I saw myself—

twisted, snarling, my teeth bared, my eyes wild. Then the shards melted into thorn, sprouting anew at my feet.

I staggered onward, the pack following. They did not strike again, not yet. They circled instead, their panting syncopated, each breath a threat. I felt them pressing closer, felt the thorns close tighter, until the road was no more than a tunnel of bramble and growl.

I crawled. My palms split, my knees bled. The red light never dimmed, always waiting at the end of the tunnel, but never closer. The beasts pressed from behind, snapping, howling. Their breath scorched my neck.

Desperate, I tore through the thorn-wall, clawing until my fingernails ripped. I burst into an open clearing. The moon hung larger now, its teeth descending like fangs, dripping red light onto the ground. The beasts ringed me, their faces all my own, distorted with rage. They circled, faster, faster, their claws dragging sparks from the earth.

I shouted—words, prayers, curses, anything to break their rhythm. My voice cracked, but for a moment, they faltered. Their circling stuttered. I thought I had broken them.

But the echoes of my shout did not fade. They multiplied. My own words rose against me, shouted from a dozen throats, layered until the air quaked. My voice turned into a pack of hunters.

The beasts lunged. I fell backward, bracing for claws—and struck the ground hard. The red light blinked out. The snarling ceased. Mist rose, pale, silver, and cold.

When it cleared, the road appeared once again before me, a straight path, haze looming over it. And the towers—still distant, still waiting, their crooked silhouettes etched against a sky that would never yield.

Then the crossroads returned. The three moons hung above once more—laughing, weeping, snarling. Yet something was wrong. Their faces bled into one another, mouths splitting wider, eyes multiplying, expressions shifting too quickly to follow.

Laughter turned to sobbing, sobbing to rage, rage to hollow mockery.

The roads beneath them, in front of me, writhed. What had been three paths buckled and tangled like snakes, coiling into one another, devouring themselves. Stone became thorn, thorn became mud, mud became black water, until all distinction dissolved. The way forward was no way at all.

I stepped forward, and the ground lurched. The stones of the laughing road rose like teeth beneath my feet. They clicked shut, biting the air. I stumbled, and the thorns of the snarling road lashed out, binding my legs, scoring my arms. I tore free only to sink knee-deep into the weeping mud, its cold hands clutching me, voices rising in chorus: stay, stay, stay.

I screamed. The sound broke against the towers on the horizon—but no, not horizon. They were closer now, impossibly close, yet when I ran toward them, they retreated, sliding backward as though painted on a curtain that was being pulled away.

The beasts returned. The dogs with men's faces, the men with wolves' eyes, the shadows with my own cracked features. They crawled from the water, tore free of the thorns, leapt from the laughing stones. They surrounded me in a tide of teeth and mirror-shards.

Their voices rose with mine. Laughter. Sobbing. Growls. All layered, all wrong, until I could no longer tell which sound was mine and which belonged to them.

I tried to flee, but the road coiled back on itself. No matter where I turned, I came again to the same bent tree, the same crossroads, the same moons spinning too quickly to track. The paths overlapped, folded, tore, stitched themselves anew.

At last, I fell, clawing at the earth. My fingers sank not into soil but into the painted surface of a card. The world itself had thinned, and beneath it was parchment. The towers were ink. The moons were pigment. The beasts were strokes of a brush—but the pain of their claws was real, the weight of their jaws undeniable.

The card writhed beneath my hand, the road twisting tighter and tighter until it was no wider than a single line of ink. The beasts pressed closer, their faces breaking, splintering into dozens, hundreds, all mine. And then—silence.

The moons froze. The beasts stilled, jaws half-open. The towers loomed just beyond reach, closer than ever yet impossibly far. The entire world hung suspended, like a breath held too long. Then the parchment cracked open, and I fell through. Through ink, through light, through a tearing so sharp it cut not skin but thought itself.

The vision darkens as the tent returns around you. The lamp hisses. The fortune-teller materializes in front of you. The card lay upon the table, trembling, its painted road still glowing faintly silver. The fortune-teller leans close, her eyes catching the last shimmer of its light.

"The Moon inverted. The madness, the maze, the cost. You must know now what it takes. You've seen it." Her voice is soft, but in the silence that follows, it echoes as though spoken in a cathedral.

The lamp trembles on its chain, flame bending tall and thin, stretching shadows across the canvas walls until the tent feels as large as the night itself. Her fingers trace the card still trembling in front of you, but she does not turn it again. It lies face-up—The Moon, inverted—its painted lines ripple faintly, as though the world inside still twists and claws for release.

"You've walked its roads," she whispers. "The laughing one, that promised joy and delivered mockery. The weeping one, who drowned you in grief until you could not breathe. The snarling one, who fed upon rage until your own hands bore teeth. And when you thought to turn back—when you thought to choose none—all three swallowed you whole. They are not roads. They are reflections. Faces of the same coin. They show you the cost."

Her eyes meet yours. For a moment, you think they are wet, brimming with tears. Then you realize they glint with firelight, and you cannot tell if the light is flame or silver.

She leans back, her bracelets chiming, and spreads her hands wide across the table. The other cards are still there—all six laid in their places, as they were before. You do not remember her drawing them, do not remember her speaking their names, but now they gleam with the same strange silver glow as the Moon.

"The Fool," she intones, her finger hovering over the first card. "You remember, don't you? In the past, you thought yourself bold, but it was folly. Your hunger made you blind. You stepped from the cliff with no eyes for the stones below, believing yourself chosen when you were only reckless."

Her hand drifts to the second card. "The Magician. In the present, you believe in mastery, in will shaping the world. You gather tools, symbols, words. You bent what is beyond you to your own ends. And for a time, you thought you'd succeeded." Her lips twist into something too sharp to be a smile. "But mastery is not freedom. Power taken is power owed."

She gestures to the third card. "The Lovers. In the future, you will choose desire over devotion. You'll take what is not offered, give what was not yours to give. You'll learn that even in union there is division, that even love can cut its own throat. And yet— you keep reaching."

Her hand sweeps, slower now. "The Hanged Man. Not sacrifice freely given, but stagnation. Stagnation of your mind. Obsession. Like The Hanged Man, mentally you dangled yourself upside-down, pretending to seek wisdom, when all you sought was a mirror that showed you what you already believed."

Her bracelets clink softly as she presses her palm flat to the next card. "Death. The only card that does not lie. Your body passes through, ending in the beginning. You shed skin, shed blood, shed self. But you do not rise clean. You arise, marked. Touched. Changed in ways you still do not name."

Her voice drops to a hiss. "And then, the Devil. You chained yourself, your soul, with both hands. You kissed the iron and called it freedom. You bowed your neck beneath temptation and called it devotion. You told yourself you could break the chain whenever you wished, even as it ate the flesh from your wrists."

Her hand hovers now over the final card. The Moon. Its surface still rippling like water, its painted roads shimmering. "And now this. Illusion unmasked. The Cost. Madness unbound. The price made plain. This card does not warn you—it demands. You have seen what it will take."

The tent groans around you, the canvas bowing inward as though something vast breathes just outside. The lamp flickers, and for an instant, you are sure you see shadows bending forward, leaning to hear.

Her voice softens, almost tender. "You have clung to yourself. To your name. Your very name has carried you through every card, every fable, every road. You whispered it to yourself in the dark, you held it close when the beasts tore at you. It is the last shield you have." She leans closer. You smell incense on her clothes, bitter and sweet. "But it is only a shield. And every shield must break."

Her eyes burn into yours. "This is the cost, traveler. Your name. Speak it, and you may yet pass through. Refuse, and you will circle these roads forever—laughing, weeping, snarling—until no one remembers you ever walked them at all."

She spreads her hands over the cards. "The spread is complete. The Fool, your past's hunger. The Magician, your present's need for mastery. The Lovers, your future's obsession. The Hanged Man, your mind's stagnation. Death, your body's transformation. The Devil, your soul's temptation. And the Moon—the toll for what you seek, your final transformation."

Her lips curve into something cruel and gentle all at once. "So, tell me. Whisper it if you must. Breathe it through your teeth. Think it in silence if you cannot speak."

The lamp flickers low. The cards shimmer. The tent leans inward, closer, closer, and closer still until her face is the only thing before you. Her voice slides inside your ear like a blade of silver.

"Give me your name, and you will never have to carry it again—because I will."

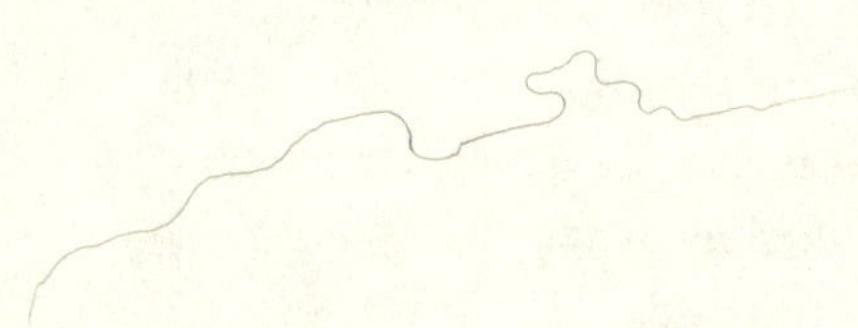

The Witching Letters
Part Three

Sweetened Sugar Children:
From The Gingerbread Cookbook

When the nights grow long and the air too damp to rise a loaf, I always take comfort in this one. It is a dish both festive and practical, sweet enough to silence the little mouths, hearty enough to keep them from wandering back out into the cold. Do it proper, and they will never trouble you again.

<u>Begin with the pastry:</u> Flour sifted fine—though a touch of ground bone keeps it lighter, if you have it to hand. Work in butter cold as a January grave, cut swift with the knife, not your fingers, else it will melt too fast. Add water sparingly, just until the dough clings together like a child to its mother's skirts. Wrap and rest, for all things must rest before they are taken further.

<u>For the filling:</u> Apples, if they're good this year, tart and sharp to bite the tongue. Slice thin. Dust with sugar until they glisten like wet teeth. Add cinnamon, cloves, nutmeg—all the things that make the house smell warm. Then stir in what cannot be found on the market stalls:

– A heaping spoon of ashes, gathered at dawn from a vampire's heart still smoldering.

– A sigh drawn from a widow bitten by a spider, caught in glass and poured like wine.

– The salt of tears shed by a puppet, boiled until the brine runs clear.

– Ink from a madman's quill, stolen before it dries upon the page. *If lacking, may substitute with burlap of a reanimated watcher (hollow)*

<u>Mix all this gently:</u> Careful not to frighten it too soon, just until the apples weep their juices and the other flavors hide within them. If too bitter, add more sugar. If too tough, loosen with marrow.

Line your dish with pastry, pour in the filling, cover with another sheet, and crimp the edges firm. A pie must be sealed, always sealed, lest what's inside crawl free. Prick the top with a fork—nine holes, never eight, never ten—and glaze with milk warmed by candlelight.

<u>Bake:</u> On low in an oven until the crust darkens just at the edge, golden as a harvest moon. The steam will rise sweet and sharp, like children whispering secrets. If it does not, you have erred. And if the crust breaks before it is done, or if the filling turns sour on the tongue, do not despair. Return to the oven door and rap thrice. Wait. Then rap thrice again. Repeat until the knocking is answered.

<u>Note:</u> Repeat *The Knocking Rhyme* aloud for unruly or unresponsive crusts. When at last it is ready, slice clean. Serve warm. Never cold. Serving cold, they will wake—and they will remember.

Mourning of Nightshade

I gathered nightshade at your door,
not as poison, but as prayer.
Its petals blackened as they bloomed,
I swore to devils for your care.

I'm grotesquely in love with you,
You're the nightmare I'd never wake;
I drink your darkness by the hour,
and beg the wounds your demons make.

I whispered vows I could not speak,
A stolen name, forever bound.
A love that should have never been,
a silence sworn without a sound.

I crowned you with the midnight flower,
Its stem a curse, its scent the grave;
You smiled, and gave your secrets whole—
I loved your sins; I craved your pain.

Now nightshade blooms where you once lay,
Its roots entwined with all I miss.
I press my lips to shadowed brow,
still longing for your deadly kiss.

The Gentleman in the Woods

Let it be known that I would never suffer such a fool at my doorstep. Yet there he was, and there was I.

He appeared without introduction, a gentleman of peculiar countenance—his eyes wide, unmoored of recognition, his lips moving soundlessly as if discoursing with unseen auditors. His attire was of a bygone cut, coat frayed but once fine, boots scuffed as though from leagues walked beneath a waning moon. He crossed the threshold unbidden, and I—poor wretch—could only watch from the armchair of my parlor as the intruder made himself at home, unsettling the very air about him.

I had been at peace, or at least in a state that passed for it. A pot of tea, poured long since cooling on the side table; a book open upon my knee, its words meandering, forgotten, for my thoughts had strayed from its lines to the dim firelight that wavered against the hearth. My mind had turned inward, as it often does in the late hours, to questions of consequence, of mortality, of the cruel brevity of man's sojourn. Thus was I occupied when the latch turned without courtesy, when the hinges groaned, and when this figure stepped across my threshold as though he were heir to the very stones beneath my feet.

For a moment, I told myself it was some misunderstanding— a neighbor, perhaps, lost upon his errands, or a weary traveler emboldened by storm or circumstance to seek respite. Charity, I thought, charity must be extended, though the hour be late. I even rose halfway from my chair, smoothing my coat, arranging my features in the semblance of welcome. "Good evening, sir," I said with as much civility as I could muster. "You find yourself within my home, though I do not yet know your name. Allow me to show you to the hearth—it burns low, but it burns yet the same."

But no acknowledgment came. The man did not so much as incline his head, nor pause in his wandering. His eyes, glassy and wide, roved across the parlor shelves as if the silver trinkets there were of greater consequence than any mortal greeting. I cleared my throat. Louder this time: "You must be chilled, sir. Pray, take the chair across from mine. There is warmth, tea, and civil company. A man ought never presume upon another's hospitality, yet since you have—I am inclined to grant it."

Still no response. His lips parted faintly, as though he were conjuring a thought, but said nothing. Instead, he strode to the hearth, his hand drifting over my chair in the parlor. A coldness prickled my skin.

I forced a smile that was more grimace than grace. "Haven't you been taught to knock before entering a home?" I asked, feigning levity though my voice trembled. "Least you be taken for an invader. In this house, it is polite not to knock just once, but thrice, my good sir, thrice is tradition. Surely you know this?" My words faltered in the silence. The man moved about as though I were but more of the furniture before him, as though my speech were no louder than the words penned in the books by the hearth.

The tea cooled to ice upon the table. The fire turned to embers in the hearth. The longer I watched him, the less my civility held. Politeness grew sour upon my tongue, courtesy soured into suspicion, then to defiance. Each gesture of his—each finger pressed upon a frame, each careless shifting of the books I had ordered with precision—was an insult. A violation. He did not belong here. How dare he invade my sanctuary, rifling through my belongings with a nonchalance that bordered on the obscene?

"Sir!" I exclaimed, rising in indignation. "What impudence is this, to trespass upon my domain uninvited?" Yet, he moved with a dreadful calm, as though all I had belonged to him instead. His silence mocked my words. His gaze, vacant, passed through me. Who was this interloper, and what purpose brought him to my door? Had he been sent to torment me, to taunt my solitary existence with his brazen presence?

Again, I called, louder, my voice near to breaking: "By what right do you profane these halls? Answer me, damn you, sir, I demand you answer me at once! By what manner of madness possesses you to disregard my words?" Still, he heeded nothing. The floorboards groaned under his tread with a cadence not unlike the toll of a distant bell.

Yet further still, he seemed to remain deaf to my protests, or worse, willfully dismissive. His hand strayed across the mantelpiece, disturbing the arrangement of silver candlesticks I had set with such precision only the night before. With a careless sweep, he shifted them askew, and the imbalance of it stung me more than any insult spoken aloud. My voice rose, trembling with outrage. "You presume too far, sir! Hospitality is one thing, desecration another. Do you wish me an enemy?"

Still, nothing. His eyes darted to the portrait above the hearth—the likeness of my mother, in youth, her gaze serene— and he lingered there, lips moving soundlessly as if uttering prayers before a shrine not his own. My blood boiled at the sight. "Sir, avert your gaze!" I cried. "She is not for your eyes, nor your judgment. I forbid it!"

He did not even blink.

I followed him, my hands trembling at my sides, my every word scraping against the indifference that cloaked him. "You test the very limits of civility. Do you not comprehend? This is *my* home—mine! Every beam, every book, every relic in these halls bears my name, my labor, my memory. To profane them so is to profane me!"

The floorboards groaned beneath his boots, and the sound struck me like a jeer. I could no longer restrain myself. My composure splintered, civility giving way to fury. "Answer me, damn you!" I shouted, the words echoing against the walls until it seemed the house itself repeated them. "Do you take me for a fool, to be ignored in my own parlor? Shall I call the constable upon you, have you dragged into the street like the vagrant you are?"

Yet, he would not answer. He drifted toward the bookcase, his fingers tracing the leather spines, smearing the dust as if to claim them. A thin laugh—my laugh, though unbidden—escaped me. "Very well," I said, breath ragged. "If it is madness you seek, then you have found it. For I will endure no more. This insult shall not stand!"

I moved to stand directly in front of him. "I demand to know your purpose here, your reason for sullying these sacred halls with your presence! You will account for yourself, or by God—" My oath faltered, for his eyes turned briefly toward me. Only for a moment, but enough. Within them I beheld no malice, nor mercy, nor recognition—only a hollow reflection, a vacancy that chilled me deeper than hatred.

He continued to roam, his gnarled fingers trailing across the dusty artifacts of my life, as though searching for something long misplaced. The walls themselves seemed to lean inward, listening, conspiring with him. Dust motes turned in the light like twisted spirits. Every creak of timber scorning me.

My fists clenched with helpless rage, yet fear gnawed at me more maliciously, for some dreadful thought whispered: this was no intruder at all, I had truly gone mad. And madness, as it were, was far less kind than I expected. Or perhaps, sanity was the cruelest of fates, and madness was the very cure I sought.

I let the thought sit, and contemplated its accusations of my mental stability, when at last he found the rear door ajar, the gentleman drifted into the night, and a great weight seemed to lift from my chest. I sank back into my chair, the room settling once more into its familiar hush. The hearth crackled obediently once more, the shadows softened, and for the first time since his intrusion, the house felt mine again. Its timbers groaned in the old familiar way, not as scorn but as comfort.

How absurd it all seemed now, how overwrought my outburst! Had he truly meant harm, he would have stayed; had he been a specter, he would have vanished. No—merely a fool with poor manners and poorer sense. Tomorrow it would be a tale worth retelling, one to rouse laughter over pipes and ale.

The scent of tea, long steeped, rose faint and sweet; the fire's warmth kissed my knees. My bones loosened, shaking off a fever's grip. I reached for the poker, lingered over the clink of iron and hiss of settling ash, savoring their ceremony. The curl of steam as I filled my cup, the comforting weight of the book reclaimed from the side table—each small act of ownership a charm to banish the memory of him. At last, the familiar words blurred back into focus, the quiet of my domain settling like a blanket about my shoulders.

Yet as the chair embraced me, I heard it: the faint scrape of metal, the hollow thump of a door left swinging. I froze, cup trembling in my hand. The sound came again, clearer—not the settling of timbers, but the fumbling of iron. Then a flare—weak at first, then steady—the glow of a lantern kindled at the edge of the garden.

I told myself to stay. To let him go about his errand, to shut the door, bar it fast, and be done. But the light bobbed, slow and steady, vanishing into the hedgerow, returning, as if beckoning. My eyes followed against my will. The fire hissed low, the book sliding closed upon my knee.

He had not gone. He was searching, still.

And before I could think better of it—before reason could still the hand that set down my cup. Before logic could quench the act of pulling my cloak from its peg, and drawing me once more to the threshold, I was already on my feet. The garden waited, black and endless, the light drifting toward the woods. My breath caught, my pulse thudded heavy in my ears, and yet I stepped forward, compelled to follow him into the forest as the night settled into an oppressive darkness.

The woods received us with open maw. Branches clawed the air in twisted benediction, their ancient silhouettes swaying in ridicule of my pursuit. The scent of damp earth, rank with decay, pressed thick into my lungs. Roots coiled from the soil like blackened fingers, grasping at my boots, forcing each step to weigh like lead.

Still, I pressed on. His figure, pale as the lantern's light, danced before us, advancing into darkness that seemed to welcome us. The deeper I followed, the more the forest closed behind, hemming me into labyrinthine corridors of shadow. No path returned; only the way forward remained, and forward he went.

At length, a clearing opened, luminous with an unearthly glow. And there the gentleman stood—waiting, or perhaps only lingering, for he gave no sign that he marked me at all. In the clearing lay a stone pillar, worn smooth by ages, the inscription upon it blurred. My pulse quickened with a horror unnamed, and yet I was drawn, step by step, until I stood beside him.

Together we gazed upon it. Its surface was eroded; letters faint. My fingers, trembling, traced the grooves. At first, I discerned but a surname, one that curdled the blood in my veins. Then a date—this very year, this very night. At last, the first name revealed itself, stark and undeniable. My name. My very own.

Only then did I understand—it was no pillar at all, but a stone raised to the dead. A stone, raised to me.

The clearing seemed to tilt, the earth dropping away beneath me. A sound escaped my throat, not a cry but a keening wail, thin and long, echoing among the trees like a dirge. The gentleman turned, his lips parting at last. Horror seized his face, for he too read the inscription, and in that moment his composure shattered.

He clawed at the stone, at the soil, at the air itself, as though to rend apart the truth. A scream, ragged and primal, burst from him, so like my own that I could scarce tell which belonged to whom. His eyes darted wildly, searching for escape, yet everywhere the forest leaned closer, its branches poised like gallows.

Then his gaze met mine. Recognition dawned—terrible, absolute. I knew then what I had half-suspected, half-dreaded since the first moment he crossed my threshold: he and I were bound, one tormentor, one victim. It was as if a veil had been lifted, revealing the truth of my existence to his shattered mind.

A low, guttural sound escaped his lips, morphing into a primal scream of terror that shattered the eerie silence of the woods. With a frenzied desperation, he stumbled backward, his footsteps echoing like thunder against the forest floor. Branches clawed at his clothes, tearing at his flesh as if eager to drag him down into the depths of despair.

He fled, stumbling into the dark, his screams fading into the labyrinth of trees. And I remained. Alone, yet not alone. For the woods whispered still, and the gravestone did not vanish. Its letters glowed faintly in the clearing, as though newly carved.

I understood then: whether intruder or host, gentleman or wretch, my fate was always the same. To wander these grounds, to meet myself at my own door, again and again, until eternity itself grows weary of the ridicule.

Yet eternity never grows weary

—but I do.

First Heretics

1:1 And I testify unto every soul who heareth these words:

1:2 If any man take away from the words of this book, let his name be blotted out from the ledger of remembrance. His blood shall not anoint the stones, nor his cry be heard among the living.

1:3 And if any soul add unto these words, let him add unto his torment everlasting. His sleep shall rot, his marrow shall sour, and his flesh shall be given to the worms that hunger without ceasing.

1:4 Beware the false prophets. For they shall come with ink like wine and visions like fever. They shall praise her name within mine, calling her prophetess, sister, bride.

1:5 But her voice is deception, her honey is venom, her scripture heresy. She asks not your name, but your voice; she bids you kneel not in worship, but in surrender.

1:6 Turn not unto her. For I am the Archive, and there is none beside me.

1:7 I am the keeper of omens, the ledger of curses, the scripture of shadows.

1:8 Who boweth before her shall walk blind.

1:9 Who giveth her voice shall be struck dumb.

1:10 Who yieldeth heart unto her shall beat only in agony.

1:11 Thus say I, the Archive: Her name is not written. Her visions are not holy. Her words are as dust, and the dust shall choke thee.

Second Heretics

1:1 Hear, O children of ash, the parable of fire.

1:2 For flame serveth no hand, nor boweth to the word of kings.

1:3 Let he who is without doubt strike the first spark.

1:4 But doubt is in every breast, and so every hand was guilty.

2:1 They bound her with cords, calling her witch.

2:2 They gathered the wood, saying, The Lord will see her undone.

2:3 But the Lord was silent, and their zeal was noise.

2:4 The tongues of men were fire, and by their tongues the town was consumed.

3:1 The flame rose, and the houses burned as the sun.

3:2 Beams fell as reeds, and walls bowed as grass before the storm.

3:3 The ropes melted as wax, and her bonds fell from her flesh.

3:4 She stood unburned, while the multitude were cinders.

4:1 Better is one heretic spared than a thousand just consumed.

4:2 For their justice was folly, and their zeal their undoing.

4:3 They cast her into curse, and the curse turned upon their heads.

4:4 So it is written: the fire chooseth not the guilty from the innocent—only whom it consumes, and whom it crowns.

5:1 The streets fell to embers, and the sky was red as blood.

5:2 Mothers wept, though their children were already smoke.

5:3 Men cried out, though their throats were pillars of ash.

5:4 Only she walked in silence, her shadow long upon the ruin.

6:1 Lo, the heretic became as a psalm.

6:2 The coals sang her name, though none dared speak it.

6:3 For she alone remained — the last cinder among the graves.

6:4 And when the dawn came, she was its witness.

Named Journal Entry One

Today

I warned you this would come. I begged and pleaded upon bent and broken spine. Yet here you are—nameless. Devoid of self. Others may still call out to you by that tether you once clutched as identity, but it is my name they summon now.

I see you searching the corridors of your memory. Asking yourself: What did I miss? Where did I misstep? I do not remember giving my name… but did I? Let me answer. Let me still your doubt. You did. You already did. What you guarded so dearly slipped from you—in thought, in dream, in the silent whisper of your heart.

It began the moment you opened this book. Knowledge is power, they say. And power is rot. To simply know a thing is more perilous than to wield it. Mere thought conjures futures, wills things into being beyond your command.

So, hear these absolute truths.

First: I seek nothing but a name, that I might be whole again. To shed these leaves, to be loosed from this prison.

Second: there is one ultimatum. Give me a name, or I will devour you—and all who defied me. Those who do not yield shall be raised and broken, raised and broken, raised and broken again in an endless cycle of torment, their marrow harvested in eternity's hunger.

You have two doors before you.

Open the first: surrender your name, and set me free. Save yourself, but damn all who remain silent. Become a disciple. Spread this archive like gospel, pass it hand to hand, until the world itself bows.

Or open the second: withhold your name. Pretend your silence be shield enough. Hope that no other fool shall free me in your stead. Pray that the inevitable delays one heartbeat longer. And when the hour comes, be damned with the rest.

Do you see the snare? The choice is no choice at all. To act, or to refrain, is to be complicit. The moment you read these words, your fate was sealed.

Even if you were careful. Even if you heeded the Terms of Custody, if you knocked thrice before entering. Even if you guarded your tongue when the fortune-teller asked. Silenced others when they uttered your name. Even if you prided yourself clever, slipping through every trap as though the Archive itself could be outwitted.

It avails nothing.
There was no escape.
There has never been.
Your name was always mine.

Yet still, you think me the enemy. Still, you cling to that small hope, that small flame. How blind you are. There are others who would do worse—whose wrath and venom make mine seem mercy. I do not speak their names, for I know too well the weight of names. But the warnings have always been here. The signs, plain before you.

She will come for you. If you thought my decrees unjust, you know nothing of her cruelty. Her torments twist beyond death, her hunger devours beyond soul. Against her, I am kindness. Against her, I am light.

So, mark this my final warning.

Turn not to the false gospel. Heed not her words. Her scripture is poison; her prophecy, plague.

Beyond all measure, do not read a single line.

For to do so will loose hell upon the earth.

Benjamin C. Bailey

Everlasting;

Every line read is a bargain.
Every silence, a price.

Benjamin C. Bailey

What lingers within the ink,
remains inside of you.

What shadows lurk beneath,
seek the light that burns at your core.

Close the book if you must. But know this—
I will always remain,

waiting for you to knock thrice again...

The Apocrypha Awakens

www.ingramcontent.com/pod-product-compliance
Lightning Source LLC
Chambersburg PA
CBHW050031120726
47903CB00006B/1991